Praise for story collections by V.S. Kemanis

"Rich in metaphors and intensely provocative descriptive passages, these stories are to be tasted, savored, enjoyed and read over and over again. *Your Pick: Selected Stories* is a powerful tribute to this author's mastery of the art of creating not just a good story, but a story that needs to be read many times to appreciate the full power of its presentation." — *Readers' Favorite*

"Eleven compulsively readable short stories... Anyone who appreciates supple writing and fine storytelling will enjoy every minute spent reading these stories... A good deal of the pleasure in the collection comes from the writing itself. Kemanis knows how to build a story and keep it going." — *Foreword Reviews* on *Love and Crime: Stories*

"[Kemanis is] unarguably gifted...a great talent... There are stories here that I think I will remember forever. They've stayed with me in the weeks since I read them and make me smile even now as I call to mind their wonderfully flawed characters, their gentle humor, their twists and surprises and, without exception, the compassionate insight at their core." — *SP Reviews* on *Dust of the Universe*

"V. S. Kemanis is certainly one of the most intelligent writers I have read, writers of classics included. Her insight into human behavior is truly unusual... These are believable stories and believable characters... Unwaveringly fascinating." — *The Kindle Book Review* on *Everyone But Us*

"Quietly effective... Perfectly paced and brimming with mood and insight into our darker moments... Kemanis pulls off the difficult trick of imbuing the humdrum with a subliminal disquiet." — David Antrobus, author of *Dissolute Kinship*, on *Malocclusion*

Also by V.S. Kemanis

Dana Hargrove Legal Mysteries

Thursday's List
Homicide Chart
Forsaken Oath
Deep Zero
Seven Shadows
Power Blind

Story Collections

Dust of the Universe, tales of family
Malocclusion, tales of misdemeanor
Love and Crime: Stories
Your Pick: Selected Stories

Anthology Contributor

The Crooked Road, Volume 3
The Best Laid Plans
Me Too: Short Stories
Autumn Noir

Visit
www.vskemanis.com

Everyone But Us
tales of women

V.S. Kemanis

"Cactus Flower" was originally published in slightly different form in *Iconoclast*, and the following stories were originally published in slightly different form in these print collections by the author: *Women I've Known, Stories*: "Women I've Known," "Poodle Lady," "Wrinkle Free," "Cushion," "Pianissimo, Fortissimo," "Sissy and Me," "Priscilla and I," "The Walking Club," "Cactus Flower"; and *Gray Zone, Stories*: "Ninety Degrees," "The Cost of Ice Cream," "Hard Sell," "Not This," "Call Me Back," "The Missing and Uninvited," and "Everyone But Us."

Everyone But Us, tales of women
The Kindle Book Review Awards 2013 Nominee

ISBN-13: 978-0-9965909-1-4
ISBN-10: 0-9965909-1-9

ℛ **Opus Nine Books**
•New York•

For my darling baby girls,
now amazing young women,
Lillian and Evelyn,
with love

.

CONTENTS

&ℴ *Women I've Known*

I SAW HER—the first time—in Cartagena, under an arch on the Calle de la Amargura. Sure of her course, she walked toward us on a line of infinite points, one of them happening to be me. Her gait was easy, her head steady under the weight of a basketful of brown-green plantains, at least a hundred of them. Her black hair, as long as mine, fell thick and heavy past her solid brown neck and the scooped neckline of her faded cotton dress, ending at the small of her back.

If I had to choose one word to describe her, it would be "purposeful." She was on a mission, one of those daily, necessary ones, something that defined her, adding to her store of contentment.

She continued in rhythm, putting one foot in front of the other on the line we shared, her eyes fixed and unwavering on a point somewhere beyond me until we were no more than ten feet apart, our collision suddenly inevitable. Her eyes slid easily onto mine, quickly off and on again for a second look and a timid smile with a sliver of white behind full lips.

She hesitated and skipped a single beat of her

rhythm. I gazed at her shyly for the moment of that beat. Her face contained every inhabitant of her land, the African slave, the Muisca, the Spanish conquistador—a blend at once indigenous and alien.

She quickly recovered her rhythm, found a new, parallel line to my right, and passed me without another look.

I turned to my companion, Preston, and said, "I have such a funny feeling. I think I know her."

Preston twisted his head over his shoulder to regard the woman's backside, shaped like a three-part hourglass with that basket on top. "The woman with the bananas?" he asked.

"Plantains. Yes. That woman."

He looked at me with his sea green, opalescent eyes, lowering one eyebrow in the manner of men who have no doubt of their handsomeness. "But this is your first time in Cartagena. Or so you said."

"Yes."

"Then it's impossible. That woman belongs here."

We walked on quietly, without touching, while I harbored my thoughts, assured of their seclusion and his lack of interest.

At thirty-two, I was on my own mission of sorts, although I didn't fully realize it at the time.

Preston, like so many others before him, was my facilitator. He had money, and he had time. And he was willing to do, essentially, what I needed or wanted him to do.

I cared about him, of course, but had long since

dissuaded myself of the notion that I must love every man I was with. Love, in fact, is impossible in a relationship between two people who possess and venerate cleverness and physical beauty.

I have the qualities that attract men like Preston, although nothing can be attributed to my environment or upbringing. I'm an accidental beauty, the product of a long line of fleeting, unsatisfactory liaisons, east meeting west, north meeting south. But my heritage, with its potential richness of culture and tradition, delivered only a void, a mixture of fragments amounting to nothing.

Not that I cared. Or so I told myself every time my questions went unanswered. I didn't even notice that I was different until third grade, when a kid on our court-ordered school bus glared at me accusingly and demanded, "What *are* you anyway?" Even then I was smart enough to know not to encourage such insolence with a response, half thinking that anything I said, no matter how accurate, would still be incorrect.

Whatever I am, some would describe me as rare, exotic, and dark. I'm a mixture of my mother and father, who were, in turn, improbable mixtures of their own. Mother: Japanese and Botswanan. Father: Swedish and Colombian. Their halves were not by any means pure, and through the years my mother hinted at ancestors who bring every corner of the world into my blood: China, India, the Caribbean, South Pacific, Russia, Egypt. My knowledge of them and their cultures ends there: in hints and wondering.

In Cartegena, Preston and I walked barefoot on the beach

at sunset. Something about the moist, thick heat made us touch. I held his hand, imagining my grandfather's.

"You know," I told Preston, "my grandfather was from Cartagena."

Preston opened his eyes wide in surprise and smiled at me the way a father regards an errant child. "And so it's a grandfather that beckoned you—not this 'enchanted' spot with its 'magical history.'" He mimicked my words, ripping them off my dreams like cellophane gift wrap. He lowered his right eyebrow in the usual way and asked, "When do you plan to visit grandpa?"

"I've never met him. I don't know where he is, or if he's dead or alive."

It was the most I'd ever told Preston about my family.

I was still holding his hand, which had reverted to being uniquely Preston's hand in the middle of his mimicking. I didn't mind. It was a good, warm hand in some ways. Protective.

On the way back to the hotel, we walked the streets of crumbling seventeenth century façades, feeling the beat of a Cumbia drifting low through narrow corridors from its starting point in a distant café. I opened my pores to the dust of ages, my feet treading an inner layer of the stones that had once supported my ancestors.

When we got to our room, I allowed Preston to have me in the way he liked. But I wasn't left without my pleasure, ascending with his deep-voiced, plentiful exclamations of my beauty. "My God! Your skin, your hair. Renee!"

* * *

I never knew my Colombian grandfather, nor his son, my father, who left us when I was three. My mother spoke very little of him, apparently because there wasn't much good to say.

My sister—my identical twin—died at birth. No other brothers or sisters. But beyond that, a gallery of unknown relatives stretches back through generations and sideways in layers upon the generations of my mother and myself. I met not a single one but saw some pictures, heard a few stories from my mother's lips. Of her parents, she told an improbable tale of Africa and Asia colliding in California, a quick, taboo love affair and brief marriage. Fantasy or reality, I clung to it.

My mother liked to show me a red and yellow kimono she kept tucked in a closet, covered with plastic. "Your grandma, my mother, gave me this. Beautiful, isn't it?"

"Where *is* grandma?" I asked one of those times, when I was old enough to think of the question.

"Oh, she went back to Japan, before I had you."

"Why?"

My mother hesitated, her face showing long-forgotten emotion. "Well, she'd broken off from my father long before that, and I suppose once I was grown and could take care of myself, there was nothing to tie her here. So she went back."

"Oh." Nothing to tie her. "And what happened to your father?"

"He's probably back in his country. I really don't know."

* * *

After three days in Cartagena without discovering the reason I had come, we departed for Tokyo. Preston asked no questions. As always, he was game to follow my whim.

"Let's go to Tokyo," I said.

"I love Tokyo," he said.

I never felt the need to explain, and he certainly couldn't see the origin of my idea in my face, that amalgam of every race and culture. My brown, almond-shaped eyes, with just a trace of a fold, might have suggested Asia, or might have suggested somewhere else altogether.

But his solicitousness was, as usual, a sign of his broader purpose, which revolved around himself at center. His need for me was something I'd known in others. I was an image enhancer, an alluring appendage to attract positive attention in any setting: recreational, social, quasi-business.

"I've been to Tokyo a number of times," he said. "I can show you around, maybe even meet a contact or two."

With Preston, business was always quasi. His location made little difference; he traveled with all the latest communication devices. Born into solid wealth, he was a carefree player in high finance: buying, selling, merging, splitting, going public, bankrupting, shelling.

I took little interest but, of course, showed him the opposite, especially in social settings. I hung on his words with rapt attention and filled his spaces with well-placed, intuitive questions, lending an aura of intelligence and sophistication. No man really wants a dumb woman, nor will he tolerate a threat to his intellectual, outer world among men. Preston reveled in his business secrets, intimating by look and phrase that the things he couldn't tell me were infinitely more interesting than the things he revealed.

In Tokyo we ate raw fish without our shoes on and danced under strobe lights wearing our shoes until two in the morning. People pressed in on all sides, our heads higher than most of theirs, as if the gods had been considerate of my claustrophobia and reserved a layer of air just for me.

I thought of my mother, four inches shorter. She was, and still is, beautiful, perhaps more beautiful than I. She's darker, her hair kinkier, her nose flatter: a kind of beauty less accepted by the dominant culture. She used her beauty to get what she needed. A string of men provided us with clothing, food, and shelter, always just enough. She settled for a small, white stucco in the flats of Oakland, California, a five-year-old Chevrolet parked in front, never rising above that.

Lucky for both of us, she didn't have another child. Plenty of miscarriages, I learned later. The burden of carrying twins at an early age had worn out her uterus. Lucky, I say, for what little love she could give would have been rubbed to threadbare if worn by more than one child. I was frequently no more than her after-thought, the recipient of leftovers.

Things started to change as I approached puberty. More often than not, her men were attracted to me. I dodged them successfully and chose my own boyfriends. I learned her game and played it well, improving on it. Why settle for corn flakes and chicken when one can have eggs Benedict and filet mignon?

My mother saw herself in me and resented my oblique cunning, my mastery of her example. But like everything else, her opinion of me showed only in the slightest shadings of expression under a consistent exterior of benevolent indifference.

From fourteen on, the words I uttered most frequently in her house were: "I'm going. See you later." For a while, she would respond: "Don't stay out late." But soon, our communication dwindled to waves and nods and dropped off altogether as she stopped looking up from her glass of Gallo or the television set.

On the day I left for the last time, she sat with her latest man in the living room, the two of them low into the cushions, forehead to forehead, giggling. I walked right past them, carrying my oversized bag. I didn't need to take much with me. Where I was going, I would be given what I wanted.

Stopping at the front door, I said goodbye with a silent wave of my hand. She didn't look up. I walked out.

I was sixteen, almost seventeen.

In Tokyo I saw the woman again. In a fish store.

Tired of my insulation from everyday life, I'd convinced Preston to accompany me on a trek through the outskirts. Somehow, we found ourselves in an area that felt like suburbia: rows of apartments, small stores.

The overwhelming smell of fish drew me in. I tugged at Preston's hand. He followed.

The cramped space was alive with housewives on their daily errands, for despite Tokyo's cosmopolitan glow, the women still buy food on the day they serve it to their families. The woman I recognized stood at the fish counter ordering her selection, leaning forward and pointing her left index finger with assurance, yet polite restraint. A small baby clung to her back papoose style, a toddler hung on her right hand. The toddler pulled. She grasped his hand firmly with authority, giving a purposeful, gentle command through the strength and warmth of her fingers.

I stopped short, regarding her profile. She felt the heat of my eyes and turned her head. Our eyes locked and disengaged. I imagined I saw a stretch of her lips, a smile.

She was different than the rest. Slightly taller, slightly darker, her shoulder-length hair less metallically straight and black—almost wavy—her eyes rounder than most.

I'd seen her before, I was sure of it. She was at once the woman from Cartagena and impossibly not her. She was a woman I knew.

"You're staring," whispered Preston.

I didn't budge.

"Come on," he said. "Let's get out of here. We'll *reek*."

"Wait."

He smiled. "Yes, I know. She's a friend of yours."

I turned to him, amazed at his intuition. Perhaps he'd been listening in Cartagena. "Possibly," I said, and turned back to see her once more.

She looked at me again. By this time, her face should have shown discomfort, even concern, but her features were relaxed, slightly inquisitive. I smiled. She returned the smile—I was sure of it this time.

Preston gently pulled me away, escorted me to the street. "Ah, that's better," he said. "Fresh pollution. I'll have to stop dressing for these occasions." He lifted his thousand-dollar lapel.

We walked a few steps in silence. Then, without conscious consideration, I told him, "My grandmother is from Tokyo." Later, I understood why: Preston had to be let in on my subliminal plans. He was not the type to be easily deceived, even if I could say, quite truthfully, that I had little notion of what I sought.

He gave a full-throated laugh and stopped, turning me by the shoulders to face him, the two of us planted like alien art forms in the midst of a suburban street teeming with Japanese housewives and preschoolers. He stopped laughing and lowered his eyebrow. "A grand-mother you've never met?"

"Yes."

"And don't know where she lives, or *if* she lives?"

"Yes."

He placed his thumbs on my temples near the corners of my eyes, which he examined like an owner inspecting his prize thoroughbred, searching for the source of his previously held belief. The women scurrying around us were too polite to give us more than fleeting glances.

Then he said something that was difficult for him to admit: "You surprise me. I like that."

He dropped his hands and turned me by the shoulder, then pushed me gently along the street, his hand in the small of my back.

"Where are we going next?" he asked, his eyes

shining, looking straight ahead.

"Botswana," I said without hesitation.

His stride unbroken, he didn't look at me and said nothing.

Being beautiful isn't easy. A truism to be scoffed at. But some behaviors between people are simply unavoidable, predictable, inescapable.

After four or five years and a string of men, I suddenly became independence minded. While success-fully avoiding enslavement as a condition of entitlement to their material gifts, I gave them the smallest possible measure of what they demanded. In exchange, I was a wealthy woman at twenty-one, but only if I remained in a state of attachment.

So, I broke all ties and tried the obvious choice: modeling. Despite my beauty, or because of it, success wasn't guaranteed. My looks could not be categorized, my allure was too daunting, or too distracting, I couldn't be sure of which. And soon I found, even at my modest level of achievement, that success came with a price: male attachments of another sort.

I changed my plans, convinced I was smart enough to make it in the corporate world even without a degree, training, or experience. I'd fooled men before, and I would fool them again.

With connections from the modeling world, I talked my way into a management position in a cosmetics and health aids firm, a job integrating research and devel-opment with sales. In the beauty industry, a certain amount of glamour was expected, but brains, I figured, would be the deciding factor in my success. I would know the products, learn the regions, study the chains, anticipate the trends, second guess the buyers. My team, the workers below me, would revere my business savvy. My superiors would recognize my contribution to the firm's profits and reward me accordingly.

But my ideas were never implemented, never even heard. I conveyed them and fought for them time and again, while many men (and women) apparently listened with small smiles on their lips, their eyes lost in my hair or face or figure. My clothing and hair style made no difference. Even the plainest business suit screamed in vibrant exultation at being displayed against the push of my magnetic form. My hair, up, invited the fantasy of lips pressed to creamy nape. Down, it caressed my shoulders in the way their hands might cup and curl under my blouse.

After a year, I left the firm without remorse or bitterness but much the wiser, resigned to pursue my true calling in life. I was, and would always remain, someone else's luxury item, an exquisite, expensive decoration in the lives of those who could afford me.

Hours after the implication of my African plan had set in, Preston said, "I suppose we all have a little bit of everything in us."

I said nothing, but he needed reassurance.

"Another grandmother?" he asked.

"No. Grandfather."

"With Tokyo, or…?"

"Yes, with Tokyo."

"Then it's Cartagena and somewhere, someone else."

"Yes."

"Don't tell me now. When the time comes." And in his eyes was the enjoyment of not knowing.

That look told me I'd been right about him all along, about his well-submerged zest for adventure. But he used his convenient cover: "One of my companies is seeking markets in Africa." Botswana, with its stable government and growing economy, presented an opportunity.

We got our shots and bought expensive white cottons and khakis for our African adventure. Stepping off the airplane in Gaborone, I was hit with the smell of heat, sweat, and dust, shocked into wondering, too late, at the purpose of my quest. My face, once considered brown, was suddenly pale. I'd been away from my mother and other dark faces for too long.

But my initial discomfort was quickly dispelled, shown to be purely self-imposed, a reaction to the place, not the people, who were open and accepting. As I looked about me, I saw the injection of Brit and Boer into the blood mix, the lighter shades blending in as easily as a swirl of cream stirred into black coffee. And, as I noticed this, I began to imagine, became certain in fact, that I would see a woman I knew in this place.

This time, I looked for her instead of passively waiting. I searched for her in every face, and the more I searched, the more I began to fear I would sabotage my own objectives.

Within a day, Preston became bored with the town, all business opportunities sized up instantly in his mind with a single glance. It was his turn to surprise me. "Let's go on a photographic safari," he suggested.

I was caught off guard, something that never happened. I'd underestimated the adventurer in him.

"I've seen giraffes and elephants in the zoo," I told him, thinking only of my own needs: to see the people, to feel myself in them, and now I knew, to see *her* again.

"You look nervous about it," he said, stroking my hair. We were in bed. "You're a little scared."

"No, it's not that…," I started to protest.

He pulled me closer. "You don't have to worry. It's perfectly safe. We stay in the truck." His hand moved to the top of my head again and gently smoothed my hair, following its course to my shoulders, down the length of my back. I trembled for him—to preserve his fantasy. The trembling came easily. I'd been forgetting my end of our implicit agreement, and his reminder filled me with resentment. But I couldn't risk being left stranded. I hadn't finished what I'd started.

"And the truck drives away when they stampede?" I asked, putting the child in my eyes and voice.

"Yes. There's nothing to worry about."

"All right then."

And so, we bought big cameras and got in the back of an open truck with several other tourists. We crept up on big animals while we clicked and grew sweatier and dustier, and I grew more irritated at Preston, this new aspect of him that Africa seemed to be spawning. As his fascination with the hunt swelled, so did his primal urge to protect, to be Man to my Woman. On his cue, I exclaimed and pressed hand to heart at all the appropriate times, thinking all the while what an interesting death I might have under a herd of stampeding elephants.

Back at our hotel the next day, Preston's adrenaline receding, he turned to me, looking for his savior from boredom. "We can do better than this," he said, referring to our four-star accommodations, which, in Gaborone, fell far short of Preston's needs. He could rough it for only so long. "It's time for you to tell me where we're going next."

Laughing, I tried to change the subject, but he wouldn't back down. "I count three grandparents. There should be another, a grandmother. Where is she? Or where is she not?"

"Sweden," I said, and his face beamed with relief. Soon, we would be back in civilization and understandable English, living the high life.

I had only a little time to find her, maybe half a day or less. Preston moved quickly. After he made the arrangements on his phone, I suggested a walk. We went to the Mall, a shop-lined esplanade in the center of town, where hawkers peddled their wares. I was drawn to a neat pile of palm-leaf baskets with geometric designs, woven by Tswana women. I picked one up, put it down again, straightened up, and saw her, and then saw her again in the face of the woman next to her. Their features, so similar but not identical, told me they were sisters. Their complexions, slightly darker than mine, were the outward sign of mixture.

One of them stooped to pick up the basket I had just held. She admired it and showed it to her sister. They were only two or three feet away from me. Their clothes distinguished them as professionals: modern, neat, and tailored, unlike the ill-fitting skirts and blouses worn by so many women in Gaborone.

I stared blatantly. Preston, slightly behind and to my side, gave an audible sigh and crossed his arms across his chest. The woman holding the basket suddenly stopped talking and looked at me.

"You wanted this one?" she asked in heavily accented English, her face open and friendly. The question fell from her tongue loosely, as though she was accustomed to free, uncalculated expression.

I stammered a bit, my eyes fixed on hers, my mouth finally forming the words, "No—no thank you." Preston's shadow bore down on me, and I ripped my eyes from the woman to judge his reaction. He looked at her, looked at me, looked at her again.

"Good!" She laughed. "I like this one!" Her sister smiled broadly, the two women simultaneously displaying their shared heritage of familial warmth, a bond between them.

Smiling at them for the last time, I tore myself away without waiting for Preston's lead. We snaked through the crowd.

"Don't tell me," he said. "Those were your third cousins, twice removed. Your mother used to show you pictures."

"You could be right," I said. "But, no, I've never seen pictures."

"We'll just pretend then. Will that make you happy? They resembled you a bit, you know."

My surprise was dampened by the mild interest in his voice, dragging under the weight of his blasé intonation. I knew then that he had begun to tire of (what he regarded as) my game.

In Stockholm, as Preston gradually drifted away, I felt like the Swedes during their daily, creeping descent into darkness, newly begun, yearly repeating. It was late October and colder and darker than we wanted it to be. Preston spent many hours on his phone, many hours not looking at me.

His drifting didn't alarm me. I was qualified to say I was well used to it in him, for although I'd known him only two months, he was the man I'd been with for sixteen years. I was experienced, hardened, immune— things I tried to prove with my sharp tongue and burning eyes.

I paced the thick carpet of our suite, my evening heels stabbing holes in its bush. I halted, drumming hard, red nails against mahogany. He said, "Just a minute," into his cell phone and looked up at me, one eyebrow lowered. "Something wrong, Renee?" he asked me.

"It's 8:15."

"Oh?"

"You've forgotten. Our reservation was at 8:00. You're not even dressed."

He looked away for a moment and turned his eyes on me again. "I think you're the one who's forgotten. We'll go when I'm ready. You can do what you want until then. Go out and look for another lost cousin." He looked down and talked into the phone again.

I started to leave, stopped, went back into the bed-room and changed. A beautiful woman in an evening dress attracts too much attention. I peeled off my outer layer of cold black sheen, wiped the red from my lips, and pulled my hair back into an austere bun. I covered my body in thick clothing, hiding it as best I could.

His mouth still going, he followed me with his eyes as I stepped out of the bedroom and walked toward the front door. Our eyes locked. I pressed two fingers to my lips and blew a kiss. He kept talking, his eyes staring vacantly at me as I left.

I hopped taxis, roamed the city. Shopped at a department store until it closed, ate in a modest café, went to an American movie and left in the middle, sat in a dark corner of a piano bar. I pretended not to look for my "lost cousin," suspecting my motive in every one of my actions, hating it, looking at faces, abruptly avoiding curious eyes.

By the time I returned to the hotel, I had no hope of seeing him again. Nor any desire. I looked for and saw, almost immediately, the note lying in the middle of the coffee table. A single piece of paper, unfolded, thick, a cream color, softly absorbing the blue ink of his fountain pen. Next to it, an envelope. There was always an envelope. This one contained one thousand dollars in cash and a plane ticket to California. Preston had been called to an "important meeting" in New York and (regrettably) would be unable to accompany me home.

Shrinking to the carpet, I became a single piece of its wool fiber. The floor stretched infinitely to walls that slid off the curve of the earth.

Finally, I walked to the bedroom, tried to sleep, could not. Packed and checked out before dark had ended.

At the airport, I was unlucky. A six-hour wait until the next flight to San Francisco. I considered picking another destination but had no choice really. In San Francisco I maintained an apartment.

Sitting in the airport cafeteria, numb to my surroundings, I became certain at last of my search— rooted in a hidden dream—remaining uncertain of its meaning or objective. And then, another woman I knew sat down at the table next to mine. A man took the chair across the table from her.

Clarity blasted through the fuzzy edges of my world, rendering her face in relief against a recessed backdrop. She sipped a cup of coffee and looked into the eyes of her man. He stretched a hand toward hers, fondled it on the tabletop. Two gleaming wedding bands.

I was staring again; I couldn't help it. Like me, she was a woman accustomed to staring eyes. Her beauty was unique, remarkable, and not distinctly Swedish, not be-longing to any one race or culture.

She turned her head slowly. Our eyes met. Only a few feet separated our small tables, making conversation possible. My mouth groped for words. She smiled at me and waited, seeming to understand the significance of my struggle.

"I'm sorry," I said finally, pursing my lips briefly to calm my quivering mouth. "Is it…is it possible we've met before?"

Her face remained calm and pleasant—omniscient— but devoid of recognition. "No. I don't think it is possible," she said in near-perfect English with the slightest, lilting accent. "Have you been to Stockholm many times?"

"No, this is my first time."

"Then we did not meet before. I do not travel much. But now," she beamed at her husband, "we are going to the Canary Islands. Our marriage trip."

"Your honeymoon?"

"Yes," she said, still looking at her man, and she said something to him in Swedish. For her, our conversation was over, but I couldn't turn away. On the verge of tears, my eyes opened wider to her as if she could dry the moisture in them or soften the knot of despair in my chest.

She couldn't avoid my eyes. Without a trace of annoyance or alarm, she turned to me again. "Are you from the United States?" she asked softly. Her husband regarded me quizzically.

"Yes, but—" I was suddenly ashamed, fearful that my tears would spill.

"Are you on your way home now?"

I nodded and said nothing.

"Where is your family, your home?"

I fumbled for my bag under the table, found it with my hand and stood, awkwardly bumping the table, toppling the Styrofoam cup with the remainder of my tea. "Excuse me," I said. "It was so nice to…well, goodbye!"

On the way to my gate, faces in the corridor shimmered in waves behind my tears. In my mind, the only visible faces were theirs: the woman balancing the basket of plantains, the housewife holding her children, the woman brushing shoulders with her sister, the recent bride with her new husband. Task, purpose, family. All of them beautiful, different, alien to their lands, yet belonging.

These were women I knew—had so convinced myself of that belief—when all they had to do was look in my eyes to see through my illusion. They'd been trying to tell me something with their open looks and polite smiles. Trying to tell me that I'd never met them and didn't know them. Didn't really know them at all.

ဢ Ninety Degrees

ONE DAY I CAME home and Al was watching TV in the living room with someone, looked like one of his buddies from work. Both still had on their sweaty tank tops and jeans coated with dust. All that dirt on the seats of their pants to push down into the furniture, not that I'm such a great housekeeper but it bothers you sometimes.

Al's friend was a little different though because when he stood up (he got up when I came in) the seat of his pants looked a whole lot cleaner than Al's. His armpits less sweaty too. Later I learned it's because he's working the backhoe most of the time and not down spreading the gravel.

"This is Pike," said Al, not looking away from the TV.

Pike nodded his head at me, standing there. He almost looked like he was going to put his hand out, but he didn't. "So, you're Tammy," he said.

"Wouldn't be anyone else, I guess." But I smiled. I couldn't help seeing he was good looking. His hair was a little long and he had these small curlicues around the edges of his face and a diamond stud in one of his ears.

"Nice to meet you," he said.

I just smiled again, and he sat down on the couch. Al was on the Lazy Boy. I decided to reach in front of Pike for the cigarettes and lighter on the coffee table. I felt his eyes looking at me, but I didn't give him the satisfaction of looking back. I just wanted a cigarette and it was a good enough reason to keep me in the room. Not that I wanted to see the game. One of those preseason games, the Patriots and someone else, everyone sweating in ninety degrees pretending they're getting ready for the fall. I wasn't about to sit on the couch next to Pike and there wasn't anywhere else so I lighted the cigarette and propped up on an arm of the couch. That way I could reach the ashtray on the table if I had to.

There was a touchdown and Al let out a hoot. Pike hooted and whistled too, but not quite as loud. "Hey, Tam, get us some beers, will you?" Al still didn't look my way, all part of his Man of the House routine.

There was an empty beer bottle on the coffee table in front of Pike and an empty on the floor where Al's arm dangled down from the side. So he knew how to get his own beer when I wasn't around. That's what made me mad. I ignored him at first, but then he said it again. "Hey, Tam! We're getting dry here."

"Get your own goddamn beers," I said, still smiling because Pike was sitting right there.

"I'm fine," said Pike, and he crossed his hands in the air and sliced them apart like flattening a shirt on an ironing board.

I looked at Pike and kind of laughed. "Acts like I'm his wife."

"Really, nothing for me at all. Thanks." He smiled and his teeth seemed very white, but their skin gets so dark out there in the sun all day, even if you're in that little cab of the backhoe most of the time.

I felt kind of bad then, because I almost wanted to get Pike a beer, but he *did* look like he meant it when he said he didn't want anything. Finally a commercial came on and Al got up to get the beers himself. He didn't look at me then either.

While Al was out of the room, Pike said, "My TV is on the fritz so Al invited me over. Hope you don't mind."

"No, why should I? It's his TV." And it was. If we split up tomorrow, that's the first thing he'd take.

"This is kind of an important game."

I couldn't see how anything preseason was important, but I didn't want to offend him, so I said, "Only game I watch is the Super Bowl." By then, Al was back in the room, handing a beer to Pike.

Halfway through, I was getting hungry and my hip was cramping where I was propped on the arm so I went to the kitchen to start cooking. I could have eaten at MK's but I was so sick of it. Al knew what I was up to; you can hear everything in our little apartment. He yelled at me over the roaring crowd: "Pike's staying for dinner!"

"Oh," I said, but I doubt he heard me. I stood there looking down into the kitchen sink for a minute before I went to the freezer and pulled out two TV dinners. They *were* watching TV, I figured.

That was a long job, months that might stretch to years. They were repaving at least forty miles of interstate, with orders to keep going that summer no matter how hot it was. Al used to come home stinking like a caveman, cussing, dripping on the floor, complaining we lived in an oven. "Just because you don't want to go fifty-fifty on AC!" I didn't think it was that hot and I wasn't going to spend my money on an air conditioner that you use only a few months, even if Al said he could find a good one for two hundred, making my share only a hundred.

I was in a job I didn't particularly like either. I really blew it when I left Smokey's where I'd been working for seven years and everyone knew me to take this job at Mom's Kitchen, home cooking and "Baking Done on Premises," and family dining and all that, a big step up in prices from the diner, so I figured, naturally, the tips are going to be much higher.

I'm on the job only a couple of weeks when I can see the tips aren't going to happen, and the base is the same so I don't have any extra money to show for the aggravation of working with a couple of people I'd call real snots. My schedule was all screwed up, sometimes working breakfast and lunch, other times working dinners. And I wasn't wild about the Dutch girl outfit with the white ruffley apron, even if Al and I had fun with it a couple of times, me wearing it without the dress underneath. Two times is still sexy, but it gets old the third time around.

I could've come home every day doing my own complaining, but his was always louder and then he would've complained about my mouth. "Bitching and moaning," he'd call it.

That's one good thing happened when Pike started

coming around. Al's moods lightened up a little. Still there, but less irritating. During commercials he had Pike to complain to, and they knew what they were talking about because they'd both been there. The sun burning them up, that lazy-ass flag girl causing accidents, the boss moving so-and-so from graveling to blacktop. "Guess I'll always be a no-good gravel man," Al would say, and Pike would try to coax him to go to heavy equipment school. So, there were some good things about having Pike around and that's why I never said anything to Al about it.

Actually, there was one girl at Mom's who wasn't half bad. Slow times, we'd take cigarette breaks together. Her name was Margie.

One day around this time we were out back smoking by the dumpster. With all these no-smoking laws, that's the only place Al would let us smoke. Can you believe it? My boss's name is Al. I have an Al at work and an Al at home telling me what to do. That's how Margie knew I had an Al at home because I mentioned the bit about their names being the same.

"So, what does your husband do anyway?" she asked me. It was at least ninety and the dumpster was stinking with waves floating out the top but we had to have a smoke.

"My old man you mean?" Couple of years ago I started calling Al my "old man" because the word "boyfriend" sounded stupid. I'm twenty-nine now and still can't decide which word sounds better.

"You're not married?"

"No, just shacking up." That also sounded kind of stupid. I pretended to wave a fly away between us but really I was looking at Margie, trying to see what she thought of the whole thing. Most people I meet completely agree with me, there's no reason to have that piece of paper, especially if you don't want any kids, and Al says he never wants any little brats even though I'm keeping an open mind on it. For right now anyway it's best to keep our freedom.

But Margie might've thought different. She was older than me, maybe thirty-five, divorced with two kids, ten and twelve. She'd gone the whole traditional route, it just didn't work out for her. And she was devoted to those kids. She'd been working at MK's long enough that she could choose her shift, the earliest one Monday through Friday, so she could get home as early as possible and also have the weekends with them.

"So, your old man, where does he work?" she asked. I still couldn't tell what she was thinking.

"He's in highway construction. Right now he's working on the interstate."

"That big mess out there?" She nodded in the general direction.

"Yeah."

"Bet that's a union job."

"Right, it's union."

"Good pay and benefits."

"Pretty good I guess. He's just a gravel man though."

"Gravel?"

"You know, the layer of gravel under the asphalt. They dump it and he spreads it."

Margie dragged hard on her cigarette, dropped it, and toed it out on the ground. She didn't say anything for a minute and I thought she was about ready to go back in. But then she said, "You know, whether you swore in front of a preacher or not, you're still a wife doing the cooking and cleaning. Only difference is, you miss out on his job benefits." She looked at me, not like I was stupid exactly. Maybe I just felt that way. She looked at me like she knew what she was saying. Still, I had my arguments.

"But I don't need anything. I get medical here."

"Sure, but his medical is better, right?" I had to kind of nod at that. "And if anything happens to him, you're nobody. You get nothing."

I thought of Pike putting the backhoe in reverse, Al standing behind. The flag girl messing up and Al clipped by a speeding car. Things can go wrong. I hadn't thought of the money.

But nothing like that ever happens to me. If we got married, more likely I'd end up divorced than widowed. Legal fees, no benefits. No alimony from Al. That's what I told Margie because she had a point in some ways but I had a point too. Then I said something I felt bad about later because Margie's been so nice to me compared to the others. "Getting married didn't get *you* anywhere," I said. Then I tried to take it back a little. "I mean, if he's still alive and kicking, you can't force him to pay you."

She didn't look angry; she just looked like what I said was nothing new to her. "He sends me a check some-times. And I have the right to go after him if I want. I can get him arrested. It's just too messy and I don't want to drag my kids through that." She didn't look at me and turned her head a little. That's when I saw she was hurting. "You're right, though," she said. "It would've been a whole lot better if he'd've died."

After that, I was constantly feeling like "the wife." Margie had put this idea in my head and then Pike was doing things to show Al for what he was. Even that first night.

After they finished their TV dinners, Pike came into the kitchen during a commercial. I was sitting at the table, eating a sandwich. Pike was carrying the forks and foil trays and saying, "Where's the garbage?" I pointed to it and he went and dumped the trays. Then he went to the sink and rinsed out the forks and put them in the strainer. I just sat there watching him. He finished and walked from the sink to the table and said, "Thanks for the food. Those fried chicken dinners are my favorite."

"Glad you liked it," I said.

"I'll get the empties." He winked and his diamond flashed a sparkle.

The commercials were still going, so he came back with the four bottles and rinsed them out at the sink. While he was rinsing he said, "You recycle these, don't you?"

Sometimes I do and sometimes I don't, but I said, "Sure. Thanks." And he winked again as he passed by on the way back to the living room.

I started cooking real food after that, macaroni and cheese and hamburgers. I couldn't feed a man like that just TV dinners. Every time he'd clean up later, even though I was messing a lot of pans. Usually it wasn't too bad though because I tried to clean up as I went along. I tried to keep the mess down because I felt a little funny about it, Pike coming into the kitchen later, usually during the commercials, cleaning up after me. Still, it was nice.

Usually they'd be in front of the TV. There was the football preseason and the baseball end of the season and when there wasn't a game there were the sitcoms. A lot of times I ate in the kitchen and took their dinners to the living room. Pike would set up the TV trays and get the forks and napkins. Al wouldn't say a thing or lift a finger.

That was when things started to get regular, but still there were days Pike didn't come over, and some days I didn't know whether he'd been there or not. Whenever I worked the dinner shift I left the apartment at three thirty, right before they got home.

But one day after the lunch shift I walked in the front door and heard voices but the TV wasn't on. I walked into the kitchen and Al was leaning an elbow on the counter with a beer dangling off the other hand and Pike stepped away from him and looked up at me like he'd just been telling Al a secret. I didn't hear what they said. Just those low voices, a little different than I'm used to because they were always so loud. At least Al was anyway. He could make up in loudness for two of anybody.

Pike gave me one of those smiles when I walked in. "Tammy! How was your day?" He was like that.

"Oh, great. A little brat knocked his milk over on me." I pointed at my skirt where it was still wet. "And someone's been stealing my tips. I know who it is but I can't prove it."

"That's tough, Tam," said Pike. He looked like he

cared. Al didn't look one way or the other, but at least he didn't say anything about "bitching and moaning."

"Yeah, well…," I said.

"That's tough. But Tammy's a tough girl."

"Yeah, I'm tough."

"Tough Tam." He smiled and winked. Boy, that Pike could wink.

Then we started talking about dinner and Pike said he'd cook. My jaw might've dropped a mile but I put my hand over it.

"Hard to believe a man can cook?"

"No, not really."

"The best chefs in the world are men."

"Go right ahead." He *did* have the confidence for it.

So Al and I sat at the kitchen table and drank beers while Pike cooked. First, he poked around the kitchen to see what we had. Not much because Al hadn't given me his food money that week and I hadn't done the shopping for a while, but Pike found some crazy things to do. Like put the canned corn and cayenne pepper in the eggs and crumbled-up shredded wheat in the salad. Other things were just normal, like the chicken noodle soup and the frozen fries he baked in the oven. Actually, everything turned out pretty good and a whole lot better than MK's.

The kitchen was hotter than ninety from all the cooking and our little table seemed real filled up with three people around it and all the dishes Pike was using. Dinner plates for the eggs and potatoes, salad plates, soup bowls, tall glasses for iced tea, a plate of sandwich bread in the middle next to the tub of margarine, the ketchup and salt and pepper.

We sat there sweating around all of it but smiling and laughing. Even Al.

"This is a lot of stuff," I said, not meaning to be critical.

"Variety is the thing," said Pike. "I always like a little variety." I made a point then and there to be more various in my cooking next time.

"It's real good," I said. I liked the soup the best but didn't say anything because all he did was open the can and heat it.

"You sure can burn," said Al.

Pike looked at Al like he appreciated the compliment. "Yeah, variety is it."

We talked and laughed a lot. Al told a story about someone during lunch break dumping a blob of chocolate pudding in someone's hard hat and what it looked like when he put it on.

"That would never happen to you," said Pike. He turned to me. "This man doesn't wear his hard hat."

"No kidding."

"Never. I tell him to."

"He won't do anything you tell him."

"Never."

"But don't worry. His head is already hard enough." Pike and I laughed.

Al piped up then. "It's too damn hot to wear that thing."

"Doesn't matter to me," I said.

"Don't care if your old man gets hit with a two ton brick. What'd I tell you Pike?"

"If you're dead, you're dead. I won't collect a thing

one way or the other."

They both looked at me then, and maybe we'd had a few too many beers but we just burst out laughing all over the scrambled eggs. I never had much of a family so I'm no expert, but something felt kind of family-ish about the whole thing, more than just if me and Al were sitting at the table together.

After dinner, Al got up and went into the living room. Pike started clearing the table.

"You cooked, so I should clean up," I said.

"No, I'll do it. You never make a mess like this." But I started clearing too and doing things like wiping down the counters while he washed the dishes. Truth was, I wanted to be in the kitchen with him instead of in the living room with Al. I heard the TV blaring in there. "Where'd you learn to cook?" I asked.

"I watch my mom. Sometimes I cook for her."

"Oh. You visit her?"

"I live there. I'm in between apartments right now."

I didn't say anything for a while, just started wiping down the stove. In a way it made sense, Pike living with his mom, even though I never would've thought it up myself. Finally I said, "Anyway, you can come cook for me anytime." I laughed to make it like a joke so he could take it however he wanted. "Al doesn't do any of this stuff."

I was right up next to Pike because there's only about a foot of counter between the stove and sink. He turned his head to look at me. My face felt greasy and damp and I know it looked that way. "But he does other things for you—am I right?"

I just looked in his eyes. They were the lightest color brown I'd ever seen.

"And he does those other things well, no?"

I smiled but couldn't say anything, feeling greasy and wishing I'd gone to wash my face.

Later that night after Pike went home, Al jumped on me, but it was different. As usual, he wasn't looking at me, but he wasn't looking at me in another direction. I finished before he did, and then it seemed he just gave up and rolled over.

The whole time I kept seeing Pike's face and wondering if he did those other things well too.

I was thinking about him so much I was getting real curious. So curious that I even took the long way around to work one day. I took the interstate.

I was on the dinner shift and didn't have to leave home until three thirty but I left an hour early to give me the time. I figured if Al saw me I could always say I needed to do some shopping at the mall which was right off an exit near where he was working. If he really noticed me, I could wave and say I was just passing by to say "hi." Nothing wrong with that.

When I got close, I started to regret it. Traffic was tied up for two miles and I'd be late for work. I put on the radio and hummed along, trying not to stare at every man in a hard hat. Along the traffic jam there were just a few, most of them concentrated up ahead where the flag girl was slowing us down.

When I finally got up to her, I couldn't believe it. This was the flag girl they always talked about, had to be, because I didn't see but one other girl there and she wasn't flagging. This was the "lazy-ass" flag girl but I didn't see a lazy ass. Her ass was moving and everyone was looking, and you bet, the cars slowed down, not to keep the construction men safe but to get an eyeful of her. That was the part I didn't get. Why Al and Pike never let out a hoot when they were talking about that girl.

We narrowed down to one lane to the side of the paving crew. Heat was rippling up from the ground. I knew I would go right past them and be so close they could see me but they didn't seem to be looking at the cars. They had their work to do. And I was right. They didn't look in my direction and I'm sure they didn't see me.

First I saw Al with the other gravel spreaders out with their rakes, smoothing a pile of it into an even layer. Dust and sweat everywhere. Al wasn't wearing his hard hat and his back was to me up until I passed him and had him in my rearview. He didn't look up.

Just ahead of him was Pike up in the backhoe, moving back and forth between a huge pile of gravel on the side where he scooped up some in the shovel and then back to the gravel spreaders where he dumped the load in front of them at a good enough distance they didn't get clobbered. I kept my eyes on him, it was easy enough going so slow, and he was into his work, moving those levers and handles up in the cab, the muscles on his bare arms flexing. He was in my rearview for a while after I passed him until the car behind me honked and I had to speed up.

All the way to work and even during work I was

thinking about his arm muscles.

Sometime after that, when I was on breakfast and lunch with Margie, I told her about Pike. Truth was, I'd started getting a little obsessed, but I wouldn't tell her that. I just kept it to some of the good things, like his cooking and cleaning and acting like he cared about me, while I left out the dreams. Some of the dreams were just me and Pike, some were with the three of us together. It was all getting pretty skanky. But I wouldn't say things like that to Margie.

Margie wasn't too impressed with Pike. All she said was, "Now you've got two men to shop and cook for."

"But Pike cooks."

"Once."

"He'll do it again. He likes to cook. He cooks for his mom."

"His mom?" Margie thought that was a good one. "His mom doesn't cook a lick and that's why he comes to your house. Now you have *two* men waiting for you to come home and cook."

I didn't really see it that way and I told Margie so because I could just as easy tell them to go out for pizza.

"But you haven't."

"No, but..."

"What you should do is just not be available. I mean, you've got a life too, right?"

"Right."

"And Al's spending all this time with his buddy, so why don't you go out and spend some time with your friends?"

I could see her point, and so right then and there I asked Margie if she wanted to go see a movie with me or something. I'd been meaning to ask her anyway. But then she went on and on about how hard it was to get a sitter and how Cathy, I think that's her name, is really an immature twelve-year-old and so Margie doesn't feel comfortable yet leaving her there alone at night with her little brother even though some of her friends are already going out and babysitting themselves, but why don't I come over to her house for dinner? She'd like the company and it would be just the women and kids, no men to bother us and we could pitch in together and whip up a meal easy as can be.

I ended up accepting the invitation for that same evening, and so, while I was still at work, I called home and left a message on the machine for Al (I almost said something about what was in the fridge to eat but thought, screw it, he and Pike can fend for themselves). Margie gave me the directions and went straight home after work, and I stopped at the supermarket first to get half the things for dinner, some Italian bread and lettuce and cukes for salad. She already had the spaghetti, a jar of sauce, and the cheese at home because that's the only thing she can get her kids to eat.

When I got there I really could see why she had mentioned the bit about Cathy being so immature. The girl was a real whiner, and the boy, B.J., was a pain in the ass, always teasing the girl and taking her things until she started whining to her mother again.

The dinner tasted good but I ended up losing my appetite what with the two kids grabbing the sprinkle cheese at the same time and fighting over it and screaming, Mom he did this, and Mom she did that, and with B.J.'s face full of red sauce from shoveling the noodles into his mouth worse than Al does. A real eye opener. Made me wonder why Margie wanted to rush home every night.

Later, when the kids were in the other room watching TV, Margie said she was sorry for their behavior and explained it was kind of an "off" day for them because Cathy had a big disappointment that day not making it into the "A" swim team which goes to compete at the state level and B.J. had gone to the nurse at his summer camp complaining of a headache from God knows what.

All in all, I could take Margie a lot better without her kids but I didn't say that and just left at nine o'clock, saying I was sure she'd have to give those kids a good night's sleep what with all the problems they'd been having that day. When I left, half of me was saying to myself that it was early enough for Pike to still be there, if he came that day, but when I walked in the front door, all I heard was Al in the bedroom talking on the phone. I heard him say something like, "We have to talk about this," and "Tammy's home," before he hung up and walked out of the bedroom into the hall where I was standing.

"Have fun?" he asked kind of accusing me. But his voice wasn't as loud as usual.

"I was just at Margie's house," I said. I don't know why I thought I had to explain myself. Anyway, he dropped it without saying another word and looked almost like he couldn't care whether I was lying or telling the truth. He actually looked kind of bad, walking around in his shorts with his hair plastered in funny directions like he'd been lying down. His eyes were bloodshot too.

"Did Pike come over?" I asked.

Al looked at me like he was about to get angry. "No, why should he?"

"I don't know." I shuffled off to the kitchen then stopped. The whole thing was strange. "Something happen between you two?" I asked.

Al looked annoyed and shrugged his shoulders. He went back into the bedroom and I went into the kitchen for a snack because my appetite was back. I hadn't eaten all that much spaghetti.

The next morning I should've slept in to get a little extra rest because that night I was back on dinners and would leave late, getting back home around midnight. But I got up at five thirty. For one, I couldn't sleep with Al all over the bed. Those hot nights were the worst, him sweating all over the place and laying his big hairy sweaty leg on top of mine when he's so asleep he doesn't know what he's doing. That was bad enough but around three in the morning after I finally got to sleep for a while he was completely gone. Not in the bed. I got up to go to the bathroom and he wasn't in there either or in the living room or kitchen. Completely gone.

It made me wonder where he was, not that I cared so much because the way things had been going I think I was questioning the whole live-together situation as it was. Maybe I should've told him we had to get married and lay down some rules or that was the end of it. Maybe all I really wanted to do was come on to Pike and see what came of that.

They say you want to come on to your old man's best friend sometimes not because you really want the best friend but because you want your old man's attention. You're hurting for some reason and that's the only way you can think of to let him know that. I hadn't figured it out one way or another. It almost seemed to me that I really *did* want Pike.

I went back to bed and slept a little but finally got up at five thirty and couldn't fall back asleep. I had no idea where he was, not that I cared. And it was one of those eerie not-quite-in-yourself days all day and through the evening when I was working because I constantly had this feeling that something was gone.

I was dead tired when I got home around midnight and first thing I knew when I walked in the door, I wasn't alone. I heard the voices and almost like giggling sounds coming from the bedroom. I dropped my handbag in the hall and started to walk to the bedroom door. There were some more quick noises and a squeak from the bed and all of a sudden Al was out in the hallway, closing the door behind him. His hand was in front of him holding a towel gathered up and wrapped around his waist and his hair was pushed in funny like the night before, but he looked completely different, better, a little smile on his lips and clear, wide-awake eyes. The skin on his chest and arms was sweaty.

"Wait a minute," he said, blocking the bedroom door.

"What's going on?"

"Pike just got out of the shower and he's changing."

"Pike?"

Some more noises were going on inside, and then Pike opened the door, a big smile on his face. He had no shirt on but at least he was wearing his jeans, still dirty from the day's work, and he was sweating too. This was sweat on both of them, not water from the shower. Behind him, through the open door, I could see the bed in a total mess, the covers half on the floor.

A bunch of things were rushing in my head. I thought of all the other times I'd come home at midnight, Pike not there, me wondering whether he'd been to the apartment that night while I was gone. I tried to remember what the bed looked like.

Then I remembered myself on the interstate looking at Al's back and Pike's arm muscles, and all of a sudden I imagined Al climbing up into the cab with Pike and Pike steering the backhoe in a U-turn around my car, doing a complete one-eighty, the two of them riding away in the opposite direction from me.

Pike saw my mind jumping and he smiled at me. "Hi, Tam! How was your day? Sure is hot."

"Must be at least ninety," said Al.

"More like a hundred," said Pike.

"Can't be more than ninety," said Al. "I can't take it much hotter than that."

They were both looking at me with those glittering eyes like I was a joke.

"Too hot for me," I said, and I turned around, sure I was headed somewhere, not knowing exactly where, but as far as I could get.

"Wait a minute, Tammy!" said Al like he meant it, but it was too late.

"Wait, Tam. Al still loves you," I heard Pike say. "That's the problem, he still loves you…"

But I was out the door by then.

✑ The Cost of Ice Cream

A WOMAN PUSHED her cart through the produce section in the supermarket. At hand's reach, inside the empty toddler seat, she'd arranged the newspaper specials and her wobbly, flaccid purse. She moved slower than other women her age—she'd declined considerably since her husband's death—yet, at eighty-seven, she was still well and agile enough to shuffle through her marketing, provided the cart never got too full. And it never did, now that her shrunken body and appetite exerted only modest demands.

Still, eat she must. The senior bus had dropped her with three other ladies from their building, ones she didn't much care for, women with different appetites and tastes, so they'd parted ways in the supermarket, nothing to discuss. Her special friend, not feeling well that day, hadn't come along, but had given instructions beforehand: "I'll be fine, really I will, if I can just do some cooking later. Please pick up a chicken, a very small roaster, the smallest they have." She'd handed her a wrinkled five-dollar bill with the suggestion, "Bring back as much change as you can."

Thinking of her friend, the woman interrupted her own needs and fretted a long while in the poultry section. Standing there, considering the chickens, she felt an itch under her chin and a drop of water on her cheek and remembered the plastic rain hat atop her head. Despite the annoyance, she wouldn't remove it while shopping. The effort—the untying and folding, and later the unfolding and tying up again—was more than she could handle, and she didn't want to risk tearing it, wasting the fifty cents she'd spent on a hat that could serve for at least three or four rain storms. So many wet, miserable days, stiffening her joints.

Time grew short. Head blurry, she had difficulty keeping a schedule, and it made little sense to look at her watch, a relic from an earlier life that frequently went unwound. But she was reminded of the passage of time when one of the other women, one of the three, strolled by the meat counter with nothing better to do than remark behind her back, "You know, it's twenty-five minutes to twelve already," before ambling on again.

Pickup time was noon, and the store was busy, and decisions were tough, so she didn't need the added worry of time limits, especially since the bus driver was under strict orders never to leave without completing a head count, as if they were on a grammar school field trip. Six times out of ten it didn't matter anyway—he was the late one. Still, if he was made to wait for her, there would be the unpleasantness of encountering his narrowed, puffy eyes as he leaned forward to look down the bus steps, fat belly sandwiching the wheel.

The chickens, all of them, were too big, most of

them more than five dollars, a few less. Her friend loved plenty of leftovers, sandwiches for days, but still, one of these roasters would be too much, wouldn't it? Half of it going to spoil. Perhaps a package of chicken parts for less money, but no, that just wasn't the same as a roaster, and her friend did so love a whole, roasted chicken. She thought of her friend's face, the lopsided smile, marred by the stroke.

She put on her glasses, threading the stems under the rain hat and over her ears, and sorted through a heap of slaughtered birds, looking at the weights and prices. It took some time, moving them one by one, using two tremulous hands for each, placing them individually on top of the chicken breasts, ruining the butcher's deliberate organization and knowing she'd have to put them all back again. There, at the very bottom, was the least expensive one at a price of $4.26.

Her decision made, and the fowl reorganization accomplished, she pushed away and looked down. At the bottom of her cart, next to the chicken, was a single head of lettuce and two bananas; the rest of her shopping, and more decisions, still lay ahead. She needed a quart of skim milk, a can of tuna fish, and sandwich bread. Corn flakes, and a particular brand of cranberry juice were on sale, and she was sure, with careful planning, that the fifteen dollars in her purse would cover all these things, with the hope, in the back of her mind, for something sweet besides. Ice cream bars, vanilla with a hard shell of chocolate.

The usual items, the ones she always bought, weren't difficult. But, as so often happens, the sale brands weren't immediately visible. Time and again she consulted her newspaper, looked at the photographs, read the brand names and sale prices all typed neatly in small print inside the rectangular coupons bordered with dotted lines and little icons of scissors. She tried to match the descriptions with what she found, thinking that the most likely cereal box seemed too small, convinced that the appropriate juice brand was out of reach on the top shelf, finally asking, nicely, a tall gentleman, if he could reach it for her. With time surely expired, she made one last stop in the frozen section, picked the sweet she wanted, and started for checkout.

She would be late, she knew, and she wasn't a spiteful person, but after all, how many times had *she* waited? How many times had she finished her shopping on time, only to stand outside with melting ice cream, waiting for that man to return from a trip to the donut shop?

At checkout, she chose the shortest line, settled in place, and looked around for the other women from her building. They seemed to have disappeared, nowhere to be seen, but presently she spied two of them, emerging together from a checkout further down, bagged groceries in their shared cart. They'd gone together and had finished together. The third woman was some distance off near the exit door, sitting on the window ledge next to a cart with two full bags, her expression set in a grimace of waiting, waiting for them. The other two were now slowly pushing toward her, arranging their cart in the aisle out of traffic's way, deciding where to sit—this side or that?—pulling skirts in around thighs and lowering themselves one notch at a time. With a final jolt, they were down on either side of the first woman on the ledge.

Three crows, perched and waiting. Through the floor-to-ceiling plate glass window, the old woman saw the bus driver, just pulling up.

A woman pushed her cart through the produce section of the supermarket. She moved with the speed and dexterity of youth, sinewy strong at forty from regular exercise. Her cart was near capacity, the added items threatening to topple. She always shopped for produce next to last, even though it was the first section in the store, to prevent squashing the tomatoes and bananas under a pyramid of beverage cartons. Frozen foods were last, a successful plan if the wait in line wasn't too long.

She moved quickly with little thought, accustomed to the weight of the cart and the weight of maintaining multiple lists in her head, adroit in the art of accomplishing the impossible in five minutes or less. Apples, oranges, bananas, broccoli, beans, potatoes, lettuce, cucumbers, carrots. She needed every kind of fruit and vegetable, added to the mound of every other kind of food, maximum ten percent junk, the treats, rewards, and bribes. Cost didn't matter. Food was food, and it must be purchased in sufficient quantities and eaten up and more bought and eaten every couple of days without stop, the money not a concern, not when it came to food anyway. The children, now ten and thirteen, their mouths opening on bottomless wells, didn't stop eating and she wouldn't stop buying. It made little sense to study bargain brands and sales. She hadn't the time for it, and the few dollars saved in nickels and dimes could easily be made up elsewhere. One less trip to the movies.

With two half-gallons of ice cream balanced on top, she searched for a line and found the best one, behind an old lady wearing a dime-store rain cap, only a few items in her cart and one other person ahead of them both, going through checkout now. She debated, glanced about for acquaintances or neighbors, and finding none, picked up a tabloid from the rack near checkout.

Five minutes later, in the middle of a two-headed baby, she became aware of her mistake. It was the old woman's turn, just eight or ten items in her cart, but she was the impossible kind, the type of person to hold everything up. To begin with she was slow, having difficulty leaning into the cart to retrieve her groceries, and to compound the delay, she interrupted this work after placing just two items on the conveyor. A problem had arisen with regard to a chicken.

"Do this separate," the old woman was telling the man, pushing a dripping chicken along the conveyer to the scanner. "This is a separate order."

"Okay," said the clerk, that single word betraying a heavy accent. He might have understood or not, might have simply been in the habit of mouthing "okay" to everything, for he bagged the chicken and scanned the next item on the conveyor, a head of lettuce, without closing out the order.

"No, no," admonished the old woman. "The chicken is separate. Here." She was holding out a limp bill, hand trembling. "Give me the change separate."

At last the clerk seemed to understand, and he voided the lettuce from the sale as the young mother, behind the old woman, glanced about at the remaining checkout lines, wondering if she could, even at the eleventh hour, find a better one. But in the midst of this search, another customer pushed a heavily-laden cart up behind her, making an escape all the more awkward.

"Please," said the old lady as the man scooped at the coin tray in the register. "Put the change in the bag with the chicken." He turned and attempted to press a fistful of silver into the old woman's hand, but she refused it and reached for the bag, fumbled with the sticky plastic, and opened it with a rustle. Her glasses were thick, distorting her eyes into the likes of insect globes under a microscope lens. "In here, please! Put the change in here."

The clerk deposited the coins, and the old woman laboriously, with arthritic hands, attempted to twist the ends of plastic into a little knot while the clerk turned to the register and ripped off the receipt. "Here," he said, holding the bit of paper in midair next to the woman as she concentrated on the knotting activity. "Here," he kept saying, as she pushed the chicken bag to the very end of the counter.

Finally, she turned to him. "Oh, dear!" she said, with a look of dismay. "I'm afraid that must go in the bag too! That *must* go in the bag!" She took the receipt, reached for the bag, and attempted to unknot her careful work, while the clerk scanned the lettuce again and stood waiting.

Hearing the metallic clink of change in the bottom of the chicken bag, thinking of the coins resting in a pool of blood and juices, the mother of the ravenous children remembered a day years ago when her daughter, too young to understand, reached up for a raw poultry leg on the kitchen counter. She had pushed her daughter's hand away, and now she felt a similar urge toward action but suppressed it, remaining silent and watchful. The clerk waited, the mother waited, each of them glancing now and again at the groceries in the old woman's cart.

Frustrated and failing in her efforts, the old woman settled on stuffing the paper receipt, twisted and crumpled, through a small hole at the top of the bag, then turned to her cart. She sighed and pushed a whisper-fine crinkle of gray under the edge of her hat before leaning over the cart for the remaining items.

The younger woman thought of helping, thought of the awkwardness involved, the difficulty of squeezing alongside and around her own cart in the narrow aisle to position herself for the task, thought about the issue of permission: whether she should ask first or simply pitch in with a cheerful comment of entitlement, hoping to appear benevolent rather than selfish and intrusive. Either way, she risked a response from the old lady, something faltering and time consuming, perhaps indignant or unpleasant. Any time gained in the helping would be squandered in uncertainties over protocol.

The old woman's breathing came harder now, and her hands shook with the effort under the pressure of watchful eyes. She didn't seem angry or bitter, only flustered and worried, perhaps growing tired of life, making her fragility appear all the more delicate and worthy of careful consideration. Patience was required— the young mother understood. Old people and children required patience.

Tabloid still in hand, she twisted her wrist to glance at her watch. Quarter past twelve. Distracted, now without any hope of learning the fate of the two-headed baby, she placed the magazine back on the rack and punched a finger into the side of a cardboard ice cream container, testing for softness. The clerk scanned the items as they came, stopping after each one to wait for the next: a quart of milk, two bananas, a loaf of bread, a can of tuna fish, and a box of ice cream bars.

Slow as it was, all seemed to progress smoothly, yet an aura of foreboding hung in the air. Two items remained in the cart, and the old woman hesitated, becoming paralyzed with confusion or indecision. She reached for one item, a plastic bottle of juice, then abandoned the effort and reached for her newspaper instead. Placing it on the counter, she pointed with a knobby finger. "This is the coupon for the juice," she said, "and this one's for the cereal," then turned around and reached for the bottle from the bottom of the cart.

The clerk, having difficulty looking at the old woman, glanced everywhere else, his eyes momentarily resting on the mother, next in line. He gave an embarrassed little smile as his eyes met hers, but he looked away immediately, speaking into the air: "Cut it. You must rip it out. The coupon."

The old woman, absorbed in her task, reached for the cereal box and didn't seem to hear the clerk: "You must…"

The younger woman worked hard with her patience. What a silly rule—cut out the coupon!—and what a lazy clerk, failing to do this small thing for the old woman while she struggled with the cereal box, lost her grasp, and let it slip from her hands to the floor. At last, the young mother was presented with an appropriate Good Samaritan deed. Released into action, she squeezed around her cart and stooped to pick up the box, placing it on the conveyor. The two women, in silence, exchanged pleasant expressions and nods, a light shining from the bug globes of the older one.

In the interim, the clerk had deigned to examine the newspaper specials under his nose and flashed gleaming eyes between the coupons and items on the conveyor. "Sorry," he said. "These coupons. No good."

The old woman, flustered and bent, leaned into the counter and peered down through her lenses, holding the frames back with three fingers to keep them from sliding off her nose. "What's that?"

"This." He pointed to the juice coupon. "Wrong brand. And this." He pointed to the cereal coupon. "Wrong size. You have fifteen ounce, but you need the twenty-two." She looked at him in confusion. "The bigger size," he said, louder.

"I looked at every one, and these match the pictures. See here?" She pointed.

"No, no, that is not. Different brand, you see? And read this! Twenty-two ounce, it say right here. See?"

"But if these aren't right, you don't have the right ones on the shelf. I looked. How can you advertise something you don't have?"

"I don't know, maybe we had it before."

"How can you do that?"

"Look, lady." He scanned the items. "The computer

say nothing else. See. Juice, $3.59, not $1.99. Cereal, $2.69, not $1.19. See?"

"$2.69? But how can the smaller cereal be more than the larger cereal?"

Yes, the young mother thought. Yes, how can it be? This quibbling over pennies!

"Not on sale. Look, if you want, I get the manager."

The old woman said nothing, eyes downcast, then glanced out the front window before turning to the clerk. "Add it up. Maybe I have enough." She opened the clasp of her purse and pulled out a wallet. "How much is it?"

"$17.69."

"Here." She handed some bills.

"This is $15.00. You need $17.69."

"That's all I have."

"Not enough." He shook his head.

"With the coupons though…?" Her voice trailed, feeble and defeated.

"I have to take something off here." He swept an arm about, motioning.

The ice cream, the younger woman thought. The ice cream should be taken off, the most expensive item and the least healthy. Butterfat to clog old arteries. That's what should be done, a certain voice said, while a competing image came to mind: the old woman sitting alone in a yellowing kitchen, gnarled fingers ripping into the paper wrapper, trembling lips opening for the ice cream bar, a messy bite, a smile, shingles of chocolate sliding down past balled-up knuckles, landing on the tabletop.

Without further thought, the young mother reached for her wallet and searched the billfold for singles while her rational self, tired of grappling with the larger issues, refused to focus on the propriety and consequence of her actions. What did anything else matter? Intrusion or not, she wanted the old woman to have everything she desired, and quick, before the ice cream melted into waste!

"Maybe I can help," she said, leaning forward with three bills in her hand.

The old woman looked at the money with a question in her eyes.

Suddenly embarrassed, the younger woman hoped for a way out, but it was too late to retract the offer. "What I mean is," she said, "it's such a shame about the coupons. Here, why don't you take this? Please."

To her surprise, the old woman did not protest. She opened her hand for the bills, and their fingers brushed for the briefest instant during the transfer. "Can I send it back to you somehow? Maybe I should get your address."

"No, don't think of it! I want you to have it. This is good food here."

"Well, thank you," responded the old lady and looked no further upon her, turning to the clerk with the extra money.

And the transaction, its completion, went smoothly after that.

The old woman's friend, after all, did not seem to mind about the cost of the chicken. "I'll have plenty of leftovers," she said, looking pleased. "There's so much here, why don't you come to dinner tonight?"

"I will," said the old woman, noticing then that she'd

been hoping for an invitation. Evenings, at dusk, just when she closed the blinds against creeping grayness, she was reminded of so many things. Her husband lying abed, stick thin and frail, and better times, his face animated, sitting across from her at dinner.

Back in her apartment after making the delivery, she thought of the ice cream. She'd placed it in the freezer before going down the hall with the chicken, and now, after a long chat with her friend, the ice cream would be hardened up again, recovered from that ordeal in the checkout line and the bus trip home, the many minutes of exposure to higher temperatures. She thought for a minute and didn't see any harm in having an early afternoon treat. It wouldn't spoil her appetite for the chicken dinner, hours later. No, it wouldn't.

She took the package of six ice cream bars from the freezer and labored at opening it. The cardboard flaps were always glued tight. So tight. She fumbled and pressed and pulled without effect until, in a sudden spasm of strength, she ripped the cardboard box open, scattering the six bars in a hodgepodge on the kitchen table. She paused to regard the disarray, and her eyes filled with tears. The box was ruined.

She carried the paper-covered ice cream bars to the freezer two at a time—two and then two and then one—leaving the last one on the table. By then her tears had spilled over and were flowing from under the rims of her glasses, down her cheeks, soaking into crevices of worn skin.

Unable to move, she stared at the ice cream bar on the table. Her eyes shifted onto the broken cardboard box, the tiny vase with three wilted daisies, the plastic napkin holder. All these things were resting on her little square table with the two chairs shoved underneath. Two chairs.

The ice cream would taste delicious, she knew, but just then couldn't bring herself to believe it. She felt queasy, unable to receive it. Leaving the ice cream bar on the table, she shuffled into the bedroom, and without thought, went to the bedside stand and picked up her favorite framed photograph. She stared down into it. His eyes held encouragement, and so she returned to the kitchen, determined to have her treat, and sat down at the table, where she propped the photograph in front of her, just beyond the ice cream bar.

Her tears had stopped but her cheeks were still wet, and her mouth wasn't eager, as it usually was, for the sweet taste. She gazed down into his eyes, big and brown and warm even in this fuzzy photograph, which wasn't a true likeness and didn't adequately catch the depth of his character, or so she'd thought at the time, now unable to trust her memory completely.

"Something happened today," she told him. "Maybe that's why I can't eat the ice cream."

His eyes encouraged her to say more.

"We were about to get on the bus and the store manager came up. He came right up to me! He was following me from the checkout, and he said, 'Lady, please don't do this again.' And I said, 'Do what?' And he said, 'You know, this is the third time, and I'm worried the customers don't like it. This is the third time you've done this.' He was talking so nasty. I didn't understand, but now I remember. He was right, there were other times. But he thinks—oh, I know it from the way he was talking!"

Her lips trembled, and she felt the tears coming again. Still, he looked up at her with that warmth, a frozen second of his life. *Kitten.* His favorite name for her.

"Edgar! Have I? Have I done this on purpose? I'm always so careful with the coupons!"

I love you, Kitten.

She touched the paper wrapper, pulled the ice cream bar toward her, hesitated, and looked deeply into his eyes, wanting to know where they'd gone, wanting to go there with him.

Eat the ice cream, my love. The woman wanted you to have it.

She pinched the end of the wrapper and started to tear it, still not wanting to eat.

Kitten, you deserve this. You deserve so much.

Water dripped from the end of her chin onto the paper, and she tugged and ripped until it lay completely exposed: the perfect shape of the ice cream bar, the oval edges, the hard, smooth shell of chocolate. She handled the stick, lifted the bar, and bit into it, tasting nothing but the salt in her mouth, but she took another bite and swallowed with a lump in her throat, and bit again and again, doing it for Edgar, eating until the ice cream was gone.

When she was done, she looked down at the empty stick, feeling unsatisfied.

Later this evening, with her friend, the chicken would taste better, she thought.

❧ Poodle Lady

THE MOOG WAS sounding exceptionally good, all the bugs worked out by the tech/musical crew (meaning Curly). Mademoiselle Francine, righteously satisfied with improvements now long overdue, put on her finest show yet in her twenty-odd years with Circus Armado.

Ruby sparkled in the cancan, her two front fluffy wristlets flung high. No one in the audience seemed to notice that her many-layered petticoat had begun to fray.

Topaz and Emerald strutted sexily around the sombrero in the Mexican Hat number. Topaz, black and gold vested, all macho. Emerald, stunningly ruffled in red, a single rose laced through bicuspids and canines.

Diamond and Sapphire galloped in sync as Roy and Dale, hind legs transformed underneath slightly tattered cardboard horses. Curly hit all the right buttons, sending "Happy Trails to You" into the air just as Diamond and Sapphire touched center ring, then lowered the volume as they cantered homeward, daylight waning, music fading—sunset. Perfect.

"Let's hear it, Ladies and Gentlemen! All the way from Paris! Mademoiselle Francine and her Precious

Gems!"

Francine scooped up Ruby and returned to the ring for her glory, a sudden gust of wind splaying the two pink ostrich feathers atop her head. Applause, this time lasting longer than Ringmaster Gordon's words, swelled on the rise of a warm July air current, a clap of thunder sounding in the distance. They'd beaten the storm too. Perfect.

"Things are going well, my love." Francine, back in her trailer, crushed little Ruby to her sequined breast, the others jealously panting. Ruby, the toy, was her obvious favorite, but the rest knew better than to bark or even yip. In afterthought, Francine glanced their way, flinging a large, pink smile. "Yes, my darlings, you *all* did well this afternoon! You make your Mama proud!" Tongues dripped with the knowledge they would dine well tonight. But not too well—Francine wouldn't let their diets go by the wayside.

Gordon knocked and entered without waiting for her response. As the tinny door slammed shut, he yanked off his ringmaster's tails, revealing a sweat-ringed white shirt. Francine stubbed out the freshly-lit tip of her filtered 120mm slim and swiveled around from her dressing table. She was ready for him.

"Good crowd," he said, pulling his shirt up over a ledge of fat supported by a red cummerbund. The Gems looked up at him expectantly, wagging. Sometimes he sneaked in treats to keep them on his side, even though Francie didn't like it.

Francine gently settled Ruby on top of a satin cushion, toed off her spike heels, and rose to meet

Gordon. They'd been doing this now for twenty years, always the same, always after the last show of the day. It was best then. But today it would be better, and she planned to take advantage. She had a few things to ask.

Gordon inched forward, his feet searching for solid floor beneath an ever-shifting, living layer of animals, costumes, and props. Topaz jumped playfully to his waist. As the only two men in the room, Gordon and Topaz shared a kind of affinity. "Hey, buddy," said Gordon. "Ladies keeping you busy? Down. Down, boy, not now! I got other things to do." Francine turned a glowering eye on Topaz, sending the dog, tail between legs, into the corner.

The ringmaster reached his goal, grabbed Francine's sparkling, netted shoulder, and delivered a wet kiss. Smiling, she pulled away before the next. She would work some of it in now, some later. "I'm *sure* we got the contract!" she rasped, her voice deep from years of smoking. "Their scout was in the audience. I'd know that puss a mile away."

Gordon gave his one-sided smile and curled the end of his moist handlebar. "You're pretty confident, baby."

Francine lifted an index finger to his temple— something she knew he liked—and delicately ran the plastic tip of her two-inch pink nail down the side of his face. "Gordy darling, you know I've never performed better." She batted thick, false lashes.

"All I'm saying is, don't count on it. Those fucks from Grove have been turning us down for five years now. Turned down for jugglers. A fucking juggler act!"

"You know this is different. I just feel it. We'll get it,

and then things will change." She lifted her eyebrows suggestively. "After the Grove County Fair it'll be Westminster, then Tanner! No more of this, this…"

"Piddly-ass garbage!"

"Like I've been telling you, Gordy. Times've changed. People lost touch with quality. They don't want to pay for quality. Just give them something cheap, something fast and flashy. Jugglers. Where's the art in that? Where's the beauty? I give them style, quality, beauty—"

"No doubt about it, Francie. You're quality all the way. And the Armados. Artistry and skill."

"Yeah, well…"

"But you, Francie. Quality, 'all the way from Paris!'"

They snickered. Between them, Francine had dropped the "Mademoiselle" and her phony French accent years ago, a couple of months after Gordon recruited her for Circus Armado.

"Care for a bonbon, *mon cher*? She reached behind her back to the box of chocolates she kept planted on the dressing table and rustled in the empty brown papers, coming up with a round cream, popping it in his waiting mouth. She found another for herself. They chewed, fat cheeked, eyes gleaming at each other. He grabbed her for another kiss, sweet goo still in his mouth, both of them oblivious of those ten, vigilant eyes.

Returning the kiss, Francine leaned backward with Gordon's lips still attached to hers as she groped for the cord to shut the Venetian blinds. She yanked it, and the trailer went dark gray. Francine wasn't shy of her Gems' watchful gaze or too concerned about the Armados next door. And she wasn't very ashamed of how she looked, fondly referring to herself as "full-figured forty-five." But things always seemed to go better in the dark, when she didn't have to worry about Gordy seeing the deep pink lines her costume had cut into her rolling white flesh.

When he left, she pulled out her catalogs and looked again at the items she'd circled. "What do you think of this one, Ruby? The purple will be exquisite against your white fur." She turned the picture so Ruby's large, liquid gray eyes could drink it in. A g-stringed, plumed, and jeweled Vegas showgirl outfit. "You're ready for this, you know you are, my darling." Francine had been planning the new number for months: Ruby center ring, the rest of the girls in the chorus behind, Topaz their love interest. New costumes, new music—something sexy. That lummox Curly would have to grease those clumsy fingers. "I loosened Gordy up. He likes to complain about money, but he'll get us these costumes now. And we'll get new ones and props for the standard numbers too."

Francine's vision was still half fantasy, she knew. If it weren't for those damned Armados. Gordon just didn't know how to take control, always catering to their whims and whining. As owner of the entire enterprise, Gordon's authority should simply go unquestioned, but every decision was filtered through the Armados, his stars, the key attraction. Sure, their trapeze and aerial act was daring and splashy, but what would the circus be without the Gems?

Francine had never gotten used to this penny pinching. Born under the Big Top, she grew up on the road, traveling with the three-ring circus from one major city to the next. But when her parents died within a year of each other, they left her with nothing but a few aging poodles and her eighteen-year-old wits and wisdom. Booted out of the Big Top, she started her own act with next to nothing, joining one small circus after another before latching onto Circus Armado. Always hoping for something bigger, never achieving it, Francine had resigned herself to this outdoor one-ringer, making the best of it.

There'd been good times and bad. Circus Armado once played all the biggest county fairs and festivals but had started to slip five years ago as Ramon and Julia Armado's nimbleness receded while that of their children had not yet developed. Ramon's three brothers, one by one, left the act. Then, a year ago, Ramon died, not in a romantic, circus accident, but in a stupid way: a drunken argument with a knife-wielding stranger in a local bar.

But now, there was hope. Jorge and David were young men of sixteen and eighteen, and their fourteen-year-old sister, Carmelita, was beginning to steal the show with her athletic incipient curves squeezed attractively into scraps of silvery cloth. In her aerial ballet she dangled, spun, contorted, and curled under the supporting grip of her eldest brother, David, trusting his strong wrist and fingers to save her from a fall, the embarrassment and possible injury—not death. They weren't willing to give up the net and likely never would. Their caution held them back, distinguishing them from acts under the Big Top.

With the clowns Sweet Potato and Pumpkin to

round out the show, that was it. One quarrelsome, extended family, four trailers. Sometimes, Francie wondered how she had stuck with it so long. But then she would pop a chocolate, light a slim, and forget all about it, gazing into Ruby's innocent eyes. Her favorite begged for attention, knowing she'd receive it. Francine would lift Ruby, adjust her paste diamond collar, and stroke her smoothly shorn white middle, feeling the warmth and rapid expansion and contraction of her tiny ribcage with each panting breath.

"More extension, Carmelita. Stretch!" Julia Armado stood in the ring below, coaching her airborne son and daughter.

David strained with his effort, the skin in his hand turning white around the edges of Carmelita's grip. The young girl arched her head backward on a long neck and tugged on her foot with her free hand, pulling it up an extra inch until the point of her big toe touched her forehead. Her other foot pointed straight to the ground, completing the creation of a large "P" with her body.

"That's it! Stretch!"

Sweet Potato and Pumpkin, in largely orange costumes minus wigs and noses, sat outside their trailer with Curly, all three puffing rank cigars. The clowns felt no need to rehearse their ancient gags, nor the sound technician his musical cues. But Francine impatiently eyed her wristwatch, tapping her toe just outside the ring, obedient Gems lined up nearby. The Armados were ten minutes over, as usual, and Gordon always let them get away with it. Always. She couldn't rehearse on the side.

He knew that. Her Gems needed the ring for their sense of perspective and spacing.

Francine snapped her fingers and Ruby, Topaz, Emerald, Diamond, and Sapphire stood at attention, awaiting the command. With a tiny twitch of her finger, Francine told them to heel as she strutted out to the center of the ring. Another gesture and they sat in a line, waiting as she arranged their hoops, balls and step stools.

Julia, ten feet away, threw Francine a hateful glare. "Once more, Carmela. David, pull her up. Up! Do it over again!"

Francine snapped, pointed, nodded. Topaz, Emerald, and Diamond hopped onto the graduated stools, front paws up. Ruby and Sapphire, one at a time, leapt through the hoops, low, then high.

David pulled Carmelita up, readjusted, dangled her again. "Gordon!" Julia yelled. "Gordon! Where the hell are you?"

The ringmaster, rumpled and unshaven, emerged from his trailer. "What's all the ruckus?"

"Gordon!" Julia motioned with her head, beckoning him to come closer. Carmela dangled, ad-libbing during her mother's distraction. Francine snapped, hand high; Topaz jumped and pranced on hind legs.

When Gordon was a dozen feet away, Julia's face suddenly sparkled, drawing on her faded, dark beauty. "We haven't finished, Gordon. Little Carmelita needs more time," Julia muttered under her breath as her eyes darted toward Francine in silent complaint. But the sight of Francine's oblivious face sent Julia's voice higher: "Little dogs everywhere. We can't have that poodle lady distracting us." Francine shot a glaring look their way.

The ringmaster, eyes pinballing between the two women, raised his hands as if to hold them at bay. "All these years, Julia, and it's still 'poodle lady.' Have some respect." His eyes paused on Francine to gauge her reaction. The poodle lady stood resolutely, hands on hips. "Francie," he addressed her. "We have plenty of time before the show. Just give them a few minutes."

Francine didn't budge. The Gems were glued tight, eyeing her expectantly.

"For Chrissake Francie! The little girl is hanging up there! Just give her a few minutes. She's trying something new."

Francine pursed her lips, swiveled, and strode off without giving a command. Fluffy ears flounced as the confused poodles looked first toward Francine's retreating form, then at one another. After a moment of indecision, each one individually took a hesitant step, then another, until all twenty legs were a blur of motion like spokes on wheels making their way back to the trailer, back to their mistress.

"Ladies and Gentlemen! All the way from Paris! Mademoiselle Francine and her Precious Gems!"

Electronic noise from the Moog. Maybe ten people clapped, three or four babies cried. They had to do better than this: the Putledge Township Independence Day Festival.

But after the show, Gordon had only bad news. Grove had turned them down again, and none of the other big fairs were coming their way. August would be deadly. Of course, this meant no new costumes, no new numbers.

"Gordy, I was meant for better than this. Those Armados are jinxed. I've had it. I'm getting out." The nervous tension in her trailer was high, the air doggier and smokier than usual as her skittish poodles looked on, their faces uncertain.

"You can't do this to me Francie."

"I don't need this anymore. Circus life stinks. We've got better things to do." She pulled out her usual threat. "I'll open up my shop. Collars, accessories, coiffures. I'll make a bundle, you'll see. Who needs this stinking life?"

"Francie, the circus is nothing without you. Nothing." Gordon knew how to turn on the charm when he needed it, but this time his usual tricks didn't seem to work. Francine was beyond consolation.

"Empty words, Gordy! Put your money where your mouth is! If I'm so important to you, where are my costumes? Tell me that!"

"Now, Francie, I told you before. It's not in your contract. Save your money. Get your own costumes. I don't have anything extra for that."

"There'd be something extra if *they* were asking. Anything for those Armados. Julia bats an eyelash and says 'poodle lady' and you jump. Is that in their contract? They get my rehearsal time? Anything they want. Anything. I'm sick of it!"

"That just isn't true. We've had all this out before. I have to make sure everything goes smoothly. That's a dangerous act, Francie. Dangerous! You've gotta give them some space, some time, you've gotta calm everyone's nerves. That's my job. I can't have any disasters, any falls—"

"Let the girl fall for once! What's going to happen? So, she falls in the net once. Big deal! Maybe it puts a little excitement in the show. But you let my little Ruby go out there in *this!*" She grabbed Ruby, still in her cancan outfit, and pressed the dog hard to her bosom. "I'm ashamed to go out there like this!" She fingered the frayed edges of the costume and Ruby gave a high-pitched yelp. Francine loosened the vise of her grip. "I'm sorry, my sweet! Mama didn't mean to hurt you!" She glared at Gordon. "Get out!" She pointed to the door. "We've got packing to do."

"Wait a minute—let's work this out. We've always been able to—"

"Get out of here, Gordon. Now!" She dropped Ruby, who led the others in circling the intruder.

Gordon retreated, making his way through dogs and dog things. At the door he turned to face her, one hand on the knob, the other on his handlebar, curling the end up toward a pudgy cheek. His eyelids drooped sleepily, his voice oozed: "Think about it, Francie. Think about what you'll be missing." And he closed the door firmly behind him, sending a small shudder through the trailer.

Francine collapsed at her dressing table, head sinking into a pink-toothed claw. Tears threatened, but she was too tough to cry. She bit them back, not soon enough to prevent the welled-up moisture from loosening an eyelash. Aiming nails away from eye, she clamped the lash with sides of index finger and thumb, ripping it the rest of the way off, then popped a chocolate and grabbed a fur-filled brush.

"Come here, my love." Francine motioned. Ruby obeyed, jumping lightly into her lap. "One good thing about all this." She brushed, teased, and fluffed. "I've always groomed you myself. We're better than any of those beauty shops. We'll make a mint."

Despite its intensity, or perhaps because of it, Francine's latest outburst cooled more quickly than the last. Her emotions, on a high-powered roller coaster, had been boiling and melting at increasing velocity of late. First nothing, then everything, seemed right.

She had nowhere else to go, really. No money. Nothing but the Gems, and she couldn't possibly sell them. And Gordon… Well, where could she get another one of him?

After grooming the dogs, she looked in the mirror and pulled off the second eyelash. Her cheeks sagged a bit, her eyes were puffy, a black line had started to thicken beneath her bleached French bun. She looked past it all into her blue-gray eyes, still with their youthful allure and sparkle. Sure, there were plenty of men in the world, and she could have any one of them. But Gordy had some-thing special. Did she have any complaints really? Didn't he come to her trailer, faithfully, at the end of the day? Always easy and pleasing. Just enough—without the noose.

And so, only half an hour after he'd left, she was ready to make up. It was her move. "Stay here, my loves," she commanded. The Gems knew the routine.

But Gordon had miscalculated, wasn't in his trailer. She went wandering into the ring, out again, around

Sweet Potato and Pumpkin's trailer, back to her own, around the corner, into the alley between Gordon's and the Armados', around the end and—she froze, pulled back. They hadn't seen her, she was sure. And maybe, if she stayed in the shadow, they wouldn't see her if she peeked around the edge, just a little.

Backed up against the trailer, Carmelita smiled shyly at Gordon, who leaned into her with his hand on the trailer next to her face. He whispered in her ear, she dropped her head, he lifted her chin with an index finger. He looked into her eyes. She giggled, returned the look, then lowered her lids. His fingertips slid easily down her neck to her collarbone to the edge of her low-cut costume, slowly tracing the border from one side to the other and back again. His fingers paused somewhere in the middle, threatening to descend.

A gasp exploded from Francine's tight throat. Gordon's head turned. He jumped back in alarm, releasing his captive, who ran to the door of her trailer.

Francine and Gordon managed not to speak through the process of packing and moving their trailers to the next fairgrounds in another county. The red and white ring was fixed into their new dustbowl in late afternoon under a ninety-degree dry heat. The fair would start the next morning. Shows at 10:00, 1:00, and 4:00.

She could have run, could have split off from the caravan, but was immobilized by a new kind of terror. Her bluff had never been called. She imagined a look of triumph in his eyes as they exchanged silent glares during their set-up at the new site. He hadn't gone to her, hadn't attempted to explain. If this wasn't enough to make her quit, then she was left with nothing—nothing to hold over him.

Follow the contract, he wants. Everything by the book. Well then, she had half an hour in the ring that afternoon, after the Armados, another half hour early the next morning, after the Armados, before the fairgrounds opened to the public.

Francine stood with pups on the sidelines watching Julia and family, certain they would encroach on her rehearsal time, as usual. Carmela had entered the ring in the shadow of her brothers, successfully avoiding Francine's gaze. Let Gordy have the little tramp, Francine told herself as she eyed the young curves.

Carmelita grasped a rope and was pulled up in the air, her back arched, her feet pointed hard as arrows. Firm flesh, cut neatly, divided sharply by the lines of her costume into visible parts, imagined parts. A precocious flirt, thought Francine. Why hadn't she seen it before?

To them, she was only the poodle lady. The poodle lady glanced at her watch, became impatient. She picked up one of her hoops and tossed it in the air, catching it neatly. Her Gems sat panting, wagging in the dust. Francine rolled her eyes. She would have to bathe them tonight.

Up went the hoop. She caught it, held it two feet from the ground. "Topaz!" She gestured with a finger, and through the hoop he went. We can do this here, she thought. They'll never get out of that ring.

Julia shot Francine a warning glance. Carmela was preparing for her spin, one hand gripping, one foot twisted into a hanging rope held by Jorge on the ground next to the net. Francine twitched her finger, and Emerald took her turn. "Gordon!" yelled Julia. Jorge began to spin the rope, slowly at first, gaining momentum, as Carmelita used her free hand to pull her leg up in a split. The rope spun. Jorge's naked chest muscles bunched and glistened. Francine gestured, Sapphire jumped. "Gordon! Where are you? Gordon! Get out here!"

Carmelita spun like a tornado. Francine motioned. Diamond attempted a jump, hitting the edge of the hoop and knocking it from Francine's hand into the ring. Distracted, Jorge took his eyes off Carmelita for just a second, no more, and his timing was off. The rope jerked. Carmelita flew like a silver bird, mouth open in a noiseless screech. Her legs hit the net and the rest of her toppled forward onto the hard ground below.

Immediately, Julia and sons surrounded their fallen one. Francine commanded the Gems to stay and walked alone, slowly, toward the wailing mass of bodies. "My baby! My little one!" from everyone, mother and brothers indistinguishable.

Francine peeked over to see Carmelita's face contorted in pain. The creamy skin of her beautiful face was twisted in agony. At once, Francine understood the emotion behind the family outcry. The sight of pain in a child's eyes can rip through the heart. And Carmelita's eyes were those of a child.

By then Gordon was outside, announcing that he'd called an ambulance. He ignored Francine as he walked straight past her, seeking out the injured girl. Francine turned to go. As always, they didn't need the poodle lady.

As she returned to her trailer, images rushed through her mind, each swiftly replacing the other: the pain in Carmelita's eyes, Gordon leaning into and touching the girl, and, years ago, another man Gordon's age, eyes gleaming, pushing a young blonde into a corner of the tent. A teenage Francine. Another girl who'd learned the hard way, too young to know the full meaning of "yes."

Later that night, Gordon knocked on her door, this time waiting to be let in. "She'll be all right," he reported. "Just a broken arm. But it'll take months to heal before she's back in the ring."

Francine stood mute, thinking of the Armados, that heap of heaving, wailing bodies. A tight-knit family. A clingy bunch. And it occurred to her then what she stood to gain from all this.

"You realize they're blaming *you*," Gordon said. "Claim you threw that hoop into the ring on purpose. They think you've had it in for them for months now, always bitching about rehearsal time."

Still Francine didn't speak. Wasn't Diamond the one to blame? Finally she spoke, her usual throaty bark lowered to a whisper: "You know me better than that."

"Yeah, well, maybe I do, maybe I don't."

"I'm glad it's not worse than it was."

"We still have a hell of a time ahead. They don't want you in the show. They want you out. But what kind of circus is that? Mama and two boys. Two clowns. It's nothing without you, Francie."

"What've I been telling you?"

"We have to go on or we don't get paid. Everyone has to be ready by tomorrow. I told the Armados you couldn't have done this on purpose. I told them that but, you know, I don't know…"

"You think I was out to get her."

"Well, yeah…"

"And not out to get you."

"Me?"

"You, Gordy. You. Who did the chasing? I'm supposed to think it's the child's fault?"

"Child? Come on, Francie. Take a look at the girl."

"She's fourteen."

"It's her birthday next month. And she's been flinging it around in my face for months."

"She isn't old enough to know what she wants. God knows she doesn't really want the thing *you* have in mind."

"Hey, whatever, Francie. I can see you're jealous. I'm flattered, really, but it wasn't what you think. All I'm saying—a man can't close his eyes."

"I'm telling you to *open* your eyes. You know the difference, Gordy. You wouldn't have tried a stunt like that with Ramon around." Gordon shrugged and his eyes glazed over with supposed indifference. Equally indifferent, Topaz sauntered across the room, stepping on the ringmaster's big toes along the way.

Francine felt her pulse quicken with a swell of power. She delivered the assault. "Ramon would have put you away if he saw you near his daughter. And what about those sons of his? That same hot blood, only more of it. Just think what they'll do when they find out what you're up to with Carmelita."

Panic in his eyes, Gordon twirled an end of his mustache with deliberate ease. "Who says I'm up to anything with Carmelita?"

"One good try deserves another."

"It's not what you think." Cool tones entered his voice. "The girl was flirting and I said something back to her. You think I'm gonna throw away what we have, baby?"

"And what *do* we have?"

"Everything. All our years together." He came closer and touched her shoulder. Topaz took another stroll across the room, pausing between them to sense Francine's mood. "I know you're mad now. Maybe you even have a right to be. But sleep on it. Calm down. I'll take care of the Armados. Do the show tomorrow, and after that, I'll be over to see you, baby."

He kissed her on the cheek. She stood stiffly, arms crossed. But she waited. Said nothing while he dropped his hand, took a step back and shuffled through shifting bodies to the door.

"It's not that easy, Gordon."

The ringmaster turned.

"Seems I have a choice to make."

"Yeah, sure, Francie. I've heard it before. And you always stayed. And you know why? Because there's no other place for you to go. This is your home."

"Not now. Not with the Armados blaming me and wanting me out—you think I can stay after all that?"

"Go then! Get the hell out!" He put his hand on the doorknob and waved the other at her in disgust.

"There's just one thing I have to do before I go. I'm not leaving without warning them first."

"About what?"

"About you and the girl."

"Hah! All of a sudden you're little Carmelita's Aunt Francie!"

"Oh, *they* won't see it *that* way. No, to them I'll be that jealous witchy poodle lady!"

"And that's why they won't believe you—"

"Sorry. Wrong. Now, after the accident, they're more likely to believe me, don't you think? It explains everything. The reason I happened to throw that hoop into the ring when their little girl was dangling in the air. I'm just a jealous witch. But they're gonna know that *I'm* not really the one to blame. It was all *your* fault for chasing the girl in the first place."

She'd hit the mark. His face showed it.

"But maybe they'll just forgive and forget, right Gordy?"

David, Jorge, and Julia did admirably well without Carmelita's aerial ballet. Her beauty—arm-length cast and all—was of use to them on the ground. Without shame, they turned Carmelita into a curiosity, a new attraction: that young aerialist who'd suffered injury at the whim of fate, an unforeseen equipment failure causing her to fall. Soon she would be back in the air with her brothers. Gordon's announcement was met with splashings of applause, a few hoots and hollers.

But to Francine, there was no doubt who stole every heart. Ruby was a showstopper in her new Vegas costume, purple plumes accentuating her adorable fluffy derrière. They'd pulled everything together in just a couple of weeks. Maybe Curly was still a little unsure, but the Gems knew their stuff. A sexy number. Who cared that the audience was a bit sparse? Francine could see the smiles intermittently behind waving paper programs, the few diehards in the folding chairs fanning at the August heat. There would be bigger and better audiences to come, she felt sure of it.

After the last show, Gordon knocked and entered without waiting for permission. As the tinny door slammed behind, he yanked off his ringmaster's tails, revealing a sweat-ringed white shirt. Francine stubbed out the freshly-lit tip of her filtered 120mm slim and swiveled around from her dressing table. She was ready for him.

"Good crowd," he said, pulling his shirt up over the ledge of fat supported by his red cummerbund. The Gems looked up at him expectantly, wagging.

ℬ Wrinkle Free

ALMOST SAD REALLY. No more than six attended Donna's party. Rumor had it she'd invited at least fifty women. Only women. A solidarity thing. She invited everyone she knew from the racket club, the League of Women Voters, Christian Charities, mothers of Sabrina's high school friends, and her fellow animal lovers from APE.

No one who doesn't belong knows exactly what the initials stand for. Animals and People for Eternity, or Animals are People Everywhere. Something like that. I became aware of Donna's involvement quite by accident a couple of winters ago, when I arrived at a charity function wrapped in my new black mink. Makes you feel quite the executioner, fishing for compliments from a person who sees only butchered animals on your back.

Donna's a woman with a kind heart. Always volunteering for this cause or that. The animals. The orphans. The disenfranchised. That's why I had to wonder when I received her invitation. The idea seemed entirely too vain. Having the procedure done is one thing, but a "Coming Out Party?"

Many people were obviously turned off. Look at the numbers: six out of fifty. Of course, many had legitimate excuses since it was the height of the Caribbean vacation season. Who can stand Manhattan in February? Everyone is away. Henry and I had just gotten back from St. Thomas. What a mistake to go in January, to come back to this—the cold and slush. How do we get into these yearly habits? Next year we should go in late February, on the cusp of spring.

Without an excuse, I thought of manufacturing one, but I'm terribly bad at lying. Instead, I tried to get past my disdain for the concept. There must be something besides vanity going on here. Donna always means well. Look at all of her causes, the ways she fills her empty time. Philip travels so much, and Sabrina is going off to college next year. This must be her way of coping, a rite of passage if you will, inviting us over to share in it. She was entitled to our support, but only six showed their faces. It was sad, really.

You've got to give her credit. She sent out the invitations even before the procedure, not knowing the results. Curiosity was my guiding star. I asked Monica to go with me because I couldn't stand the thought of facing Donna alone if I was the first one. What would I say to her? The truth? What if she looked a disaster?

On the way over, Monica and I were joking. Maybe she's going to wait until we're all there, make a big entrance, and unwrap her bandages like the Invisible Man. A cruel joke, with no basis in fact. It had been a month and the bandages were removed after a few days. We wondered though. Wouldn't she have canceled if things hadn't ended well? Maybe not. Her solidarity idea applied whatever the results. We were curious to see.

Monica and I were fashionably late of course, but I could have died, we were still the first ones. The maid Olga, looking like a Scandinavian import, opened the door and led us into the empty living room. The place was dead, a tomb. Spotless. Everything dusted and gleaming. Donna's Steuben glass collection. The Steinway with the cover propped up. The slick parquet floors and white rugs and all the Danish contemporary furniture in white and off-white.

Donna has an eye for design, but I've always been afraid to set foot in her place. I like comfort, more of a lived-in feeling; my apartment is darker, decorated in the English manor style. In Donna's, you get the sense of walking into a white sand desert without your sunglasses on. They say the brightness helps fight depression, but maybe it did the opposite with her. Every blemish and line is visible under that track lighting. Anyone would wish for the knife! Monica came up with that one as we stood in front of the big mirror over the glass statuettes, waiting for Donna.

But who needs knives anymore? Incredible what can be done with lasers. Absolutely amazing. Donna walked in about ten minutes later, Monica and I still the only ones. In sleeveless, full-length, flowing white, she looked and walked like an angel. She's striking in white because she keeps her tan up all year. Of course her face, after this, is not tan. Her doctor strongly recommends against the lamp for another month at least. She floated toward us, lighter than air. A different kind of walk. You'd think she'd had surgery on her legs. Removing a layer of skin must have made her feel lighter. Peeled.

"I'm going to be peeled," she used to say after she'd made her decision. She told us exactly how it's done. The surgeon aims the laser at the wrinkles and zaps them off, one dot at a time. The tip of the laser is about the size of a pencil head. He zaps and zaps and zaps, a million zaps per wrinkle. The top layer is burned off, leaving the inner layer of skin, new and pink. It heals and grows back smooth.

Immediately after the procedure the patient is a mess, like she just stepped out of the rubble of Hiroshima, all puffy with peeling skin and scabs. It must be a shock to see. At the party I asked Donna, "When you took the bandages off, did you dare to look right away?" She did. She bit her lip and lifted that mirror. You've got to give her credit.

Luckily, not long after Donna entered the room, the others began to arrive. Connie, Diane, Maxine, and a woman named Lara from APE. That was it. Me and Monica. Olga passed out hors d'oeuvres, all fat free Donna told us later. We were impressed.

She *does* look younger. She's probably about forty-nine, but now she looks maybe forty-two or forty-three. Noticeably fewer wrinkles.

She said to us: "You remember my face. How could I ignore it? We all have different issues. For some women it's cellulite, for others it's a flat chest or sagging buns. For me, it was always wrinkles. I was a premature wrinkler from the age of thirty. Dry skin runs in my family. How could I ignore it? How could I expect Philip to be happy with a woman who looked like his mother? He's had a point about it all these years. And you know, he's so happy with my new look!" She beamed in triumph. Philip wasn't there to confirm. No men invited was the excuse.

As she spoke, I studied her skin, trying to avoid a direct stare. There was something about it that fascinated me. The new skin has a certain look—almost like plastic wrap pulled tight across the top of a bowl of melon balls. Turn the bowl upside down and the melon balls make soft lumps against the smooth plastic. So she's still jowly, a little lumpy, but the skin is smooth and the wrinkles are gone. On the whole, it's a more natural look than the tight cheeks and stretched mouth you get from a bad lift.

"I have a confession to make," Donna announced with a naughty little smile on her lips. She admitted to inviting a man, one man only, her laser surgeon Dr. Blount. He was a terribly interesting, terribly handsome man. So knowledgeable in his field. Of course, he was unable to attend and had sent his regrets. In surgery. "So that's who thought up the idea for the party!" I said. I was trying to make light. The tension in the room at the beginning was very high. "He wants to meet your friends and examine our wrinkles!" Well, the joke fell flat. I was never so embarrassed. Donna even seemed to take offense. "No, no!" she kept saying. "How could you think that? Wrinkles aren't even your *issue!*"

So then we got on the subject of what *did* give her the idea for the party. Some brave soul asked her. I think it was Lara. Donna said it was an idea that had just come to her, flowing out of her whole philosophy of life. And her therapist had given his okay.

"I'm not a person to hide," she said. "I couldn't just disappear for a month and pretend nothing was different, all of you looking at me and wondering. Believe it or not, some people are against cosmetic surgery! They forget all the valid, psychological issues and just say, 'never!' The whole implant thing caused a big scare. Women started thinking, 'I should just be happy with *me*. If there's a problem, deal with it in therapy.' Well, I went as far as I could go in therapy. It wasn't enough. So I'm having this party to get everything out in the open. You don't need to gossip or whisper! I have nothing to hide! This is the true me, spirit and soul, unwrinkled beneath that aging layer of skin. I'm proud of it, and I'm announcing it to the world! I'm Coming Out!"

Well, there wasn't a dry eye in the room. We were proud of her too. She *did* look happier, it seemed to us then.

Everyone loosened up a little after that. Olga came out with some champagne and we made a toast. There was a wedding-like feeling, everyone very happy and bubbly. Until Sabrina came in.

No one noticed her until she was in our midst. If Donna floated, then Sabrina stalked. Seeing mother and daughter together, one could only think: here stand Good and Evil. Donna, all in white against a full-body halo of brightness. Sabrina, the only dark thing in the room except the piano. Dressed in black from neck to toe, pierced and slashed. Two delicate gold loops in her nose, one in the left eyebrow. Three parallel lines engraved and raised in her right cheek.

The facial markings were a shock to see, even though Donna had told me about them months back. Apparently, tattoos are now passé. Sabrina's tattoos weren't visible under her clothes, which covered most of her body (winter is good for some things, I suppose), but in her face she'd carved the latest manifestation of teenage ritual, the sign of her totem. Who or what Sabrina's totem was, Donna hadn't a clue.

My first thought, of course, was, why hadn't that school of hers kicked her out? Were all the students allowed to carve and embellish themselves in this manner? The headmistress must believe fiercely in the value of individual expression. That, or Philip's money.

The initial scene was very awkward. As soon as Donna saw her daughter, she pulled her aside and spoke to her, not ten feet away from the rest of us. Everything could be heard. Donna was all smiles, but her voice was like shattered glass. "Please, Sabrina," she said. "Whatever you do, don't show the pictures. I won't have you spoiling my party! This is *my* day!" That kind of thing. The girl nodded halfheartedly and came over to us, rather sulky at first.

"Would you like to make a contribution to FemGen International?" she asked in her quiet, morose voice. Like a warmed-up mummy. Maybe I'm a sucker for causes, but she seemed to be looking at me more than the others. Or maybe she remembered the days when she was a normal little girl, when I used to accompany her and her mother on shopping trips to Saks.

"Excuse me for saying so, but I'm not familiar with the organization," I admitted.

She lifted her eyelids, those liquid round eyeballs protruding like a codfish. "FemGen was established to fight the practice of FGM around the world. Here. Take a look at the brochure." She shoved one my way and started to distribute others among the ladies.

"Not the one with the pictures!" shrieked Donna.

"Don't worry, Mother."

I glanced at it, my eye jumping to a phrase in bold letters: "female genital mutilation." A practice followed in many cultures, Africa, Asia, the Middle East, now done in the United States by immigrant groups. Operations on little girls to remove sexual pleasure or possibility—sewing them closed until married—little sewn-up virgins. After marriage, the desire to cheat sliced away. Two-year-olds. No anesthesia. Complications. Even death.

"A lot of women in these cultures are now fighting back," said Sabrina. "But most of them still do it willingly. For their *men*." Her eyes shot sideways toward her mother. "Education is needed."

Well, what could I do? I wrote a check on the spot. Several others contributed as well. Sabrina accepted our money with a little smile on her pale lips. She seemed about ready to slink back to her bedroom when she stopped and said, "Did Mother tell you what Daddy did after her operation?" Her smile became twisted. "Did you tell them, Mother?"

"Sabrina! Leave us ladies to chatter and go back to your room."

"My father is away right now. Did you tell them? He's on a cruise, somewhere in the islands. With his secretary."

The color rose to the surface of Donna's peeled skin. A fatal flaw in the procedure, I feared—Dr. Blount had gone too deep! Every tiny capillary was visible, red, and throbbing.

Her eyes opened wide and the eyelashes fluttered, as if she would faint.

"You don't know what you're talking about, Sabrina! He's on a business trip."

Sabrina wouldn't look at her mother. She stared directly into my eyes and said, "Mother did her face for Daddy, you know." Those three purple scars were raised angrily on her cheek. With a sneer, she turned and left the room.

Donna's white dress deflated and she crumpled, dropping to the couch. "That girl! What can I do with her? She comes up with these things. She has evil thoughts. Nothing but evil thoughts!" Donna's head fell into her hands and her shoulders began to shake. "I'm so humiliated!" she sobbed.

The rest of us were still standing, dumbfounded, with one question on our minds. Was it true about Philip? Of course it was true. You could see it.

I was the first to move. I sat next to her and put my arm around her shoulder. "Don't let Sabrina get to you. Look at the positive side. She inherited one of your best qualities. She's found a cause and she's fighting for it. I mean the FGM thing. What she said about Philip—"

"It's all true! And how can you blame him? The way I look!" She was near hysteria. We could barely make out her words.

Her sobbing and our silence seemed to last forever. I

was thinking fast. We had to help her feel better, and somewhere, I'd read about a method. It couldn't hurt to try.

I helped Donna to her feet. "Come with me, Donna. We're going to help. You're going to say your affirmations." I glanced around at the rest of the ladies. They seemed to know exactly what I meant, or else they sensed the power we held and knew it was good. I can't describe it. We were one. A universal, cosmic thing, seven female spirits united.

With my arm around her shoulder, I led Donna gently to the big mirror over her statuettes, while the others crowded in behind us. The walking calmed her. The red capillaries receded. I took out my hanky and dabbed her eyes.

"Look in the mirror," I told her. She resisted at first, but after a while she complied. Seven faces were staring back, Donna's in the middle. "Don't mind us," I said. "Just look at yourself. See how beautiful you are? Repeat after me: I am beautiful."

"No." She shook her head.

"Say it, Donna! You know it's true!" The others started to encourage her.

"I am beautiful," she said.

"Look into your eyes. I am beautiful and strong."

"I am beautiful and strong."

"I am strong. I don't need any man."

"I am strong. I don't need any man." She lifted her head and stood up tall. It was starting to work.

"I am Donna."

"I am Donna."

"I'm wrinkle free!"

She slid her fingers over a satin cheek, smiled, and repeated the words.

❧ Hard Sell

I WANT YOU. I want you, Michael.

I need oven mitts to pick up these sunglasses, and what a dumb thing that was, leaving them on the car seat. Only 8:58 and already the sun is frying eggs on the black Firebird, my two-month-old baby, all mine for the lowest possible down and five-seventeen-oh-six per month, electronically sucked from my checking account on the third without fail, maybe ten seconds after my paycheck shoots in. Thirteen-forty-four-twenty-eight in, pfftt, five-seventeen-oh-six out, pfftt. You do the math. My commission money is low and unpredictable, so I'm walking the wire on the rent and raisin bran, but my brand new '99 Bird is worth it. *Need a ride, Michael?*

For a minute I'm worried they melted into the Charcoal Mist, a little puddle of soft brown turning hard when it cools, but I give a nudge and see the upholstery is fine. I'll get the car going and the AC cranking before letting them burn my nose. Besides leather, which is what I really wanted but couldn't afford, they had Burgundy Wine, Indigo Twilight, and Evergreen Forest. I went with the darkest, the Charcoal Mist, to go with my personality.

People are wary but attracted and drawn in, buying without understanding why, responding to that dark side underneath my half smile, something mysterious despite the blonde hair. That's what I'm told, even though I tell *them* there's nothing to it. Denial is almost a part of the image: that enigma, that sexy schemer saying, "Who, me?" with her crazy little grin. God knows a woman in lingerie needs something like this to hang on, while a man can simply hold up the bra and speak sex with any kind of wholesome look (*ah, that smile!*), then relax and let the orders fly in.

I'll need to scoot into the office (*Michael! We should talk…*), pick up the new samples—the Silkeze Allure (trademark) satin teddy collection—and scoot out again to appointments. Five minutes onto the freeway, right before Mulholland, it's backed up as usual, four lanes across on my side, the other side flowing free. Doesn't matter because the road is my quiet time when I get the most accomplished. I'll start my calls, do my lipstick, and if it's really jammed, some work on this broken nail before I get to the office.

I hit Mem 1 (Mindy) and send, but it's the machine. "Hey girl, answer the phone! Get up! I don't believe you're out the door already, you hear me? I don't go for it!" I wait a second to see if she's screening, but nothing. "Call me back. You know where." Mindy's a last-minute girl, jumping out of bed ten minutes before she rolls out on the road, fresh and perky. Me, it's hours in front of the mirror, ten cups of coffee. I could try her cell, but she's probably traveling her territory, out of range.

I should call Daddy, but he isn't in Mem and my

thumb won't move on the numbers. Yesterday—or has it been a couple of days?—he was on my machine. "Slow down and come out for a visit," he says. "I have a new recipe for squid," he says. My beachcomber Dad in his plaid baggies, strolling the edge of surf in Venice with that nickel-finder attached to his arm, nosing the sand. I know what he's selling: the elements, the sunsets and salt water, the "real" things he calls them while he looks at me like I've missed the boat.

I don't have time for that right now. I'm beyond therapy on this, beyond the confusion of my twenties, beyond the me-talk of the '80s and '90s and how I shouldn't feel guilty about my aversion to him, and yes, there's a commitment, so I'll call him later, definitely, when I get home. I'll call him later.

I press Mem 2 for Paul, my too-bad-he's-gay-but-that's-why-we're-so-close best friend, when I don't send because I'm getting so tired of seeing Mr. Arab Terrorist in my rearview mirror. *Michael, did you ever...?* He's driving a rented van wired for action, on his way to blow up a federal building, and the traffic is holding him up. Get off my tail. I flash him the eyes in my rearview, the mysterious, dark, down and dirty part of me, and he looks up. Oh, yeah! Our eyes meet and his are burning holes. In a hurry, are you? The timer's set and it won't be thousands buried alive in concrete, just the few of us in some twisted metal out here on the Ventura, one person to a car.

I drag my eyes back to the road and all of a sudden I'm standing on the brake to miss the car in front, but oh my God! Why does this have to happen to me? Why, why me? Screw the whiplash, it's my shiny baby, the Firebird!

I hit the pavement before Mr. AT steps from his van, so casual with nowhere to go, a big grin under the mustache, just enough to get me going even before I've taken a look, and I'm afraid to look but I do, and jeezus, it's worse than I thought, a dent wider than the Grand Canyon.

Then, just like always, the traffic suddenly frees up and cars are going thirty on either side of us, me cursing, the Arab standing dumb and clueless, wearing a Sunday-afternoon-picnic smile. His hand flicks into a pocket and I jump (*Michael, save me!*), but I hold my ground. It's a wallet. He two-fingers a business card and says so politely, in perfect American English: "Let me give you my insurance information."

I'm stunned, and he smiles even bigger because I've stopped cursing. I've stopped talking in fact. He takes out his insurance card, a ballpoint pen (metal, not disposable), and copies the information onto the back of his business card. He hands it, I look. "Michael O'Keefe, Bright Interiors Design Group." Christ! A homegrown Arab terrorist named Michael? Admitting responsibility and disclosing identity, no less. I'm smiling at him—how do you expect me to believe this?—flicking his card on my thumbnail. I give him my own card before walking back to the Bird.

Just as I'm opening the door, ready to step in, he calls from behind, "Hey!" and I turn before he can remove his eyes from my body. "Call me," he says, and is he really doing this? Brushing his eyes up and down my front, then cocking his mouth and sending a wink.

* * *

When I get to the office, I do the usual and go the long way around so I can pass Michael's desk. The door from the parking lot is right there, and it's just as easy to go right or left, so why not left? He's behind his desk, picking up panties, mauve, taupe, ivory, teal, style number sixty-two-thirty-seven, stringing them by leg hole along his bare forearm. Tan, muscled, neatly haired. Black hair.

"Hey, you," I say, feeling my smile growing an inch too wide, past enigma level. Why this? The only man I lose my cool with. I walk up close to his desk, and he's standing behind it, shrinking the pile of panties, racking them, five, six, seven. A lot of panties can fit on a man's arm.

He looks up and smiles, but his eyes are a little tired. "Hello, Brandi." I cringe at my own name which, ten years ago, seemed like a good idea and a lot sexier than Stephanie but now cries out desperation on Michael's lips. *I've grown since then, Michael, can't you see?* I'm noticing my nerves and can't help it, adjusting my purse strap, shifting from one hip to the other, the knit tight across my body. In lingerie, tight helps the sell and squeezed-in suits me anyway, so what's wrong with looking your best? We're not librarians. Michael's chest fills out his polo and he keeps racking, eight, nine, ten.

"You'll never guess what just happened. Some bozo rear-ended me and—"

"Hold it, Brandi." He's looking at the panties, not me, his lips moving, counting. Finally, he picks up the last one. "Damn! Still short. Marilyn's so stingy she'll dock me for this."

"Leaving gifts for the buyers?" I lower one side of my smile and narrow my eyes to reassert the enigma. God, I can't take my eyes off him, and finally he looks up, and he's into me for a minute, locked in and smiling. "Yeah, the buyer at Stern's." And we both laugh, thinking of that frump with greasy skin and no waist, a tape measure draped around her neck for easy access to thirty-fours, thirty-sixes, and thirty-eights. But the next minute his eyes move away and he's preoccupied again. "Gotta go, Brandi. I'm late. Three department stores are waiting."

"Departments? I'm boutiquing today." I can't seem to move. I'm thinking of that day, about a month ago, when I was standing right here on the other side of his desk in the same spot. Maybe there's something about this spot, so I'm standing here, waiting for him to walk around the desk and touch me again, four fingers on my shoulder, before walking out of his cube on the way to wherever he has to go. Needing to touch me before starting his day. That's the way it seemed at the time.

But not today. He points his pantied arm down over the throat of his open satchel and lets them slide like limp onion rings. *Damn you, Michael, look at me!* "Well..." I turn around and need to switch my bag to the other shoulder before glancing back. "See you at the meeting tomorrow."

"Right." He looks up briefly and that's the best I'll get, so I wave and keep going. Some reps claim the trick is to hard sell in a soft way, act like you could care less, and always, always indulge preoccupations. The toughest customer to win is often your best in the long run. But it's the waiting that gets you, the waiting and the doubt creeping in after you were feeling so sure about everything.

Walking up to my desk, I see that Marilyn has dropped the new samples there. "Get to know your product," she would say, but the line sheets and promo have been out on these for so long I don't need to examine them like the old days. I dump them in a bag and take a step toward the door when the phone on my desk rings. I answer it: "Brandi DePrez."

"Brandi!" A man's voice.

"That's me."

"It's Michael!" His voice is different, very sexy, the way I like it. "Michael?"

"Michael from Cintrex. How ya doin' today?"

"Oh, you. You are good."

"Hey, Brandi, not as good as you."

"I usually hang up before we get this far, but you *got* me. That takes real talent."

"This is all very interesting Brandi, but the reason I called was—"

"I'm sure you'll make it big somewhere else Michael, but I'm not buying. I'm selling, and I'm rolling out now."

"I can tell you're the kind of woman who could benefit from the offer Cintrex is making today—"

"No, I can't, Michael. I'm sorry." I hang up, pick up my purse and sample bag and go back the long way around the loop, passing ten desks, some empty, some occupied, not seeing anyone, looking for Michael, but he's gone and I'm out the door again, sneaking up on the Bird from the front so I don't have to be reminded.

Just starting out, it's time to begin my usual late calls. No way will I be able to make my ten thirty, even though traffic is actually moving. These new customers aren't in Mem, so I set up the phone list on the passenger seat, one eye on the road, one on the list, thumb seven numbers, check screen, send. "Doris? It's Brandi from Silkeze. How's things? Good! Listen, I hit a bad snarl and it's looking more like eleven, eleven thirty. Will you be there? Great! See you then." End, clear. Press ten numbers and send. "Hannah? It's Brandi from Silkeze—we had a one o'clock?" Static. I can't hear Hannah, then I lose her. Should have called from the office. Her boutique, The Intimate Secret, is way out in the valley, and I keep trying but can't get a connection.

As it turns out, when I finally roll into the Intimate Secret at three, Hannah is long gone. Instead, a man is there, unusual for a boutique like this, but not out of the question. He walks up to me and says, "Brandi DePrez? Hannah couldn't wait. But maybe I can take a look." He holds out a limp hand. "My name is Michael." I shake it, not really wanting to. He looks like the type that might enjoy trying on the samples himself. *Please, God, give me a real Michael!*

I let the samples spill, he fondles them with his milky fingers, especially the cups and gusset linings. Then he places a big order on the spot. This never happens. Says he has authority for Hannah—I don't know. I hope for the best and plan to check Intimate Secret's credit rating back at the office.

When I get home, I'm so wiped all I can do is fall on the

couch and hit Power on the remote before my thumb goes into permanent arrhythmia on Channel. I glance at the phone, innocent white plastic hiding those twisted circuits, sitting next to the caller ID box, numberless and empty.

All day long, muy mucho, I've been trying Paul and Mindy, but what do I get? My cell's been dead, and no messages at the office or at home. Mindy knows what's up, she promised to get back. Forever I've been asking about openings at her company, Electra Exercisewear, trying to prepare for the shakeup at Silkeze. It's been coming for months, and if it weren't for Michael I'd have been long gone by now. *Michael, when will it be?*

I'm remembering my last message on Mindy's machine, thinking it might have sounded a little too cranky and maybe that's why she won't call back. Paul doesn't overreact to my crankiness. I happen to know he's between lovers right now, so he has no excuse not to be responsive. Deliberately ignoring me, the two of them. I'm thumb-punching through a flickering chain of beer and depilatory commercials when the phone rings. At last, a call from one of my self-absorbed ex-friends. I don't check the box before picking up.

"Finally!" comes out of my mouth instead of hello, and then I see the box, too late. UNAVAILABLE. At least I can say this for Mindy and Paul: they don't use masking codes, they have more honesty than that. I'm about to hang up when I hear a voice I like. "Brandi! Glad to catch you in." I don't know what I'm thinking. I'm feeling a little numb and this man, this voice, somehow speaks to me.

"Yeah, you caught me." And then I know, before he says it.

"It's Michael from Cintrex! How ya doin' tonight?"

What the hell? Someone to talk to. I keep punching the remote, still nothing but corn flakes and Hawaiian vacations. "Very good. Just great. How are you?"

"Hey, Brandi, not as good as you."

"What are you, on automatic pilot? You know who you're talking to, don't you?"

"This is all very interesting Brandi, but the reason I called was—"

"Today. You called me today at the office. Ten hours ago. I drove a hundred miles and back since then. Don't you ever go home?"

"I can tell you're the kind of woman who could benefit from the offer Cintrex is making today—"

"I don't care what Cintrex is offering. What are *you* offering? *You*, Michael?"

"The savings of a lifetime. You don't have to lift a finger. We'll send everything out to you at two-five-oh-two Haskell Avenue, satisfaction guaranteed."

"Forget it, Michael. I can't use it."

"I'm sorry to hear that." His voice changes, like he's the doctor and I'm the patient on the couch. "You realize there's absolutely no obligation. No commitment of any kind. Examine it. Use it. Have the time of your life on us, free of charge. You can send it back after thirty days, no questions asked."

"But it's never what you say, and we never send it back. People don't have time to send things back. That's how you make out. That's the catch."

"No catches here. No fine print, no gimmicks of any kind."

But he won't stop talking to me. Stop is jammed and his voice is permanent, asking me over and over: Where's the real thing here? My sandcastle washes away and he's talking. *Just sand and water, Stephie. These are real things. The castle is gone, but the sand and the water and the person who made the castle are here. The real things are the only things and they're beautiful.*

Michael's been talking too, but I haven't heard him. "No, thanks, Michael. No thanks."

He's angry now and takes a new tactic—hostility. "You're missing out, Brandi. Missing out big time—"

Receiver down, big time. No matter how bad the sell is going, never, never do I move into hostility. I pride myself on that.

My hand is hovering over Mem, but I never programmed his number, so I move my finger to the pad, thinking four-three-seven-oh-oh-two-six, a number I gave to every high school boy and girlfriend a hundred years ago thinking *call me call me save me save me*. But I can't punch. *Find something real, Stephie,* my daddy's saying, like a guru. Never would he call me Brandi. My finger hangs a little longer, but I can't face one of those conversations. Not another one, not now.

I fill up the next three hours with sitcoms, micro-wave mac and cheese, and aimless wandering through my black book, such as it is. Around eleven, just before I get in bed, Paul rings. I'm even angrier now so I ask where he's been, doesn't he know I'm going through a crisis here?

I'm expecting a sassy comeback—maybe I know I deserve it—but his voice is sweet and dreamy, almost a whisper. The whole world is rosy, me included. "I couldn't call you before," he says with a secret in his voice, trying to make me curious, waiting for me to quiz him.

"Oh?" I say, not giving him the satisfaction, not right away.

"I've been busy."

"Oh?" I say again.

And finally, he can't stand it anymore. He tells me. "I met someone today."

"How nice for you."

There's a pause and a little muffled noise like he's pressing the receiver in his chest, then he comes back on. "It's okay." Paul keeps the whisper. "He's sleeping."

"I'm so happy for you. Who is the lucky guy?"

"You should see him, Brandi. He's beautiful. I met him at the club and we just connected."

"Sounds like the one. What's his name?"

"Michael."

Bright Interiors, Cintrex, Intimate Secret … or Silkeze? I don't want to know, but Paul, full of love, isn't sensitive to my needs. He wants me to know.

"And you'll never guess what he does for a living."

I hold my breath.

"He's an astronaut, an honest-to-God astronaut."

I let the breath go. "Amazing."

"There's one problem. He's going back to NASA next week. He's just out here visiting."

"So, how does L.A. compare to Mars?"

Paul isn't impressed and accuses me of jealousy, pent-up sexual frustration, and downright meanness. He always speaks his mind, and I've never been able to figure out my attraction to this habit of his, why I seem to crave his raw words and uncensored thoughts, but now, just now, I can't hack it. I'm fighting tears and don't understand why—crying isn't my thing.

But Paul has lost interest. Michael awakens.

In the morning, I find my dark glasses in the house and put them on before going out, coming at the Bird front on, trying to forget. I can't. From the back, the dent is screaming for therapy.

Today is going to be deadly. The monthly sales rep meeting is at ten, something big and nasty about to fall. My only solace will be Michael, sitting in the same room at the same table—across from or next to me? Next to sounds best. *Anyone sitting here?*

In the conference room before the meeting, before Michael gets there, I'm standing, talking to Gail, keeping an eye out while her yakkety-yak bores me to tears. "…ordered sixteen lavender," she's saying, "…such a witch…had to tell her…no stock…," when Michael comes in like he hasn't the time for anyone, crosses to the far side of the room and sits in the middle of a big empty section. Pat takes the chair on his left. "…handled it badly …who's my boss she wants to know?" I say something to Gail and I'm gone but she probably doesn't notice, she's so into herself.

I'm over on Michael's right before someone beats me to it. "Anyone sitting here?" He looks up with those eyes and shrugs, so sexy, probably the same shrug he uses when he wants the buyers to buy but wants them to think he doesn't want it. As I'm sitting down, Gail catches my eye with a glare, and all I can do is feel sorry for her.

Before I can breathe, Marilyn swishes in all business-like, setting up her charts and maps and pointer and everyone's down, coming to order, and then the news is out of her mouth. That's Marilyn. Right to the point. Department store and boutique sales are down, catalog and web sales are up. She drops us a bone: "This is no reflection on your efforts. It's just a new fact of retail life." Then she drops the bomb: "Silkeze will be under-going a comprehensive reorganization, pulling back from wholesale, beefing up direct retail and mail order, restructuring from the bottom up." Yeah, let's start at the bottom.

She moves her pointer around the map, outlining new territories, consolidating, shrinking ten down to six. Christ. More mileage, less action. I look around the table. Four of us are going to be wiped out. Gail sends me another glare, and I pull in closer to Michael, the man with the biggest figures. I suspect that Gail's figures are low, that she's going to be one of the first to get the axe.

Marilyn keeps talking, ignoring the steam coming out of our ears, the smell of sweat and road rage. In her own way, which is pretty pathetically holier-than-thou and self-absorbed, she's trying to encourage us. She has openings in the retail end and wants us all to "seriously consider a career change." A move into the gutter? Taking telephone and web orders, adding the S and H charges, stuffing bubble mailers?

A voluntary re-shifting would be easier for Marilyn, but one way or another heads will roll a month from now, giving us some time to get our sales figures up. A little healthy competition. Everyone knows this is talk: some reps, Marilyn's favorites (me, not one), have the good territories to begin with.

Finally, the tension breaks, a few cracks are made around the table, funny and nothing too disrespectful, so even Marilyn has sense enough to laugh. Then Gail pipes up: "Maybe we can take some lessons from Brandi. Learn the hard sell." I give the enigmatic grin, knowing that everyone thinks this woman Gail has just made a fool of herself, when I look around the room and see nothing but shining eyes, a blinding glare. "Yeah," says Michael loud enough for everyone to hear, and his eyes are shining too, his sexy little smile flipped upside down.

He starts laughing, and then the whole room is laughing, everyone except me. There's too much laughing, much too loud. I'm trying to find the joke, trying to smile, but I can't breathe and the noise starts to fall back into the distance while fog rolls in around the edges of the room.

Nothing to wish for except a phone call, I think I hear my cell, buried deep in my purse, waiting to be found. I pull my shoulder bag around from where it's hanging on the chair and look inside. The little green light is flickering on, on, on, ready to receive, receiving nothing.

Then, before I know it, I'm on my feet, saying something about appointments into the silent room as I make it to the door. Behind me, Marilyn says, "We're not finished, Brandi…" I keep walking, my eyes burning, knowing what I've always known, that my backside looks good and they're all looking. But suddenly, I don't want them to look and I feel sick because of it.

Back in the Bird, I put my phone list on the passenger seat and start driving, cell in my right hand. I'm looking at the list, looking at the road, list, road, trying to remember. Appointments. I must have appointments, but I can't think where.

I throw the cell on top of the phone list. Everything's swimming, waves of blur and mascara stinging, but it doesn't matter, the traffic's stopped anyway, right after Mulholland. I drag my handbag up onto my lap and fish out a tissue, wipe and blow, stick it wet and wadded back in and feel the edge of my wallet. I remember an appointment I should have made, an appointment I can make now. It's one big parking lot, so I'm using two hands, pulling the Bright Interiors card out of my billfold. Card in left hand, cell in right, I punch seven numbers and send.

"Hello, Michael?"

"Yes."

"It's Brandi DePrez."

He thinks a minute, then he knows and says, "Brandi." I can almost feel those eyes again, brushing me up and down.

"We really have to talk about my fender."

"No, we don't," he says like the stranger he is. "There's no need to talk." So cold.

But my eyes are hot again and I'm choking. I can't take this, not from my easiest mark, the surest sale I ever thought I'd made without even trying.

"But, you said…" I'm blubbering into the phone.

"You're too late. I found what I wanted elsewhere."

I'm seeing his eyes again, wondering where that interest went. "You're saying it was nothing? Nothing but—"

"An impulse. Dangle the goods, hang them next to the register, and you make the sale—"

"But you told me to call!"

"—let the customer walk out and it's too late. Out of sight, out of mind. Goodbye, Brandi. Tell your insurance to call my insurance."

The phone is dead and my cheeks are wet again. His voice is everywhere, trying to remind me. Even when it washes away, he's saying, the real things remain. He's talking, but my thumb won't move on the pad and it jumps to Mem 1. Machine. Her message unwinds in my ear for the tenth time while the snot runs into my mouth, and it beeps and I'm gagging, "Mindy, damn it, call me," boiling, rabid saliva splashing everywhere. "You owe me this. You owe me, girl." End.

A second after End the cell rings, such a loud noise I jump because I've forgotten the sound of it, it's been so long. I think it's Mindy, that she must have been screening and can't avoid me any longer. I hit Yes without thinking.

"Brandi!" Loud and strong, sucking the tears dry, making me hopeful again. I'd forgotten about this one, the last Michael on earth.

"Yes, it's Brandi."

"Glad I caught you! Michael from Cintrex."

"God, Michael. You're good. So goddamn good. How did you get my cell?"

"This is all very interesting Brandi, but the reason I called was—"

"No, Michael! You messed up. You're supposed to say, 'How ya doin' today?'"

"Hey, Brandi, not as good as you."

"You're right. No one's as good as me. No one."

"And I can tell you're the kind of woman who could benefit from the offer Cintrex is making today—"

"Maybe I can, Michael. I need something. I need something here."

"You don't have to lift a finger. We'll pinpoint your coordinates and express deliver everything out to you in your Firebird, California license tee-aye-two-five-nine-oh-six, satisfaction guaranteed."

"That's exactly it. *That's* what I've been trying to say. 'Satisfaction guaranteed.' But he didn't buy it. Why should I buy it from you?"

"Because there's absolutely no obligation. No commitment of any kind. Examine it. Use it. Have the time of your life on us, free of charge. You can send it back after thirty days, no questions asked."

"But it's never what you say, and we never send it back. You say it's the real thing, but it isn't what we expected, and still we don't send it back. That's the catch."

"No catches here. No fine print, no gimmicks. No real things of any kind."

For a moment, all I hear is traffic muffled through the glass, engines running, car horns. I wait. I'm not sure.

I break the silence with a scream: "No *what?*"

"No real things, period." So confident. But the other voice starts up again and it's stronger. We build things and start to imagine they're us. Don't lose the real things, Stephie.

I yell even louder, blasting every last tear on my cheek into atoms. "*No real things!* You've got this wrong, Michael. Something has to be real. Something is always real—"

"You're missing out, Brandi." Hostility again. "Missing out big time."

"Let me tell you, something. Never, never in my life have I ever believed that hostility sells!"

"Missing out, Brandi—"

"You're wrong about that. You've just lost the sale." I press End. We had to end this, Michael.

The crying's over now and I'm just driving, knowing where I want to go. I'm on the road about an hour, his voice in my head the whole way, soothing like the waves.

And I can see him in my mind before I get there. I'm coming in the back door—it's always open—and walking through the house, floorboards creaking, and the front door's swung wide to let the breeze in. Through the opening I see him, his back to me, sitting in his canvas chair on that salt-rotted front porch, looking out over the Pacific.

"Daddy," I'm calling, "it's me, Steph." He's twisting around in his chair, moving slowly because he moves so slowly now, and he's sending me a big, craggy, wet smile. Something real.

❧ Cushion

THAT AFTERNOON, SOMETHING happened that would change them, making them different and better, coming together like the zenith of a storm—thunder lagging then catching up with lightning, erasing the millisecond between the two, light and sound splitting the air with the power of unity.

The feeling of electricity had sparked the soupy August air all that morning, even before the first rumble was heard. As Joyce pulled into the driveway, Carmen was coming down her back steps, Vida trailing behind. The house was an old Victorian, the steps rickety and narrow. Carmen delicately touched the wood railing and twisted halfway around, beckoning Vida to come and greet their guests.

Joyce applied the parking brake and turned to look, beholding mother and daughter in a still frame: Vida, all three-year-old chubbiness stuffed into a bathing suit; Carmen, all benevolent motherhood filling out a jeans miniskirt and tight, sleeveless undershirt, bra visible beneath. The white shirt and white house shimmered brilliantly against Carmen's rich skin and the angry sky.

Joyce extracted a wiggling Sarah from her car seat, using the extra moments as distance. The freed child, ecstatic, ran up to Vida and grabbed her hands, jumping up and down with squeals of delight while the women touched cheeks in greeting, kissing the air alongside. Carmen's cheek was soft, as if covered with a fine, invisible fur, and her long, dark hair brushed Joyce's shoulder as she stepped away, smiling with brown eyes and red lipstick. Joyce had never seen her friend without that lipstick. It was part of Carmen.

Joyce managed to grab Sarah long enough to pull her play dress over her head, leaving on the swimsuit underneath. The women sat down in lawn chairs while the girls ran to the green turtle wading pool, filled and waiting in the grass.

We should let them do this now before it's too late, too dangerous, they agreed, eyeing the sky.

They fell silent, listening for thunder in the distance behind the children's laughter. Nothing yet. Though the sky was dark, the storm was slow in coming. But it would come, and it would show its fury, they knew.

Their meetings, always comfortable, had not become casual or offhand. The physical distance between them seemed to prevent it. Half an hour was not a terribly long drive but longer than Joyce had expected two years ago when the "play dates" for the children began. As a new resident of the county, and not entirely sure of the geography, she had called Carmen, a college friend from years back, and their contact began anew, encouraged by the pleasant discovery that their daughters matched in age. They met at one house or the other several times a year and talked on the phone in between, the calls becoming more frequent of late.

On this August morning they might have taken their comfort with one another for granted like they had so many times before—if it hadn't been for the storm. But there were many minutes before it was upon them and they took the time to lounge, wrists dangling from arm rests. Theirs was not a bubbling chatter but a soothing exchange of the usual stories about daughters and husbands, houses and vacations, while their girls exchanged pails of water over heads.

Kicking off sandals, Joyce wiggled her toes in the grass and settled deep into the vinyl cushions, the atmosphere pressing in but not oppressive, liberating in its heaviness, thick with moisture in her nostrils, on her skin. She clamped her limp, mousy hair in one hand and pulled it up off her damp neck while her other hand fished in a pocket for a clip. In one movement she fastened the hair in place, not concerned with bumps and imperfections in her spontaneous hairdo. In Carmen's presence she could give in to such a natural inclination without a second thought about her appearance. Were it otherwise, Joyce sensed, Carmen might take offense at a show of self-consciousness.

Carmen got up to retrieve a pail that Vida had flung into a bush. Her barefoot gait was easy and round, accustomed to form-fitting clothes like a second skin, while her thick hair swayed in one unit across her back. A perfect mélange of heritage, Carmen displayed her Spanish mother's dark beauty and warmth, her Scandinavian father's industriousness and practicality. She leaned forward into the bush, her jeans-skirt coming up high on the back of her thighs. On another woman, all of it might look contrived. On Joyce it would. She sat up in her chair and pulled at the damp material of her loose Hawaiian blouse, then stood and rearranged the waistband of her baggy shorts.

The first rumble sounded, low and still far away. The women exchanged glances while Carmen placed the pail in Vida's outstretched hand. What do you think? they asked each other with raised eyebrows.

They gathered up their girls in oversized beach towels, smothering them with hugs and rub-a-dubs, and pushed them along into the house. Wet suits, squirms, and giggles. Somehow Joyce and Carmen managed to wrestle the girls into dry clothes and send them off into Vida's room to play.

In the kitchen, the women could hear their daughters chattering in the other room. Joyce sat at the table while Carmen examined the contents of her refrigerator for lunch possibilities. The walls and fixtures and cupboards were white, dimmed to gray by the storm.

"Shall I turn on a light?" asked Joyce.

"No, it's fine like this." Carmen looked back over her shoulder, seeking agreement.

"Yes, there's something nice about the natural light, isn't there? But it's getting darker."

Another rumble, louder this time.

"Soon we may need the light," said Carmen.

They prepared lunch together, each knowing exactly what her own daughter would and would not eat. Bread, soft brown and heavenly. Peanut butter, smooth. Salad for them, green and crisp. All in a clean kitchen, orderly but well used, the food colors joyful against speckless countertops. Sparks of electricity invaded Joyce's fingertips, heightening every texture she touched. She got the utensils—she knew everything in this kitchen—and set the table, placing cotton napkins next to each plate, even the children's. Her fingertips lingered along the fold of the last napkin, enjoying the feel of soft fibers while her eyes captured the picture of the completed table. Its symmetry and simplicity pleased her.

"This all seems so easy now, doesn't it?" she mused while placing the plates of food at each setting.

"Almost too easy!" exclaimed Carmen, her eyes dancing. "We used to just hover over them, preventing disasters! Now we can talk. When did that happen? I can't remember."

"It hasn't been long. Things started to change after they turned three. Now they play so nicely together."

"Just wait 'til the second one comes."

"You're pregnant?" asked Joyce, feeling a tinge of shock.

"No, but we've been trying for a while now. I'm going to have a checkup tomorrow."

Carmen and Brent, trying to conceive. An image of them together, trying, laughing and tender, came into Joyce's mind.

She turned away from Carmen, wanting to hide the internal embarrassment, the unexpected guilt of betrayal. Among women, pregnancy was not considered a private matter. Explicit sex was, maybe, too difficult to speak of, but not pregnancy. They had talked about it, Joyce expressing her own reservations and fears about going through it all again, Carmen agreeing—or not? Now Joyce couldn't recall her friend's words or opinions in those conversations, sure of just one thing: Carmen had never mentioned her deep longing for a second child, something Joyce could sense now in the trembling beneath the casual words, the voice trailing off into a dream.

A lightning flash. Five, six, seven, seconds, and a crash. Joyce shrunk involuntarily, hearing frightened shrieks from Vida's room. The girls ran into the kitchen calling for their mommies, who scooped them up, one to one, and held them close in their laps while sitting at the kitchen table. "It's dark," complained Sarah, and then Vida, and then the two in unison, and Carmen reached to flip the light switch, turning on a ceiling lamp over the table.

Time remained before the storm would descend upon them full force. But the girls would not budge from their mothers' laps. The four neat place settings disintegrated into a jumble of two and two, side by side at either end of the table, while the two mother-daughter pairs sat across from one another, the little girls rolling their eyes, heads shrinking into shrugged shoulders, hearts drumming in anticipation before they squealed and jumped at the next bolt of lightning and the crash that followed. Somehow, they all managed to take bites in between, nearly finishing their lunch by the time the lightning moved overhead.

In the ascendancy of the storm, just before the crescendo, the little girls started to cry. Carmen and Joyce exchanged looks over their daughters' heads, laughing with salad in their mouths. Joyce swallowed. "Maybe we spoke too soon about our freedom," she said over the noise, holding Sarah tight and kissing her silky crown. She rubbed her cheek against the baby fine hair, relishing its soft warmth, lifting her eyes to Carmen.

Vida sat back into the "L" of her mother's arm, pushing against Carmen's breast and causing a tawny mound to rise above the low neckline of the white undershirt. For the instant of a lightning flash, Carmen's skin took on a nacreous hue. Her eyes met Joyce's again and dropped as she replaced the salad fork by her plate, freeing her second arm for Vida. Her arms enveloped the girl and she lowered her head, a thick curtain of dark hair falling over her shoulder and in front, partially hiding the child from view.

Searing light and a deafening crack hit at once, splitting the house in two it seemed, but the walls remained standing when they looked up from their own cringing forms, the light bulb overhead flickering, then dying. "The lights!" screamed the girls. Then one flash-boom after another came, quicker and closer together, each one on top of them with simultaneous light and sound.

They picked up their girls and walked to the living room couch, the women sitting with sides pressed together, children in laps, waiting out the worst of it. Pressing softly, damp skin in places and warm flesh under thin layers of clothing, they huddled and touched, their arms circling small bundles, the couch giving in to their backs, thighs and hips, their bodies gently flowing one into the other like the wavy layers of chocolate and cream against the glass of a fountain sundae.

Afterward, everything was pleasant, sprinkled with a lightness and gaiety that comes with the release of anticipation, tension. As the thunder rolled and rumbled away, the aftermath remained: electricity dead, branches strewn in the yard, the thick smell of rain on hot pavement seeping through the windows. Joyce hadn't planned on staying long after lunch, but the radio news station reported flooding and downed trees on the roads. Listening to the newscast, they looked at one another long and easy, Joyce unable to feign disappointment. Carmen's red lips parted slightly in a smile at her friend's wide-eyed gaze. A victim of circumstance, Joyce would be Carmen's prisoner for the rest of the afternoon.

By early evening, all major obstacles had been cleared. Lacking a credible excuse for further lingering, Joyce bid Carmen farewell with a warm embrace, pillowy softness in her arms. They exchanged kisses on cheeks, real ones without thought. Joyce packed her sleepy child into the car and pulled out of the driveway, waving to Carmen, a different Carmen, on the back steps.

Joyce was home in time to assemble a hasty dinner, humming a mysterious melody while she worked. Ted walked in. She swiveled around from the counter, just long enough to greet Ted with a silent smile.

"You're glowing," he said.

"Am I? You used to say that when I was pregnant."

"There couldn't be any possibility of that, now could there?"

He came up behind her at the counter and placed his hands on her shoulders, fingering the wisps that fell from her hair clip. He pulled back the collar of her shirt, kissed a spot at the top of her shoulder and peered around at her face. "What's this on your cheek?" he asked.

Joyce touched the skin that her friend had kissed. "Carmen," she said. "You know, the red lipstick."

Ted kissed her in the same spot, his evening whiskers bristling against her skin.

Three around table, they ate cool summer food, Joyce and Ted speaking intimately with their eyes over Sarah's chirping. Soon after dinner, the little one safely asleep, Joyce took Ted's hand and led him into their bedroom where they stripped down to moist skin and made love under the whirring of the ceiling fan.

A few days later Carmen called, and they talked about the usual things, the approaching autumn and their changing schedules, preschool for the girls, Carmen's plans to volunteer at the battered women's shelter, Joyce's plans to find part-time work. Their meetings would be more difficult to arrange. On the surface, nothing seemed changed, but Joyce still felt the difference, knew it to exist. If only she could see Carmen's face, her eyes, she would have the confirmation she needed.

A week went by and Joyce called her friend, leaving a message on voicemail. Carmen did not return the call, an occasional omission she'd been guilty of in the past, before the storm. A week later Joyce left another message, but still Carmen didn't call. The silence now seemed unusual, and Joyce became doubtful—maybe even a bit angry. But life was busy, and another week passed and she woke up one morning feeling sick, knowing immediately what ailed her and knowing that it would last for months. She was pregnant.

Days dragged, and as Joyce learned to live with the nausea, a quiet joy started to swell within her. The resentment—never consciously acknowledged—finally disappeared altogether, and she felt a sudden urgency to share her good news with Carmen. She called on a week-day morning in late September, surprised to hear Brent answer the phone after the first ring.

"Carmen is sleeping now and can't come to the phone," he said, his voice slow and heavy.

"Is something wrong?"

"I guess… She didn't tell you? It all happened so quickly. They found some lumps and, well, she just got home from the hospital yesterday. A double mas-tectomy."

Joyce fell silent, a thousand images rushing through her head, everything that Carmen must have gone through in the past several weeks. At last she spoke, hardly knowing what she said to Brent.

"Well, her mother had cancer at a young age too," he replied.

"I didn't know," she heard herself say, wondering how many things she didn't know about Carmen—how many things her friend hadn't told her and didn't want her to know.

Another long time passed before Carmen was ready

for a visit. Joyce called to arrange a time, careful to ask whether Sarah was wanted. Carmen assured her that everything was back to normal, that Vida had missed Sarah and would like to play.

Autumn was now full upon them, the air brisk and clean. As Joyce pulled into the driveway, Carmen opened the back door and stood in the doorway, holding her daughter's hand. Her face looked tired but otherwise the same. She leaned against the door to keep it open, one hip thrust to the side beneath a new, oversized T-shirt. Noticeable breasts pushed out from underneath, and tight Capris revealed the shape of her legs. She smiled with full red lips.

Joyce helped Sarah from the car and floated toward the back stairs thinking that everything had been a dream. But then they were close and slightly askew, exchanging a sideways hug and kiss rather than a full-chested one.

Carmen laughed nervously, a sound Joyce had never heard. "Don't look at me like that!" she said. "I put my falsies on just for you."

"I'm honored," said Joyce, adopting her friend's tone.

The girls were already gone, shooting past their mothers into Vida's room. The women went into the living room and sat six inches apart on the couch, feeling awkward in their nearness. Joyce was at a loss for words. Carmen could see it, so she chattered more than usual and with apparent ease and forthrightness, assuring Joyce that everything was going to be all right, that a chance of recurrence always existed, sure, but the doctors were confident they had gotten all of it and they saw no need for chemo. She was fully healed from the surgery, and now…now she just had to get on with life, and life, after all, was not about a pair of breasts, and she was strong enough to get through this…

Carmen had said many of the same things before on the phone, and the stream of words drifted into Joyce's ears and through her brain like a good weather report on a sunny day, heard every ten minutes on the car radio and fully understood, perhaps reassuring, but of little significance. The anticipation built within her until she couldn't wait, and without thinking, and in the middle of Carmen's speech, a word fell from her mouth.

"Stop," she said, quietly.

"What?"

"Stop, Carmen."

Silence, Joyce's eyes searching Carmen's blank expression.

"Why didn't you call me? I thought we were… I could have helped you, at least with Vida or the house, while you were going through all of this. We could have talked."

Carmen's blank expression gave way to shame, and she crumbled, looking down at her hands.

"I'm sorry," said Joyce. "It sounds like it's all about me, but I don't mean it that way. I just want to help, to be your friend. I'm making it worse. I'm sorry."

Carmen looked up with tears in her eyes, her mouth trembling before she could catch hold of it and speak. "I told other people," she said, "and some women came to help. They were just, you know, people in the neighborhood. It wasn't hard telling them. And it wasn't hard telling Brent. But you…every time I picked up the phone to call, I just couldn't. I really don't know why. I kept telling myself you wouldn't want to know…" Unrestrained feeling poured from Carmen's teary eyes before her head dropped and her shoulders slumped down over her chest.

A slow flush rose in Joyce's cheeks, the heat of regret, sorrow and excitement all mixed together. But the confusion suddenly vanished into a clarity Joyce had never known, and she was overcome with an urgency to show Carmen that it didn't matter, it really didn't matter in the way her friend had feared.

"Oh, Carmen!" she cried, grasping her friend's shoulders, and she came close, lowering her head to the layers of artificial padding, gently resting, then burying her face in the cushion, going deeper and deeper, finding, entering, embracing Carmen's soul.

♪ Pianissimo, Fortissimo

THEIR VOICES SPOKE to me, flowed through me. I uttered them softly, *pianissimo*. I shouted them bravely, *fortissimo*. I had my favorites, but they were never enough, and new ones came to me, quietly begging, loudly demanding. One by one I chose them, never letting go of the old ones, my favorites. Each new one gave me something the others could not: his own way of moving me, telling me how to feel and affording me the luxury of wordless expression.

These were my thoughts when I first met Bowen, but I didn't say them, for I've always had difficulty speaking, using my own voice to express myself. My chosen circle was ever-expanding yet closed to outsiders not of their world. So I thought. But all I said to Bowen was, "I'm afraid."

He understood. "If you're devoted completely to them, for me it would be like saying, 'I'm devoted only to myself.' That's ridiculous. We all need something else."

He was right. And he cured my insatiability while I continued to enjoy them all, hearing their voices and letting them flow through me, letting them use me to speak.

One day early on, when we were still at Juilliard, I was surprised to see him pick up and play, well but with mistakes, at least five different instruments. "I play them all badly but hear them all perfectly together," he told me. Then he handed me some music. "Play this," he said. "You'll play the theme perfectly while I hear all the other instruments perfectly, in here." He tapped his temple with his forefinger, just under a blond curl. After I played it, he sat down to write, adding strings, brass, woodwinds, percussion.

From that day on, we were together in every free moment, the few, our union spiritual more than tangible. I played, he composed, eleven, twelve hours a day. In between, we found each other. There was more of him to find than there was of me. His music was his voice. My music was theirs. But he said, "You exist in it. Otherwise, it would be nothing, sound like nothing. Parts of you are there, and I can hear them." I was grateful for his faith in my existence, for I'd not been able to find it on my own.

Two years later, an orchestra performed the composition that Bowen first asked me to play. Finally, I was blessed with the sound he conjured so easily in his mind.

I'm on tour again.

I walk onto the stage wearing anonymous black, my dark hair pulled away from my face, falling straight down to the middle of my spine. Whether alone or with an orchestra, I have no separate existence. My body should not be seen. I'm no more than an instrument of the voice speaking through me.

The people in the audience fade into gray. If I think of them or play for them, I'll fail. The composer, his voice, fills my mind, and I'm completely faithful to him in that moment and throughout our evening together. I'll play him, *pianissimo, fortissimo*, and everything in between.

On my first bow, a small one, the applause comes to me like a distant gust of wind high in the trees, something that won't ruffle my aspect or disturb my purpose. I sit and adjust myself on the bench, lift my hands above the keys, and wait for my cue, his voice saying, "Now."

But before he speaks, someone in the front row coughs. I hear the cough. I shouldn't hear the cough. I've never allowed myself to hear the sounds the audience makes. But I hear it and suddenly it's me, Victoria Burgess, sitting in a black dress at a piano on stage.

People from another world summon me, and I turn to look. They wait. They cough, rustle programs, fidget with suits and skirts, cross, uncross their legs. I'm alone on stage or in front of an orchestra, I can't remember. Suddenly deaf to the voice that guides me, I struggle to recognize it. Am I to play Rachmaninoff's Rhapsody on a Theme of Paganini? Ravel's Piano Concerto in G? Chopin's Ballade No. 2 in F?

Turning back to the piano, I raise my hands and let them fall into a snarl of disconnected phrases. I'm stunned but continue. My fingers are twisted and curled, playing none of the right notes, but playing. Then they become limp and mushy, unable to play at all. No strength. I cannot move them. Then pain. Then nothing for a long while.

Time, a lot of it, has passed; I have no way of judging. But now my hands feel something. No longer mush but straight as boards, my hands are bound tight. Nothing should ever bind my fingers in this way. They must remain relaxed and softly curved in moments of rest.

I resist, suspecting the worst. My fingers, long and slender, smooth and curved, nubs for nails, have nowhere to go. Once fleet and exact, they stumble and fail.

I struggle to understand, but not very hard. There's a truth here I don't want to discover.

Their voices come to me, begging, fearing the loss of their medium. First Bach, with his mathematical exactness. Then Brahms, with his romantic intonations. Then Mozart, with his precise playfulness. Then Chopin, Bartok, Liszt, Ravel, Debussy, Prokofiev, Haydn, Beethoven, Rachmaninoff.

But most of all I hear one voice, Bowen Tanzer's. His phrases play in my head, surprising me with their ironic twists, always ending the same way: turning a blind corner in the near distance, suddenly facing me head on, beckoning me back.

Bowen is standing above me, looking down. He smiles, but his forehead is bunched with lines of concern. I've seen him sit for hours, fingers tapping, forehead bunched over staff paper as he composes, but never looking quite this way. His smile now looks like a conscious device, intentionally pushed onto his lips from a perceived need—a need that would never arise in the course of his work. Only in relation to me.

I smile back, but my thought is, "Why are we smiling?" His face is all I see in a shimmering bowl of bright light. He stands above me. Something odd.

"Bowen," I say, hearing nothing. I'm sure my lips have moved, yet I hear nothing.

"Don't," he says, his fingertip touching my lips. The universe revolves around that spot of warmth on my mouth, sending my eyes back into my head under heavy lids. No part of me exists but the place he touches.

Another long time, maybe not so long.

I open my eyes. He's still standing above me with the same smile.

"Bowen," I say, this time hearing my voice. "Something's wrong. Something happened."

He shakes his head, but not to negate my words, and closes his eyes tight in two straight lines. When he opens them, his face has the same smile, the same bunched forehead, and a single tear traveling slowly down his cheek, past his mouth to his chin, a droplet hanging suspended in time, then plummeting, smashing into atoms on my nose.

I never really awaken completely. The first several months are spent in pain, more mental than physical. The scene is replayed again and again in my head. My arm swings freely, unhindered by the slight pull of my briefcase. I've been careful not to overload it with music; the extra weight isn't good for my hands, their strength to be guarded, preserved. I carry only my current work, Beethoven's Sonata in F Minor, the "Appassionata."

I'm humming the *andante* movement as I cross the

plaza at Lincoln Center. At Broadway I pause before entering the crosswalk, stopping to look, right, left, both ways I'm sure, right and left as always, and I step out lightly into the street, still humming, but a car comes from nowhere and I'm in the air.

Air is all around me but there's none to breathe. The briefcase flies away from me, pulled from my hand by an unseen force, and I'm flying after it, suspended above the ground with my arms stretched long, my internal music changing suddenly to the final movement, the *allegro ma non troppo*, as I anticipate the blow of concrete. My arms reach long for the other side of the street, and in this tangled moment of perception I imagine unscrewing them from their sockets like doll's arms and throwing them free to the other side. But instinct takes over as the ground comes up to slam me. My arms, my hands, break my fall.

I owe my life to my hands. But is it a life anymore? There's no hope and never has been any hope I will ever play again, my wrists and fingers broken in so many places that they've healed stiff and useless. Daily I bend and flex and curl them, not to play or in any hope of playing, but simply to relearn what I must to survive, to dress, to eat, to bathe. To touch Bowen.

I cry daily, sometimes hourly, but hide it as best I can.

Bowen sits, hour after hour, forehead bunched, fingers tapping next to staff paper. He scribbles, erases, scribbles, crumples the paper and throws it. He doesn't fill many sheets.

Finally, I say, "Bowen. I'm weighing you down. You

should be free of me."

He looks at me, his eyes tired and sunken. "That's ridiculous. I can't live without you." His voice sounds tired because he *is* tired, tired of struggling for the perfect consonance that once filled his head, but he doesn't mean it to sound unconvincing. Like it sounds.

My lip quivers despite hours of practice with the words I must say. Finally, as always, the words fail me. I can't use my voice to express my thoughts. How can I tell Bowen that he proved my existence, something I always doubted? He found my very being and showed me where it lay. Through the composers' voices I could speak. That existence is gone, the one Bowen discovered and loved.

I say nothing more. But he knows.

"There are other ways," he says at last.

"What ways?"

"Other ways to express yourself in music."

"There's nothing. Every instrument takes fingers."

"You should lecture. You have so much to give."

I almost laugh. "Me, lecture? I can hardly talk to *you* about music."

He looks down at his empty page, unable to meet the truth in my eyes. He knows his suggestions are made in vain.

Then I speak again, more than I'm used to, my voice shaking. "People talk about music. They lecture. They write. But it's meaningless. You know that. Do you think Beethoven can be heard and understood by me talking about his music? Do you think his voice can be heard through my words? Of course not. His music has to be played and listened to and felt. That's the only way music communicates."

Bowen looks at me again, his face just like it was on the day I opened my eyes in the hospital. All these months and his expression hasn't changed—that tiny, forced smile, meant to be reassuring. Reassuring for him or for me? His lips grope, then emit sound, a small, painful gasp. "Victoria." His eyes squeeze into those two straight lines and open again. "There's a way for you. Somehow, I know this."

Bowen finally completes a short piece of music, his first since the accident. I've made progress, now able to hold my spoon like a chimpanzee, able to dress myself through the wonders of Velcro.

He smiles more than he has, a smile turned inward in self-congratulation for his small, yet momentous, achievement. With that slender grin, he shows me the music. I can hear the theme in my head but not in his way, the thirty instruments combined in thunderous sound.

Taking my stiff right hand, he leads me to the piano. We sit together on the bench. He places the music on the stand and starts to play.

His hand misses. "Damn! That's not it." He plays, misses again, but keeps on.

I'm shaking by now, sitting on my hands to keep them from the piano.

He stops in mid-phrase, turns to me, looks at me hard.

"I can't hear it without you," he says. "Play."

Our eyes are locked in awareness of my hands,

hidden from view under my thighs. The blood, what little I still feel, is pressed out of them.

"Play!" he says again.

I have to do something. I extract my right hand, my "good" one, and raise it above the piano, letting the blood flow back into it. My index finger is poised, tremulous. I let it fall on middle C, lift it again, down on F. A weak, impious sound. My finger rests on F, then slides off into my lap.

"Play!" he yells, his cheeks two balloons of red. "I can't hear it without you. Play it!"

Paralyzed, I can't respond. I think he's going mad. Of course you can hear it without me. Of course you can, Bowen. Why this torture?

He stands, starts to pace, then breaks down in the middle of the room and drops to his knees, letting go a howl, a ripping, primal sound. I've never seen him do this and I'm scared.

He howls and sobs. He's breaking down completely and for the first time. All this time he's shown nothing but that forced smile, that single tear in the hospital. All of it held in until now.

I can't look at him, and I turn to the music, trying to focus, feeling the heat of my insides elevate to a rolling boil in my abdomen. It pushes upward on my diaphragm and tightens my throat into spasm, then just as suddenly washes everything clean and open. A hand straightens my spine, another lifts my chin, completing the inner passageway, my column of sound.

I sing! Middle C, then F. It's Bowen's voice, my own mixed with his, the notes purely felt, more beautiful than

I've ever heard them coming from me. I sing, on and on, feeling his voice deeply within me.

My voice rises above his painful sobbing. He lifts his head to regard me in astonishment. Quietly he stands and returns to the piano. By now I'm completely immersed, our voices united as he listens by my side.

When I'm done, my eyes remain on his music. I'm afraid to look at him. We wait a long time, the room absorbing the sound I've made.

He takes my chin gently with his hand and turns my face to his. "You've changed it," he says softly, like whispering in a church. "You made me see."

My chest swells and exhales in warm release.

He smiles like he used to, relaxed, without pretense. "This is my first piece for voice. Your voice."

❧ The Missing and Uninvited

"SO, TRENT UNINVITED his girlfriend. Is that it?"

"In a nutshell, yes."

One of Justin's annoying words. "Nutshell." A lawyer-sounding word, his favorite, often following one of his lengthy, methodical, monotone orations. Blah, blah, blah, blah. In a nutshell, blah.

"Have you ever met this girlfriend?" Mallory asked him.

"Charlotte? No. Never."

"They've had a fight? What did Trent say?" How inconsiderate, Mallory was thinking. Four around table was intimate, cozy, barely enough. Three was impossibly embarrassing, even though Mallory was enthralled with Trent, found him stimulating and wonderfully new after just a brief encounter, that quick exchange of words in Justin's office. Trent popping his head in, flashing that smile: "So, you're the wife?" in a sexy tone, mocking the chauvinists.

Still, it would be awkward to look at him, sitting alone at her table, while questions about the girlfriend lurked beneath the lilt of polite conversation. To ask, or not to ask? she would be thinking. To delve or not to delve? Knowing herself, she would likely probe deeply, ending in Trent's embarrassment or not, as the case might be, depending upon the strength of his character.

"Just said she couldn't make it. He was sorry. She couldn't come after all."

"Just like that? No explanation?"

"No. But it's not important anyway."

"How could it not be important?"

Justin paused before responding, his expression indicating mild resistance to her question. "Well, I doubt they're a solid couple. She doesn't meet Trent at the firm—you know, for lunch or after work—and she doesn't come to any of the office social functions. So, I get the sense they're somewhat on again, off again, that sort of thing. In a nutshell, nothing serious."

Lunch and social functions, the proof of solidity? Mallory did little of that.

"But he says he's free and would like to come," continued Justin. "We'll have him over on his own. Nothing wrong with that, is there?" He looked at her with a face devoid of social understanding. Most men were like that, Mallory had found. Something she'd learned in her profession. They failed to understand the error in forgotten introductions or poorly-timed eye contact or sitting with an ankle propped on opposite knee while wearing too-short socks under business suits. Or inviting a single individual, male or female, to dine at the home of a married couple.

"No, nothing wrong. We certainly won't cancel. It's only a picnic on the deck, after all," Mallory said, making noise while she thought. On again, off again. A man like that couldn't be averse to filling in the fourth side of the square, another female to tighten the gap. Benita came to mind. Benita Vanderlyn, Mallory's new friend, a classy looker albeit with a past, that interesting, quirky, and sad story. Another topic of conversation Mallory would strive to avoid, if she could, while sitting between two terribly interesting newish people with intriguing secrets behind their faces. Trent's on-again-off-again and Benita's—well, what would you call *that?* Something so tragic and titillating it begged disinterment.

Mallory didn't stop to analyze the plan or her motivations behind it. Perhaps it came naturally. She wasn't a social matchmaker, never had been, but her daily existence revolved around plugging holes, filling business needs with appropriate skills, linking people with complementary personalities and backgrounds. So, without once considering whether to seek Justin's approval, she called Benita straightaway. With her usual dose of self-confidence, Mallory conveyed the invitation as a sort of gentle demand, slipping in a word or two about Trent—a small hint at the significance of the event. The suggestion of matchmaking was there, oblique but unmistakable.

Benita hesitated in her shy and simple way before responding. "I, I'd love to come." A little stutter rarely evident in her speech. "Just the four of us? This man—Trent—he's single I suppose?"

"Did I mention a wife?"

"I—how can I put this? I appreciate the thought, but I don't think I'm ready for this."

"Oh, I'm not asking you to be *ready* for anything! It's just a casual barbecue, and Trent is a fun, *fun* person, you'll see. Justin *too* of course—remember you said you'd like to meet him? We'll just be a merry bunch, nothing stressful." Mallory wondered at her cheerleading. Fun, fun, rah, rah. Trent would be entertaining, but Justin? Mr. Even-Keeled, Mr. Rationality? Still, the cheery falsehoods spouted forth, something she'd done before with Benita, whose sweet sadness always seemed to inspire it. What a sad, sad girl, but a girl with such potential! It was Mallory's gift to recognize the potential in others and develop it. She'd built her reputation on that premise and the proof lay in her results, always true to her initial vision—well, almost always.

On the eve of the barbecue, Mallory informed Justin of her plan. He responded with his characteristic nod of the head, brow crunched into concentration: that intellectual mystique Mallory had once found attractive. Now, after six years of marriage, she knew it only too well. An ineffectual intellectualism—mental prowess without results. He exuded these little signs constantly, these needling reminders of her flawed vision. "Benita, sure, fine, we'll have her," he said absentmindedly in response to Mallory's belated declaration of intent.

But Justin's lack of interest didn't really matter. The plans were laid. And what could be more relaxing and sensual than a summer afternoon on the deck, shaded by heavy, big-leafed trees? Mallory couldn't deny that suburban living had its charms (even if she *did* always begin to long for the city the moment her train pulled out of Grand Central on weekday evenings).

Their home, Justin's and Mallory's, was picture perfect, straight from a magazine. "Great for enter- taining" said the real estate listing when they were looking. A large, elegant dining room and a modern, well- mapped kitchen. French doors opening onto a spacious wood deck in a private yard. If Mallory had to live all the way north like this—her one concession to Justin—then it had to be in *this* house, something way beyond their means at the time they bought it five years ago and only marginally within their means now. And perhaps forever after only marginally within their means, a constant source of strain and worry, never to be taken for granted—if recent events were any indication.

Hours before the guests were to arrive, Justin was into his routine, measuring and mixing. These were his creations, but nothing was ad-libbed, every recipe mentally recorded in perfect three-quarter teaspoons of this and one-eighth cups of that, ingredients planed straight as ice at the top of measuring implements with the sharp edge of a knife. It was Mallory's job to wash, chop, and assemble—tasks she performed in a slapdash way but well enough, relying on Justin's sauces, dressings, and garnishes to make these very ordinary picnicky dishes into culinary masterpieces.

What a shame I've no accounts with gourmet French restaurants, Mallory often mused on occasions like this, watching Justin cook with precision, exhibiting his own quiet version of zeal. He really did enjoy it. Perhaps had missed his true calling, she thought with a bitter laugh bubbling up internally under the influence of her pre- company, pre-dinner glass of chilled white wine.

They were both outside on the deck when Trent arrived, Mallory finishing the table, Justin at the barbecue setting up his utensils and that silly little plastic timer. Mallory heard the car on the driveway, heard the door close solidly, went to the deck railing, and saw a brand-new black Mercedes convertible, top down, and the man next to it, tanned, dark glasses, khaki shorts. Sun glinting off car and hair, both gleaming black, matching in color.

Mallory leaned over the deck railing at her waist, causing the fabric of her V-necked cotton shirt to pull down tight across her chest. "Hello, you!" she called. "Come around back!"

Trent looked up, removed his sunglasses. Smiled. Walked into the backyard toward the steps up to the deck. Mallory noticed his legs, muscular, pleasingly haired. Not apish, nor embarrassingly bald and shiny like Justin's. Eighty-four degrees, and she couldn't very well ask Justin to wear long pants, so there they were, all three of them bare legged, the men cloned in khaki and polos (Trent's shirt a deep lavender, Justin's a drab olive), Mallory in her vibrant turquoise cotton tee and white shorts—dangerous with barbecue sauce, but would she really be eating any-thing anyway? Still, it was a crisp, sporty look that did her well and something that Benita would unlikely copy, at least that much Mallory could predict based on her know-ledge of Benita's wardrobe, those loose, chiffony things she liked to wear. Benita, always a bit different, but some-how entirely proper looking—and prepared for every possibility. (Well, not *that* one, but how could she have ever predicted?)

In fact, it was Benita's preparedness that had led to

their meeting, six months ago, in the locker room at the health club. Mallory had forgotten to bring her socks and was muttering something to that effect under her breath when Benita, quietly but firmly, had offered hers. "Here," she said, handing them to Mallory, "I have an extra pair." Clean, not just clean, but brand new, Mallory was sure of it. Never before worn. She accepted.

And what could Mallory do, failing to wash and return them by the next Zumba class (and the next and the next) but drag Benita into the club's sportswear shop and buy her a new pair? "No, please don't," Benita protested while Mallory stubbornly repeated, "I insist." This awkward interlude was followed by an hour-long chat in the juice bar, Benita's sad history emerging over grapefruit juice. Mallory subtly elicited the details, absorbing them in silent triumph.

An interesting girl, that Benita. Too interesting for Trent? Mallory watched him ascend the five steps to the deck, his tan very rich against the deep lavender shirt. Dashing and handsome, but still quite conventional. Justin extended his hand, Trent's sprang out to greet it. A snapshot of that handshake might have passed in a poster touting racial harmony. At one time, Mallory had admired her husband's gentle, dusty good looks, but now, in the summer, and especially next to Trent, he simply looked dustier, pasty, and shorn.

Retrieving her glass of wine from the table, Mallory sauntered forth noncommittally, as if the dinner party had been entirely Justin's idea. Trent leaned slightly forward, touched her upper arm, and kissed her cheek, natural as can be. A hint of musk on his face, not overdone. He was taller than Justin. Mallory noticed that.

"So, you found us," declared Justin.

"Sure, but my *God*, what a hike!" complained Trent with a grin. "That Mountain Ridge Road—"

"I guess we're used to it."

"*Jesus.* I should've brought my shotgun. A herd of deer ran me down."

Laughter.

"At least our wildlife is prettier than yours down in the city," said Justin with a little smile that said he was attempting a joke, his voice remaining even and colorless. Mallory and Trent looked at him, not quite sure.

"How long does it take you to get to the office?" asked Trent.

"Entirely too long," said Mallory.

"An hour and fifteen," offered Justin.

"Hour and forty-five."

"Hour and a half max."

"For you maybe."

"Mallory is all the way downtown," explained Justin.

Trent emitted a single, musing laugh and folded his arms while the married couple exchanged looks of regret. Mallory jumped into the silence. "What can we get you to drink?"

"Anything cold."

"Wine, beer, something softer, something harder?"

Trent's eyes briefly roamed, spotting Justin's frosty tumbler of cola on the deck railing and Mallory's half-empty wineglass in her hand. Evaluating. "Wine would be great." He nodded toward Mallory's glass.

"Sure now? Maybe a gin and tonic? I also make a

mean margarita." She had done her own evaluating and knew he would enjoy a drink.

"No thanks. What you're having is fine."

Tactful. Still too early for anything but tactfulness.

Mallory smiled at Trent before turning, retreating, passing through the French doors into the kitchen. She breathed in deeply, quieting a flutter in her chest. Cooler inside with the central air on, but still not so sticky outside as to justify abandoning the barbecue-on-the-deck plan. She took the wine bottle from the refrigerator, topped off her own glass, took a few sips, topped it off again, then filled a clean glass for Trent. By the time she returned to the deck, Benita had arrived and was extending a timid hand toward Justin.

"Benita!" exclaimed Mallory. "So, you've all met one another?" She handed Trent his glass of wine and eyed Benita's outfit. Just as she'd predicted. Slightly overdressed in a loose blouse and lightweight, flowery skirt to mid-calf, but still cool enough and not in-appropriate. Mallory was grateful for Benita's unique fashion, something that masked her ample curves, a contrast to Mallory's style which always did the most to expose and amplify her own athletic line.

"I made the introductions," testified Justin.

"Yes." Benita gave an affirmative shake of her small oval head, sending a shudder through her thick black hair from crown to mid-back. Mallory looked at Benita, then Trent, then Benita. The same, exactly and precisely the same color and consistency of hair. Benita and Trent— and that Mercedes. It seemed embarrassingly wrong, even though Mallory's two guests were so different in other ways. How could a man and a woman with identical hair (except in length of course) possibly be right for each other? One thing so obviously the same, and another so obviously different: Trent all square-edged and self-assured next to Benita, retiring and ill at ease. How hard for her this must be! After everything she's been through, getting out socially again!

Mallory offered a drink; Benita requested a cola. After Mallory filled the order, the foursome remained ensconced around the barbecue, sipping drinks, exchanging pleasantly inane chitchat, Benita mostly quiet, Justin professorial and correct, Trent and Mallory high spirited and growing ever more so, trading comments about Justin's detailed preparations and exacting method of grilling the meat. Tongs, sauce brush, cooking mitts lined up on the left; platter of chicken and Justin's special sauce on the right; lid closed for preheating until the thermometer reached 400; timer set for ten minutes; bare chicken on the middle rack, placed with a sizzle; sauce brushed on after the second ten-minute side; timer reset for five minutes. Justin took the barbs good-naturedly, attempting his own flat-sounding repartee. "Laugh all you like. You won't be laughing when you taste it!"

"No, we'll be enshrining the barbeque!"

"And worshiping that little timer!"

Benita remained silent, her eyes dark and compassionate.

Noticing Benita's maturely distant look, Mallory began to wonder how a thirty-something group could sound like a bunch of seven-year-olds. She left for the kitchen, returning with the bottle of wine for the table, a couple of extra cans of soda for Justin and Benita. They were about to start serving.

"I have to admit, this is delicious," said Trent when they were all seated, taking their first bites. Trent across from Mallory, bottle between them, Justin across from Benita.

"The chicken's great," said Benita. "And the salads are wonderful too, Mallory. You'll have to share your recipes."

"Thanks," said Mallory, glass to lips. She glanced to the side at Justin over the top of her glass but said nothing to correct Benita. Justin didn't look at his wife, keeping his eyes cast down at his plate.

"I feel like I'm on vacation at a country resort," said Trent. "A sort of mom and pop operation."

"Mom and pop?" Mallory gave Trent the evil eye.

"You know what I mean. This is a very…married sort of thing. It's great for you two of course." He waved his fork at Justin and Mallory. "You have a great house, a wonderful yard. Just not for me at this point in my life."

"You ought to go for it, Trent," said Justin. "The life is good." He patted the top of Mallory's left hand where it rested on the table. "Green trees and fresh air to come home to."

"And a *lovely* wife, isn't that right, dear?" Mallory inadvertently bumped the table, sending plates and forks jumping as she leaned toward her husband with an upturned, kittenish face. Justin maintained his straight-spined posture and smiled. "But I suppose," said Mallory, pulling away from her husband and regarding Trent, "that you aren't any closer to marriage after recent events."

"How do you mean?"

"Well, this girlfriend we've been dying to meet. Charlotte."

"Oh. Charlene. I had thought of bringing her, but it just didn't work out. You're right, though, I'm nowhere near marriage. Not that I don't envy you, it's just not for me right now. I'm enjoying the city too much. It's the place to be when you're single." Trent took a large swallow, finishing his glass, and reached for the bottle. "But I guess you wouldn't agree, would you, Benita?" he continued, looking at the bottle as he poured.

"Agree?" she repeated, fork halfway to mouth, her dark lashes fluttering briefly.

"I mean, you're single, but you live all the way up here in the sticks, right?"

"Well, yes…"

"She's just a few streets over from us," chattered Mallory, "but like everyone else she got married before moving up here, right Ben?"

Benita flushed.

"So, you're married?" asked Trent in a dull voice.

"When she *first* came up here, sure, but now they're separated of course." Mallory reached for Benita and squeezed her forearm reassuringly. "But you're right, Trent, this is a very married sort of a place. As for me, I was always more of a city girl. I *love* the city and feel a little isolated up here with all these mommies and their toddlers." Another slip. She glanced obliquely at Benita but continued without hesitation. "Justin, dear, would you get us another bottle? There's one in the fridge. You'd like some more wine, wouldn't you, Trent?"

"Thanks, I'm fine." He leveled a hand over his glass despite the want that showed in his eyes, Mallory was certain she saw it there.

"No, really, we could use a little more. Benita, sure you don't want to join us? Please, Justin."

Her husband, grim faced, obeyed without comment.

In his absence: "That was all part of the plan when we came up here," continued Mallory, picking up the thread she had left dangling. "Move to the suburbs and have kids. Change my name to Melrose so the child won't have identity confusion. Can you imagine? 'Mallory Melrose.' I've told Justin it's nothing personal and not even women's-libbish but I'll keep my own name, thanks, Mallory Boyd. It just goes together, and there's no need to change it, especially since we have no little ones to confuse. We've been here five years now, and I could still move back to the city in an instant. Just pack my bags and go. Leave all this behind!"

She was looking into Trent's eyes, imagining a shining ray of approval in them. He was certainly returning the gaze with the hint of a thought underneath his grin: *My kind of girl*, it seemed to say.

The sound of Benita's voice cut through. "That's too bad."

"Too bad?"

"Well, that you've had trouble having kids."

"Oh! No trouble! We just haven't gotten around to it. Ah, here he comes now. Justin, I'm about empty." She lifted her glass. He poured just a third of the way up. "It was all sort of more Justin's idea anyway, wasn't it, dear? You see, having kids would ruin my career right now."

Justin paused, bottle in mid-air, then moved his arm mechanically toward Trent's glass, poured. Trent did not refuse. Justin resumed his seat behind a dirty dish, empty except for a few bones and the traces of his secret sauces.

"What is this career you'd be ruining?" inquired Trent. "You haven't mentioned where you work."

A giggle bubbled up into Mallory's mouth and threatened to burst forth. How absurdly funny! Her own Justin, never mentioning a word about her job to Trent! Of course he must be embarrassed. Had to be. The idea was inexplicably hilarious.

But Mallory suppressed the bubble, allowing its effervescence to emerge in the form of a little smile. "I'm a headhunter," she said.

"I always thought that was such an interesting word," offered Benita. "Headhunter."

Mallory turned to Benita and voiced her immediate thought. "Interesting maybe because the word almost seems to fit your situation, doesn't it?" She lifted her glass, swilled a bit more.

"But I have a job," replied Benita with polite insistence.

"Oh, sure, of course, but Trent, did we tell you that Benita is a graphic artist? She does layouts for magazines and book covers and such. It's all very creative."

Justin sat up taller and leaned toward Benita, incipient language on his lips. But Trent was too quick. "Is that so?" he said, throwing Benita the shortest of glances before returning to gaze upon Mallory. "And what kind of headhunting do you do?"

"Corporate, executive, upper management, and law.

In fact, law is my biggest area." She looked at Justin, then back at Trent. "I have a very large account with your firm."

"The way we've been growing it isn't any wonder."

"Listen to *him!*" exclaimed Mallory, feeling very familiar. "'The way we've been growing,' like he owns the place now that he's made partner. My congratulations, by the way."

Justin stood and raised his tumbler with an inch of melted ice and liquid the color of weak tea. "Yes, our congratulations. Here's to your continued success at Belknap and Stone." They all lifted their glasses.

"That's very big of you, man," said Trent as Justin sat down again.

Big is right, thought Mallory. Justin was never one to begrudge anyone anything. So big, magnanimous, and selfless. Too good for his own good.

"I suppose being a lateral hire didn't hurt your bid for partnership," she said. "And you did it in just a year's time!"

"I made it clear that my six years at Gersen Finch had to count for something. We didn't use the word 'partner,' but Steve implied it would be mine as long as I didn't commit any major screw-ups."

"Steve Belknap? You already knew him?"

"A friend of my folks."

Benita's eyes jumped from Mallory to Trent to Justin, her expression mildly befuddled.

Mallory patted Justin's hand while sending Trent an admiring gaze. "Ah, yes. Those with connections are never in need of my services." She and Trent shared a sparkling gaze. "Maybe Justin should have transferred before it was too late," she said as if he weren't there. "They strung him along for seven years, and then—"

"It's a tough call," broke in Trent diplomatically. "We have three hundred lawyers and just a few openings for partner. Why do you think we have the Senior Associate position? To hang onto the good ones, and Justin's one of the best."

Justin fidgeted, remained silent.

"Of course, I said as much to the hiring committee when I sent his name over, seven years ago," said Mallory.

"You?"

"Yup."

"You got him into Belknap?"

A moment of awkward silence.

Benita broke in. "What a lovely way to meet! Such good luck to get a job and a future wife at the same time." She was looking at Justin, her skin soft and dewy.

"Yes, well, I thought it was great luck," said Justin. "Listen, why don't we get up and take a walk before dessert? I'd like to show you the neighborhood." He stood.

"Still trying to sell me on the life, hey old man?" asked Trent with a grin.

Benita stood. "That's a wonderful idea. It's so much cooler now." She started to pick up her plate.

"No, leave it," said Mallory, waving a hand at Benita and pushing herself up from the table. "A walk? A walk he says."

"Just to the end of the street."

"It's almost dark," and "Such a lovely time of evening"—a cacophonous blend from Mallory and Benita.

Justin led the way to the deck steps, followed by the guests and finally Mallory, whose complaints evaporated once she realized that she was more or less floating, her head miles above the contact point between feet and ground. Down the back steps, out to the driveway, to the street, then four across, Justin, Benita, Trent, Mallory, then somehow Benita and Justin ahead, Mallory and Trent behind. The sun had set, and it was cooler but a bit more humid, the thick atmosphere a straitjacket against Mallory's tendency to drift, while moisture sprang to the surface of her skin, making her simultaneously hot and cold like a sweating glass of iced liquid in the sun.

Mallory did her best to ignore Justin, who immediately launched into his "tour guide" persona, directing their attention to one side of the road then the other: those two giant sycamores in front of the Morgensterns' house, the spectacular spray of dianthus at the Caronellis'. But soon, shortly after they'd broken into pairs, the commentary stopped, along with the obligatory, noncommittal responses from their guests.

With the other two ahead, Trent and Mallory fell silent—a condition rarely experienced by either one—an unspoken something inside the decent column of space between them. The silence wasn't uncomfortable for Mallory, her sensibility dulled. But she did feel Trent next to her, sensed his height and weight and breadth, all slightly more than her husband's.

They slowed, watching their feet. Mallory looked up.

Benita and Justin seemed miles ahead, their faces alternately turning toward each other and away. Lips moving. A lot from Benita's lips. So shy all evening, now a chattering doll. What could they be talking about? Impossible that she could be telling him about *that*.

"So, what's the big secret?" asked Trent with such familiarity that she knew him, saw herself in him.

"What secret?" Coy.

Trent laughed. "All this stuff you were covering up about your friend's marriage. You're not very good at keeping a straight face." She looked at his grin, the glint in his obsidian eyes. He turned his face forward, glanced at Benita's backside, and nodded his head by way of indication. Interested? Not that kind of interest. Mere curiosity.

"Oh, *that*." She giggled. "Poor Benita's had such a hard time of it. Really something." Her tongue was loosening, a surge of speech ready to spill with the relief she felt to be talking about someone else.

She began the story in a raised, hoarse whisper simply to add suspense, for the other two were so far ahead there was no chance they could overhear. "She was married a few years ago to a wonderful, wonderful fellow. You know, hardworking, good looking, upstanding, Mr. Nice to everyone, fun loving, generous, you name it—of course this is the description Benita gives. I never met the man. Corey Vanderlyn—she's kept his name. They moved into their house up here right after the honeymoon, and about a year and a half later Benita is two months pregnant with their first baby, and, and then, unbe*liev*able. He just disappears. Corey is gone. Drives off to work one morning and no one sees him again. He could be in China or at the bottom of the river or wandering around with amnesia for all we know. And poor Benita was so heartbroken she had a miscarriage, a very bloody and painful one. She's been in shock for almost a year now and tries to feel like a widow, but she has *no* way to be sure and keeps hoping that…"

A big laugh from Trent. "Sorry," he sputtered in his mirth. Mallory caught his laugh and felt a smile curl her lips. "Sorry," he said again. "It's not a funny story. So sad maybe it's funny. She's just killing herself with this widow fantasy."

"Oh, no, no. It's *not* a fantasy. He adored Benita and wasn't the kind of man to just run off, so there's every reason to assume the worst. His parents and friends haven't seen him since. I mean, there's no proof, his body hasn't shown up and he didn't seem to have a single enemy in the world, but anything could have happened, an accident, a carjacking."

"He'll show up. It's been, what, less than a year? Can't hide forever. It's nearly impossible to cover your tracks."

"Hide?"

"Come on, Mallory. A wrecked car and a body don't disappear so easily. The guy has no enemies but all at once he has a mortgage, a wife, and a baby on the way. Maybe even a job he doesn't like." Trent shook his head. "Most men in that situation would at least think of cutting out."

"On Benita? Who would ever cut out on her? Someone as sweet as Benita?"

Mallory noticed the way Trent eyed Benita up ahead, for the first time regarding her as a woman. The attraction was there. But a moment later, he averted his gaze, seeking freedom. "Yeah," he said. "Someone as sweet as Benita." Then he looked at Mallory, the attraction harder. "After all, don't women always complain there aren't enough men like Justin in the world?" Trent's eyes were taunting, teasing, urging her to shed the last bit of decency.

She returned his smile, feeling dizzy and drowning, caught her breath and looked away. Regarded her husband. Maybe Justin was abnormal. Too good. But what good was goodness if it didn't make people happy?

The distance between the pairs had diminished as they approached the dead end, the two in front pausing in the turn-around before heading back. Still talking, Justin and Benita seemed engrossed in their conversation, oblivious of Mallory and Trent, who slowed their pace to gain a few extra moments of privacy. "Maybe I understand what you're saying about Benita's husband," said Mallory.

"I thought you would." He paused and turned to her. Their eyes met. "You're dying up here, aren't you?" His voice a sultry whisper.

She returned his gaze, not shrinking this time, her eyes saying *yes*.

Justin and Benita, sensing the others nearby, cut off their conversation and looked back. "So this is the end?" Trent called out as they closed the gap. "What a great neighborhood!" He was square and forthright, using a voice that Justin and Benita would find sincere. Mallory, and perhaps only Mallory, could detect the sarcasm.

"Nice, isn't it?" said Justin, a proud look on his face. Benita at his side, face serene, nodded approval in slow motion with a languid, heavy-lidded blink.

They turned and started back, this time careful to remain a group, four across, the suggestion of their private conversations lingering underneath the pleasantness of superficial observation. The gradual descent of evening had left them near the end of a long summer dusk, still light enough to see. Justin, the tour guide again. Benita demure and correct. Trent diplomatic and witty. Mallory quieter than before, with an urgent need to pee.

They rounded a bend, the Melrose-Boyd house coming into view. The outdoor lights had come on automatically in their absence—another one of Justin's timers. Mallory noticed a strange car in the driveway, parked behind Benita's which was parked behind Trent's. A tattered, aging luxury car of a forgotten decade, a big rusty boat. Something that didn't belong here.

At her side, Mallory felt Trent reacting, growing tense. "How in the world…?" he muttered, shaking his head. A woman emerged from the driver's side. Tottering on high-heeled mules, she clicked around to the back of the car. Tight miniskirt, tube top.

"Must have peeked in my address book. Sorry about this, old man…," Trent apologized to the man of the house.

"Charlene," whispered Mallory under her breath.

"…it may get a little ugly."

The forgotten girlfriend was not looking happy, blonde hair standing in shock waves around her puckered face.

"Hello," said Justin, when they were close enough. "Hi," from Charlene, glaring at Trent, then glaring at Mallory.

"Meet Charlene, everyone," said Trent. "Justin, Mallory, and Benita." Realization of her mistake crossed Charlene's face. She switched her glare to Benita. "If you could just give us a minute?" Trent said to Justin, eyebrows raised.

"Sure, no problem."

Charlene exploded well before the others were out of hearing distance. Who was that woman, and I'm not good enough for your friends, and I embarrass you, and the like, all in hysterical outer-borough tones, while Trent, remaining the diplomat, offered deep-voiced phrases of reason and control.

Inside, Justin and Benita went into the living room while Mallory headed for the powder room and spent a long time peeing and thinking. She thought of the absurdity of Charlene with Trent. The incongruity. Trent's messy little secret. She thought of Charlene's eyes on her when she first walked up and laughed at Charlene's perception and choice. The perception of threat had been correct, but the perception of affinity incorrect. After all, it was Benita who'd been loved and left, just like Charlene. No one had ever left Mallory. But maybe that was because Mallory had always done the leaving first.

Mallory spent a moment in front of the mirror, noticing pink in the whites of her eyes, feeling the beginnings of a headache. She heard Trent come in the front door. Impressive. He'd gotten rid of Charlene in just a few minutes.

When she stepped out of the powder room, everyone was congregated in the foyer near the open front door, the guests in the preliminary stage of taking their leave.

"I apologize for the scene, old man. Charlene wasn't too happy when I called it quits last week."

"It's okay. Understandable," said Justin.

"A bad way to end a great evening!" Trent looked at Mallory, a hint of guilt under his smile.

"The dinner was fabulous," said Benita. "Thanks so much for having me." She looked up at Justin gratefully. He returned the look, lingered, his glance filled with something Mallory had never seen.

Benita and Trent inched toward the door. Mallory thought of protesting, reminding them of the forgotten dessert, the after-dinner drinks, the possibility of intimate conversation in the living room. But those possibilities were gone, no one wanted them now, at least not the four of them together, all at once, in the same room.

Trent shook Justin's hand, then turned to Mallory, touched her shoulder and bussed her lightly on the cheek. He caught her eyes on the way up from his kiss, sending a spark meant to inflame earlier intimations. She was reminded, knew she wouldn't forget, and knew this wouldn't be the last time. But for now, her head throbbed, obliterating everything else.

Justin's eyes followed Benita and Trent as they traversed the front walk to the driveway, parted with a polite handshake, and got into their cars. Mallory, standing behind her husband, turned and walked away from the front door.

"Too bad," she heard at her back. Justin's voice came out heavy and slow—from fatigue or emotion?

She hesitated before taking another step.

"It's just too bad," he echoed. They remained frozen, back-to-back with a yard of distance between them.

When he spoke again, his voice was barely more than a whisper. "It's a shame you're so disappointed in me."

Justin closed the front door quietly and went off to collect the dirty dishes.

Mallory headed upstairs to bed.

∞ Sissy and Me

SISSY AND ME are sitting in front of Kmart after school when this guy comes up and says, "I got some blow. Let's have a blow party."

We're wearing our white T-shirts and jeans and the rubber tire sandals with the cloth straps. The T-shirt has to be "X Small" and the jeans tight into your creases. Some girls don't wear any bra under the shirt, like Cindy Crawford in *Fair Game*. But me and Sissy don't. "You have to leave something to the imagination," I told her (we're both in tenth but she's almost a whole year younger so sometimes I'm almost the big sister role) so we wear one and usually that lacy kind so you can see the patterns.

We're drinking a Snapple and eating chips, sitting right up against the wall near the Kmart front door when this guy comes up. He looks like he already had a snort of that blow he's talking about and his eyes are kind of smeary. He says, "You girls are hot. Your lips already greased up, ready for the blow party." I'm getting kind of sick looking at him, but maybe he's good for something.

"You have a cigarette?" I ask him.

He pulls out some Kools, and I'm almost impressed because it's my brand, but the pack is all squished and the one he gives me is kind of messed up but I look at it and there's no tears in the paper. It won't pull if the paper's ripped, so I take it and get out my own matches in my back pocket. It takes a while because the matches are in there tight against my butt and when I get them out the cover is all squished flat together but they still work.

I take a drag and hand it to Sissy. We were dying for a cigarette. You can't get a pack in Kmart even if we have the money which we don't. We tried plenty of times even with different people behind the counter but it never works. They have their policy down good. So if we have the money we go to Hardwick's Drugs when Junior's there (that's Hardwick Junior I think) and the counter comes up past your belly button and we lean over it and he always sells us a pack. But we don't hang there too much. Nothing happening in front. Not like Kmart. We come to Kmart a lot of times after school and a lot of times when we cut.

Whatever it is, we never go home as long as we can. What do I want to see my mom for anyway? I say that a lot to Sissy almost to make her feel better because she doesn't have a mom. Or a dad. They both died when she was little and she likes to go into these head trips about how her mom was beautiful and nice to her, nicer than her grandma that she lives with. So I tell her about my mom and how it's not really so good to have a mom anyway if they act like that and you never know, her mom could have been just like mine for all she knows. Sissy's really my best friend and we hang together all the time but sometimes she gets on my nerves too because she acts so immature. It's probably because she's almost a whole year younger than me.

Like I tell her, like yesterday, I go home and my mom is crying again. It almost makes me sick. She sits in a corner and cries over that guy. He comes over every night after midnight (I know because I'm still awake, I'm a night person), and he's really loud and hairy too. I don't know what she sees in him. I can't stand him. He comes in yelling about stuff with his dirty mouth, "f— this and f— that," and I couldn't even go to sleep if I wanted to.

Sissy likes to use the "F" word too and I tell her you got to clean up your mouth. It's not feminine. And even I don't like guys who say it too much. She thinks I'm a little out of it or something but like I said she kind of looks up to me so she tries really hard to clean up her act.

Anyway, sometimes he knocks her around a little in her bedroom which is right next to mine and she might even bounce off the walls sometime and he usually stops before he kills her. Then she starts with her teeny little girl voice act. I can't see them because I'm in the other room but I know she has her eyes popped open wide with that mascara gooped all over to make those lashes really long and goopy with little globs on them (she thinks this is pretty) and blinking or fluttering I guess you call it and then he starts to laugh and she giggles and then he jumps on her for fifteen minutes. I couldn't even sleep if I wanted to.

He's always gone in the morning and she's sleeping so I don't see her and I leave. If I come home around dinnertime she's always crying with that black stuff running down her cheeks. Then around nine, ten o'clock, she fixes herself up.

That's usually when she gets in a pretty good mood and sometimes we have "Makeovers." She tells me, "Why don't you girls ever wear any lipstick? You need some color in your cheeks too and some eye shadow." She once worked at a makeup counter in a department store and says she knows everything about makeup, how to turn you from a "before picture" into an "after picture." She laughs and says we should get a camera so we can have the proof.

Anyway, I know this makes my mom happy, so I let her do it and she gets everything, I mean everything, out, the blusher, the liquid cover-up, the eye liner, five hundred kinds of shadow, the lip liner, lipstick, pencil, and her favorite, that mascara. She puts all this stuff on me, it takes just about an hour, and she says the whole time that she knows my colors. They do some kind of scientific color charts at these makeup counters like where she worked once, and they're supposed to know all the exact colors that go with your skin to make you look perfect or something.

She even does my hair too. I have long hair with a "lot of possibilities" she says but she's not really an expert at hair. She tried once but she flunked cosmetology school. So she does my hair kind of sloppy and puts all this junk on me (at first I used to try to convince her that natural is in again and a lot easier but she doesn't want to hear it so now I just let her do it), and when she's all done I look really gross. I look like a witch, but I tell her, "That's cool, Mom," and she smiles a lot.

She's almost kind of pretty when she smiles but sometimes I tell her when she's crying and all pathetic that she looks like an old hag. I mean, Cindy Crawford is thirty and look at my mom, an old hag (she's thirty-one, almost thirty-two, but I don't think Cindy Crawford is going to look like that in two years) and she just sits there all miserable with the black stuff smeared under her eyes and a cigarette stuck in her mouth bobbing up and down, talking around it (I tell her that's not feminine, take it out of your mouth when you talk and put it the right way between your fingers to look feminine), and she just cries and talks around that cigarette. "You watch out! You'll look just like me if you have a baby when you're sixteen." Then she sometimes starts screaming, "You aren't pregnant, are you? If you're pregnant you're out of this house! I'm not gonna keep you and a baby too!" And what a great house, right?

Still it would be pretty bad I guess, but I don't think I can get pregnant. I got the clap once and waited too long to get the medicine and I might not be able to get pregnant, but I don't know for sure. I heard of another girl who had the same thing happen and her doctor said she can't get pregnant. Whatever, I'm slowing down with that because I really don't like it too much anyway.

So we do these makeovers at about ten sometimes, and we do other things too. Sometimes we just talk and she tells me about my father who was a real stud and treated her right. She'll be smiling when she talks about that. But then she usually remembers to say how she messed up and started looking at other men and he left her, which makes her cry. I almost like the makeovers better.

Once after a makeover I left the stuff on my face and waited until her boyfriend came over and when they were busy in the bedroom I snuck over to Sissy's and knocked on her window. It really scared her at first. She said she thought it was this boy she was trying to ditch going to break in the window and rip her pants off like that time that made her decide she wants to ditch him for good. When she saw it was me (she couldn't even tell it was me right away because I looked so different) she was relieved and opened the window. "You look like a witch!" she says and we cracked up forever and couldn't stop laughing but we had to be kind of quiet so her grandma wouldn't hear. Her grandma's a heavy sleeper and didn't even know I was there all night, and in the morning, we went to school together and left before her grandma even woke up. My mom didn't even know either.

The guy Sissy was trying to ditch didn't ever come bother her again, and I'm glad because Sissy's really still too young and doesn't have as much experience like me. So that's what made me nervous about this guy with the blow party and everything because I don't even think Sissy knew what the guy meant. If Sissy was alone, she might do something I wouldn't do. That's why we made this agreement a long time ago that we always hang together. We don't split up. So I tell this guy, "Me and my friend have to talk."

"What you have to talk about?"

"We have to talk."

So we go off, me and Sissy, a little ways away to a corner of the building, and the guy with the blow, I can still see him standing where he was before. He's not moving. He's waiting for us. I tell Sissy, "You know what he means don't you?"

"Blow, you mean? He has some coke."

"Yeah, but he wants something else."

"Oh. I know. That's not so bad if he's gonna give us some coke."

I look at her really hard because I just can't believe my ears. She is so immature. Sometimes I think she just doesn't know anything. "Sissy." And I'm still whispering because I don't want this guy to hear, but it's getting hard to whisper anymore with Sissy acting so out of it. "That is so disgusting. You're gonna tell me you *like* that? That is *so* disgusting! He's talking about greasy lips and everything. I don't care how much blow he has. He didn't even take a bath since last year." I look over and he's still hanging over there looking at us with smeary eyes.

"Come on," I say to Sissy, and I almost have to lead her away, push her a little on the shoulder. We just walk away, and I look back to see what he's doing but he isn't moving because, really, there isn't anything he can do with all the people in the parking lot coming in and out of the store. He can't really just run after us and grab us or anything. That's what I like about Kmart. A lot happening, but you don't have to worry too much.

So we go over to Hardwick's even though it's pretty boring and we say "hi" to Junior and he gives us a pack even though we don't have enough money. He says, "When am I gonna get some of that?" and I say "Never, if you're lucky," but I smile at him and do some extra leaning on the counter to make him feel good. Then we go outside and sit on the ground in front and light up one cigarette for us to share. We like to do it that way to save them and then also one of us always has our hands free. Sometimes we braid each other's hair in those tiny braids, and we like to move the loops and posts around in each other's ears, changing them in the different holes to see how they look. I have five holes in one ear and four in the other, but Sissy only has three in each of hers.

❧ *Priscilla and I*

PRISCILLA AND I were in Pre-Company class doing center work, our legs lifted to the side *à la seconde*, when Mr. Duval came up behind and grabbed my upper thigh, rotating it to force the turnout.

Priscilla was next to me in the front row. While Mr. Duval rotated my leg, I tried to catch her eye in the mirror. Then I felt his breath on my neck and saw him looking at me in the mirror with his left hand on my waist and his right hand under my thigh. The whole episode was astonishing, but Priscilla didn't seem to notice.

I *did* look good. Priscilla and I were wearing the thin-strapped leotards with the tiny bow between the breasts, cut astonishingly low in back. Very little coverage. We're required to wear black leotards and pink tights, but the style is left up to us. Last week, when we first wore the thin straps to class, Mr. Duval stared at us a bit and rolled his eyes up under his eyelids. Maybe it *is* just a little juvenile to wear matching leotards (on purpose), but Capezio's was having a sale and we bought them that morning on impulse. I put them both on my card because Priscilla's parents never seem to buy her anything (she's on scholarship), and I knew my mother wouldn't notice. I have at least thirty black leotards and Priscilla has less than a dozen, so I bought her one and my mother won't know a thing. She says I can buy whatever I want at Capezio's because everything there falls in the category of career advancement.

But Mr. Duval's reaction, the rolling eyeballs, was simply astonishing. Uncalled for, really. Priscilla and I, even in matching styles, don't look anything alike. Priscilla usually wears glute and thigh warmers on top because she needs to sweat where she's heaviest. I have to admit, I *am* a little worried she won't make Company because she weighs at least 110—at least—and you just don't see thighs like that, even in the *corps*. I'm sorry. But she's my friend, so I don't say anything when she's eating a muffin (pretending she's picking at it) between classes instead of drinking a cup of coffee.

Mother says you should do what you can to keep a friend in this profession because everyone is such a backstabber. Mother knows from experience. I don't think she has a single friend left, unless you call those women she invites over "friends," with their big red mouths and slivery eyes.

My glutes and thighs are skinny and limber, so I don't need any help there like Priscilla does. But I do need ankle and shin warmers. My ankles take forever to warm up, and my right shin has a hairline fracture from the time a boy in Pre-Company let me down too hard from a lift in *pas de deux* class. He didn't even apologize. Honestly, I don't know how he got into Pre-Company.

So, there was only a thin layer of stretchy material

between my thigh and Mr. Duval's hand when he clenched me like a football, his thumb on top and four fingers down very near my right buttock, and he twisted hard until I bit my lip to keep the tears back. I'm not a crier like some of the girls. Mother says, "Don't ever let them see you cry!" So I bit my lip while Mr. Duval squeezed and twisted. "Out!" was the only thing he said, and his voice was different—deeper. Then I felt his breath on my neck and looked in the mirror, where his eyes were just waiting for me.

The whole thing was just a bit too astonishing, not because I was already perfectly turned out before he touched me. It was the *way* he did it. I had never thought of Mr. Duval that way before (well, that's not completely true if you count dreams which just happen to you in the middle of the night). But I always assumed he was gay like most of the rest of them, especially with that teal-colored silk scarf he likes to wear around his neck.

After class I told Priscilla. She smiled. She has this very big smile. They'll never pick her for Company with those braces on her teeth. I'm sorry. I don't have to tell her. She is *so* angry at her mother for sending her to that incompetent instead of going with the best, my orthodontist Dr. Miller. You just can't be cheap when it comes to your smile; it's one of your biggest assets. Now we're fifteen, it's our most important year in Pre-Company, the year they can pick you, and Priscilla's getting her teeth done *all* over again.

Priscilla said to me, "So, Mr. Duval likes you. Lucky, lucky girl."

"Maybe he was expressing his hatred for the entire

female gender. He practically *killed* me. His grip is just astonishing."

"Maybe. But I saw that look he gave you."

"You weren't even paying attention."

"I was too! How could *you* know? You were staring at him in the mirror. It was so lashivious."

"Lascivious. *I* was?"

"Not *you*. Him."

She smiled again like she wasn't even self-conscious about her braces or the little pieces of muffin plugging the holes in them. She took another crumbly bite while I sipped my coffee, and then she got all defensive like she does sometimes. "I'm just taking a few bites of this now and saving the rest for later."

I acted like I believed her, but she knew, and I knew, that the muffin would be gone before noon and replaced with another one she would try to pawn off as the original. I always go along with her, but we both know that *I'm* the one with the willpower.

For breakfast I usually have a piece of dry toast—no butter, no jam—but I skip it completely if I'm up a pound to 97 in the morning. Then it's just coffee, black, before and after class. By noon, I've usually perspired away the extra pound and can feel decent about a little cottage cheese for lunch and maybe a few grapes. I *do* like sweets (ballerinas are *notorious* sugar lovers), but I don't remember ever finishing a brownie or cookie. Two bites at the most—just enough sin to feel I've indulged myself.

After Priscilla said that Mr. Duval might actually like me, I started thinking about the way it felt and sort of imagined it as a lustful squeeze of the flesh. Maybe he was thinking only of his boyfriend's *derrière* at the time—how should I know? I'm a virgin and will probably remain that way until I'm forty-two. Ballet is everything to me. I'm consumed by my art. I have no time for sex (even if a boy of the right persuasion could be found).

In fact, it's rather astonishing I'm here at all, the way Mother talks. Back then, everyone was supposed to be straight, but the men were just as uninterested. Mother says the only real possibilities were, and still are, men outside the dance world but connected somehow, like doctors (we dancers do seem to require an astonishing number of them). So, you guessed it, my father is a doctor.

I know the real reason she married him and had me (don't tell her I know). Her career was going downhill, really slipping. I mean, most great ballerinas dance well enough to keep going strong into their forties, but Mother (despite the impression she likes to give) was not one of the greats. By thirty-seven, when she had me, I was about the only thing left she could produce.

And she's still producing me. At four thirty in the afternoon when I get home from the studio, she's waiting in the foyer of our apartment with her toe tapping. I swear, she must have an agreement with the doorman to buzz her when I hit the lobby downstairs so she can position herself for the toe tapping routine while I'm on my way up in the elevator. As I walk in, she reminds me (as if I didn't know) that Gretchen (my tutor) will be there momentarily and that we have English, algebra, and history to review. Every night after dinner I study for another three hours on my own. "The Company won't let you in if you're flunking!" Mother likes to remind me over and over again.

While I'm busy with Gretchen, Mother fixes me dinner, the same thing nearly every night. Lucky she only needs to cook for a ballet brat, because she never learned to cook. The usual is five ounces of skinless chicken, a measured half cup of rice or pasta—no cheese, no sauce—and five or six green beans. Mother sits down and eats with me—exactly the same food—putting up her cover as though I can't tell how she's been gaining (pigging out while I'm gone) and how her dress size expanded from six to eight. (I looked at the tags myself one day when she came home from Bloomy's and hadn't had a chance to cut them off.)

Father is never there for dinner, or rather, never there period. Whenever he is there, his beeper goes off and he talks on his cell phone (always right next to him) and then says to us, "Emergency. Gotta go." His patients are still mostly dancers, so I wonder about all the emergencies. We dancers have a lot of things that go wrong, but usually not life-or-death emergencies.

Priscilla told me once that she thought she saw my father near Columbus Circle talking to a girl in the Company (just a *corps* member), and he leaned forward and whispered something in her ear, almost touching it with his lips. "It was kind of lashivious," she said (maybe she just can't say it right because of her braces).

"O Gawd, Priscilla. Your imagination is astonishing. It was probably just noisy on the street." I don't know about my father and that girl, but I really don't care. I never see him, and I have more important things to worry about.

Priscilla's family looks, well, so normal. I met her parents and her brother once at the studio. They had all come just to watch her in class. All three of them. And all three with the same big smile Priscilla has. The thing that was most astonishing was the way they actually looked at one another when they talked.

Her mother is very sweet, really. She comes to the studio every once in a while, looking dowdy and lost. I think Priscilla said her mother grew up in Missouri (or one of those "M" states). She's not at all like my mother, who always walks in like she owns the place as if everyone remembers her. That's just the difference between me and Priscilla. That's maybe the reason she won't get in. I tell her, "You have to act like it's yours." But she just doesn't get it.

This year, they'll be picking only five of us for the Company. I'm sure I'll get in, and not just on my mother's connections. I have the longest line, the line they look for, and I have the best elevation and *pirouettes*. My feet are precise too. *Entrechat* and beats are a breeze for me. Priscilla is very sweet, very lyrical, but she's maybe just the slightest bit too heavy on her feet.

I suppose it wouldn't hurt having Mr. Duval on my side as well. That little squeeze of his and the look he gave me set off a whole fantasy, a recurring one, that was almost embarrassing. I wouldn't dare tell Priscilla, even though she'd love it. It's so "lashivious."

After I started having the fantasy, I felt sure Mr. Duval could read my mind. I kept my eyes away from his. A few days later, I got a little braver, and I looked at him, but he ignored me, totally ignored me. Usually I get at least a few corrections from him. So I took his avoidance as another kind of a sign. But the next week went by, and everything seemed normal, so dreadfully normal. It made me think that he had squeezed and turned my leg that day because maybe, after all, it really needed squeezing and turning. I've been working harder on my turnout ever since.

A few weeks before holiday break, I was sitting in the hallway with Priscilla. We were pounding out our new *pointe* shoes on the floor to soften the toes a bit before class. Out of nowhere, she asked if I would like to come over to dinner at her apartment sometime during the holidays.

I didn't know what to say at first. I've never been to her apartment before, but I imagined it as kind of messy with a lot of food smells. I could already see the dinner table, loaded down with animal flesh and mashed potatoes. I thought of myself around her parents and my mouth began to ache; they seemed like the type to expect a lot of smiling.

"It might be kind of hard to schedule," I said. "I'm renting studio space every day over the break. You're going to give yourself class aren't you? I mean, we have to stay in shape."

"Sure. But you have to eat dinner too. It was just an idea, anyway." Her mouth barely opened at all when she spoke, and for once I could hardly tell she wore braces.

Priscilla really is a sweet girl and maybe the best friend I have. So I said, "It's a good idea. I'll check my calendar and find a date." Priscilla came back with that big metal smile.

That was two weeks ago. Today is the day I go to Priscilla's, and I actually woke up feeling kind of excited about the whole thing.

Astonishing.

❧ Not This

IT WAS LAUREN'S day to achieve full lotus. An exalted feeling! Two years of Nikki's yoga classes had brought her to this. Directing them from the front of the room, Nikki lent encouragement with her cat's paw voice, padding a delicate weave around their mats. "Breathe deeply, a cleansing breath. Feel the life force within you."

Sandalwood smoked in the natural light, Nikki's disavowal of the electric switch. As always, she'd placed burning candles along the perimeter of the studio, enclosing and sheltering their shared space. In the warm shimmer of air with her eyes closed, Lauren sensed Barbara's presence on the mat inches away from hers. She envisioned the gentle rise and fall of Barbara's chest, the eyelids gently lowered, calves easily crossed, and thighs splayed outward. Soon she would return to earth and become aware.

The moment arrived. Barbara unfolded her legs and entered reality, but Lauren delayed, maintaining her position with senses alert, waiting to feel the light of Barbara's attention before she unwound her feet and returned the look. Their eyes locked and held. A swell of creation surrounded them, the energy of a dozen women—Sherri, Risa, Eve, Angel, Linda, and all the others. Lauren was blind to their physical presence, feeling the warmth of God on her cheek and a hand caressing her lips, gradually molding and stretching them into a smile identical to Barb's.

Like a foreigner, strange and fascinating, Barbara arrived with an offer, the recognition of common ground, washing away the barriers and moving toward the deepest kind of identification, a unity of feminine spirit, soul, and intellect.

This was it! Something rare, only dreamed of, and Lauren had been chosen for it, had made it happen!

After class, Barb and Lauren walked out together, Risa and Angel tagging behind. A late spring evening, eight o'clock, light fading into dusk. The euphoria remained, and Lauren hoped to share it with Barbara. She had the extra time tonight—no plans with Nate, and he wouldn't be expecting her.

The foursome lingered just outside the studio door, commenting on the fragrant spring air, the awakening it brought. And they spoke of mundane things, work the next day, families to care for, Barbara's children, Risa's husband. Conversation flowed easily between Risa and Barb, good friends for many years, while Angel listened for the most part, awkward but involved.

They wandered to the parking lot, Lauren hoping to lose the tagalongs. She loved these women, all the women in the class, but for now, she wanted to be alone with Barb. Risa might have been the one to cause a problem, but finally she announced she had to run, pausing long enough to aim an intent stare at Lauren while touching Barb's shoulder. Angel peeled off too, and at last they were alone.

Barbara turned to Lauren, her eyes alive with the unusual warmth she possessed, a heart that seemed to include all of humanity in its compass without judgment. It was the quality that had attracted Lauren to her from the start. "What a wonderful class tonight," Barb said simply. But Lauren detected a sublime thought beneath the surface of the words, an acknowledgement of the new and greater feeling between them.

Only two years ago, Barbara had been a mere acquaintance, one of Lauren's regular customers at Petals, her flower shop. Following Barb's suggestion to try Nikki's yoga class, Lauren was soon enough hooked, although the exercises did not come easily to her. She fell in awe of Barbara, the most advanced and flexible student, performing every *asana* effortlessly with full meditative quality and inward awareness.

At least, this is what Lauren believed. She'd sneaked peeks here and there, suspecting it was improper but feeling a need, so drawn was she to this example of self-actualization, an inspiring sight. "Gaze into the flame, don't let your eyes wander, breathe deeply, look inward," Nikki would say during their meditative sessions, a candle placed in front of each student. "Look within, look for the source." And then Nikki would be quiet, letting a hush settle over the room.

Lauren had found it difficult, this shift from the external world to the internal, although it seemed that everyone who had something to say about her character would remark how inwardly peaceful and calm she appeared. In the shop, she engaged contentedly in her work, shears in hand, contemplating an iris or lily. She moved gracefully through her day—this is what yoga had given her—pointing her toes as she walked, stretching into the refrigerated case for a rose like a ballet dancer. Serene, tranquil, secure in her purpose.

Dinners with Nate (they enjoyed tablecloth and candles, even at home), she expressed her thoughts in careful, ethereal prose, a quality many admired, Nate foremost. But at times it was too much for him. At times, when she gazed out beyond his shoulder as she spoke, he would complain that she seemed distant and searching. This would bring her back. This would make her wonder if she felt a void in his presence, and why, if she needed to look outward to fill that void, why didn't she look to him?

She believed the answer stood before her now. A complement, not a replacement—the companionship and understanding that only another woman could give. "It was a wonderful class," Lauren agreed with Barbara. "I felt something inside, the way I feel when I look into the lip of an orchid."

She remembered a fleeting glimpse of it this afternoon, a precursor of this evening's experience, as she tied a corsage, gazing deeply into the flower's velvety center, a kaleidoscope of yellows, oranges, and purples, thinking, *Is there such a thing as too much love? Can there be too much for one person to feel?*

Now she took Barbara's hand, wanting to recreate

the unique moment they'd shared only fifteen minutes before. Many times they'd hugged and kissed cheeks, but this touch meant more. Barb smiled warmly and squeezed Lauren's hand, but then her mouth turned slightly downward with a hint of blandness and disinterest.

"Oh, Barbara!" Lauren blurted, sensing the withdrawal and not wanting it to happen. "Can you spend some time with me tonight?" She took Barb's shoulders and pulled her close, embraced her fully, pressing against the length of her body to feel its warmth, power, and nourishment. Faces near, cheeks touching, Lauren whispered past her ear, as if it were a secret only they two could understand: "Let's be close. Very, very close! I love you so!"

Stiffness and a strange sound—a throat clearing?— and suddenly everything was wrong. Barb pushed away, adding a huff and a snort to the throat clearing, sounds that Lauren had never before heard. The loved one stepped back, eyes narrowed, all the warmth gone.

"Next time," she said, "maybe it would be *best* if you kept your secrets to yourself." She turned her back, a stranger after all.

Watching her go, Lauren uttered a primitive sound, a burst of air meant to be the beginning of a perfect phrase to repair all that was lost. Barbara kept walking, no longer loose and warm and transcendental but tight and nervous, fumbling in her bag for car keys.

Lauren's mouth hung open, nothing emerging until "See you in class!" popped out with a false cheeriness.

Barbara's response, nearly imperceptible in the descending light, was the slightest movement of her head, a shake and a shudder of disapproval. She did not turn around.

Lauren awoke from a restless night with a need to act, to reach out again, although she felt certain that Barbara would disdain any sort of contact. An odd thing to be sure of, so abruptly, so unexpectedly, after days and weeks and years of frequent and pleasant company. Yet she had no doubt of it, so evident had been Barbara's shock and displeasure at her desire for closeness.

She went to her shop, where things were busy. Mid-morning, her first free and alone moment, she looked at the clock, and knowing that Barb would be out of the house, she called and left a message. "Barb, it's Lauren," she started, but her voice cracked and she had to stop momentarily to catch her breath. Every ounce of blood had drained from her face, and she felt the slightest bit dizzy. "I just want to apologize," she continued. "I'm sorry if I offended you." She paused again, debating whether more would strengthen her case or only offer proof of an indiscretion she hadn't intended. "Please, I just hope you'll forgive me." She gently touched the "off" button and soundlessly replaced the cordless receiver, as if this outward demonstration of grace and stillness would lend more dignity to her apology.

A moment later the phone rang, jarring her from a haze of suppressed emotion. "Petals," she answered, and took another order from a customer. As it was, she'd been lucky to find a free moment to deliver her apology. The busy season was in full swing, Mother's Day coming up on the weekend, followed by proms, graduations, and weddings, and she had no help. Her only employee, a college student, had quit the week before under pressure of final exams.

Lauren worked alone in a crowded, humid space packed with vibrant blooms and a mixture of scents, the perfume of roses and the fecund redolence of moss and soil. Once so comforting, the reds and purples were blinding, the smells penetrating, suffocating. But she was grateful for the busyness, the constant movement of her hands, the innate pleasure of practicing her intuitive sense of beauty and creation, while trying to ignore the new suggestions in her surroundings, increasingly morbid and haunting.

The longer she worked, the sicker she felt. This was an aberrant existence, after all, wasn't it? A reclusive association with dead things, cut from their roots and nutrients, arranged and watered and pampered to prolong the illusion of life. She should be out in the fresh air, shouldn't she? Working the soil, seeding and nurturing plants instead of being an accomplice to their destruction, propping them up in death. They'd been cut from the earth, just as she'd been cut from the ideas and dreams that had nourished and elevated her above the tediousness of everyday existence.

That evening, she was unable to rise above this feeling of impending doom. In Nate's kitchen, after a spate of superficiality and evasiveness, he took a long, hard look at her and said, "So what's wrong with *you*?"

"Nothing," she replied, sullen.

"That's the biggest nothing I ever heard of."

Annoyed, she glanced at him briefly but had to look

away. His gaze was so penetrating it suggested omniscience, his words part of a devious ploy to reveal her chimera and the tragedy of her misguided certainty. How could he possibly know the value of the thing she'd nearly attained and lost? How could he be so sure it didn't exist?

"It's nothing," she said. "There *is* nothing, nothing more important than this," she picked up a salt shaker, "or this, or *this*," an onion, a knife. "There's nothing else in this world. Nothing."

He turned away and started to slice, then chop the onion. She stood two feet away from him, propped against the counter with arms crossed, the only sound a sharp knife through crisp onion on the chopping board.

A tear came into his eye. "Then I guess it must be nothing," he said.

The following day presented the moment of truth. Nikki held class every Monday, Wednesday, and Friday evening, and Lauren hadn't missed a class for many months. Wednesday had been the wonderful day that had turned on her, and now it was Friday.

The tone for the day was set by a message on her answering machine, the first thing she heard upon arriving at Petals that morning. Barb's voice, cold and businesslike. "Lauren." Clipped. "I received your message. For such a long time I've tried to ignore this, but you just went too far the other night. There's really nothing more to talk about. Please don't call again."

Lauren froze, staring at the machine, thinking back over the past weeks and months. *Such a long time ... tried to ignore … this. This.*

The rest of the day did not exist for her. Nearing six o'clock, closing time, she made none of her usual moves to finish up. Normally there would be no question about it. On yoga days she would clean up early, turn over the "Closed" sign, and lock the door on the hour, even if a customer sought entrance. Nate was well aware of these practices, yet on this Friday he did the unthinkable. At five to six, he walked in the door.

She looked up and there he stood in the doorway, acting as if he had a right to be there. She felt a small sigh pass through her body. She hadn't yet admitted to herself the deliberateness of her avoidance and omission. Her usual state of mind at near-yoga time, a mild form of excitement with the anticipation of release, hadn't come upon her. She'd done nothing to ready herself. Instead, she'd continued her activity, working within the same morbid fog, busily moving her hands as she'd done all day long, relying upon mechanical function, not hearing her customers' voices but allowing their needs to register in the control center of her brain.

"Not going to class?" he asked, but his presence had already announced the superfluity of his question.

"I have too much work today," she answered.

"It's six."

"I know."

"Let's go to dinner."

"I have too much work." The phone rang. "Petals," she answered.

While she was on the phone, he walked to the front door, locked it, flipped over the "Closed" sign, and turned off the lights in the front part of the store. She finished talking, hung up the phone, and started to gather up the debris on her work table, the ends of stalks and dry, shriveled leaves, nothing but dead things. He walked up behind and firmly placed a hand on her wrist, his fingers steady and warm. Her hands shook. "Enough," he said. "Let's go to dinner."

"I'm not hungry."

"Come then."

He led her by the hand into the back room where she kept a small couch for moments of escape. Hands on her shoulders, he gently pushed her down and stood again to turn off the overhead light, leaving a filtered grayness in the air, early evening sun through a high, tiny window. He sat down next to her, pressed alongside, his arm around her shoulder. "I'm not going to ask you what it is. Maybe you'll tell me one of these days. I just know something happened. I'll stick with you until it's better."

She said nothing, at once comforted and annoyed by his closeness. She did not want him to be right. He had met Barbara once or twice and did not think much of her. He would understand the strength of Lauren's disappointment but believe it to be out of proportion.

After ten minutes of silence with their lines of vision parallel and straight to the wall, he turned and kissed her forehead, lifted her chin and kissed her mouth. "I don't want this right now," she said. *I cannot because I'm a bad person, an offensive person undeserving of love.* She knew it was silly and untrue, but she said it to herself repeatedly, her senses deadened, emotions suppressed.

"I'm not asking for sex." He fell silent again. They

sat together for a long time, not looking at one another, his arm tight around her shoulder, reining her in.

Saturday morning early, Risa walked in.

"Hey, girlfriend!" she chirped, tossing her pile of blonde hair.

Lauren looked up and smiled. The greeting seemed somewhat too familiar—she didn't know Risa well—but maybe it wasn't familiar enough. Maybe Lauren didn't know what was appropriate and what wasn't and how people should act with one another and whether closeness was a good and desirable thing or a dangerous thing, something to avoid at all costs.

"How are you?" she answered, friendly but detached.

"Just great. We missed you in class last night! Took the day off?"

"No, just…" She looked at Risa, considering, but held her tongue. "Just had too much work to do."

"Then I guess you mean it." She turned and pointed. "The sign in the window."

Lauren didn't understand.

"Help Wanted."

"Oh, yes!" She'd forgotten the sign. "I could use some help."

"Well, maybe you'd consider me. I'm in between jobs right now." With brightly painted lips, Risa smiled broadly in that way she had, warm and big but almost too big, almost mocking herself and the person she smiled at. Her transparent blue eyes twinkled and caught the light in a way that always made Lauren unsure if she had winked or was about to wink. "You're doubtful, I can see. I worked in a nursery once, you know. And I'm a quick learner."

"Oh, no, I'm sure you are. I'm just surprised you'd consider it. I can't pay you very well."

Risa waved her hand in the air. "It's not the money. I want to help you out. You've been looking a little overworked lately. Everyone's noticed it." A gentle emphasis on the word "everyone," along with that smile and a slight narrowing of the eyes.

"So, everyone has?"

"Yes. You even look a little rough around the edges today. Maybe you should spend more time relaxing with that man of yours, what's his name?"

"Nate."

"Yes, Nate. How is he? He seems like such a nice guy."

"He is. Indeed, he is. Probably the nicest man on earth."

"So, when are you two getting married?" This time she *did* wink, Lauren couldn't mistake it, and there was something about her expression that wasn't entirely good-natured. But the look and the discomfort it caused were there and gone in an instant, defying certainty. Lauren just smiled and said nothing.

Silence overcame her along with a feeling of unutterable sadness brought by this reminder, the presence of one of Barb's friends, a person still in good stead. She allowed Risa to fill the silence with chatter, an endless exposition about the benefits of marriage and the attributes of her husband, a doll of a man she loved to death, but then a customer walked in, and the monologue ceased. While Lauren was occupied, Risa poked around the store, and when the customer left, they got down to business, Lauren explaining what was needed.

In short order, Risa proved her worth. She worked all that Saturday, returned on Monday and every day after that for the next several weeks. A big help. Over lunch she would relate the current news about Nikki and all the women at yoga while Lauren absorbed it all, grieving silently over her loss, harboring memories of a world that was quickly fading into the past, a dream that had been only that, a dream.

And every Monday, Wednesday, and Friday in the late afternoon, Risa would ask the same question: "Coming to class tonight?" The inquiry became a ritual, delivered with the knowing smile of a benevolent therapist, each time the look more intense, the smile that much brighter, seeming to say, *I know what your answer will be.* Lauren made excuses, her biggest one Nate, although he wasn't an excuse at all but a necessity.

Early on, after that first evening in his kitchen and the second evening on her couch, she'd poured out everything to him, her dreams, her emotions, her attraction to Barbara, the crushing disappointment. It was easier than she'd thought because he was, after all, the right person to receive her confidences. Sage, intuitive, and gentle, objective enough to see things she couldn't, involved enough to understand her needs. And he didn't believe her to be wrong, the thing she'd feared the most.

But now Risa was always there to bring her back, to remind her. All the little things that slipped out of Risa's mouth kept getting bigger along with her sense of privilege and righteousness, betrayed by the light in her eyes, the jaunty cleverness she couldn't contain. Lauren wanted to ignore it, to accept the outward friendliness as genuine, wanting to continue to love life and to love every person on earth, including this woman who'd declared only that she was there to help and who, in fact, had eased the pressure in some ways.

"When are you coming back to class? You're such a big part of that place," Risa would say in a taunting voice. "Everyone misses you. I was just talking to Barbara about it the other day," a slight emphasis on the name. "You know, I can *really* talk to that Barbara—such a *good* friend." She looked at Lauren as if to gauge her reaction before going on. "And your friendship means a lot to me too, Lauren." She paused for dramatic emphasis. "I just think it's important to say these things out loud sometimes. Good friends should tell each other how much they care, don't you think?" A look and a smile. The hint of a wink.

Horrified, Lauren returned the look with an open expression, eyes wide and loving. This reminder of Barbara's contempt—a test? How easy it would be to let anger control her. "Yes," she said, matter-of-factly. "I would agree that it's important." Important not to let others redefine her words and intentions. *I'll keep loving them. I have to love them, or I'm lost.*

Finally, on a beautiful Saturday late in June, she turned to Risa and said, "I've really appreciated your help, but the business is starting to slow down again…"

"I was about to say, maybe it's time we should cut this off?"

"That sounds like the right thing. Thanks for helping me get out from under."

"My pleasure, girlfriend." She smiled and winked, picked up her purse, and turned to go.

When Risa was at the door, Lauren called out behind her, "See you at yoga," this time really meaning it.

Soon after that, the first very hot night of early summer, she awoke to see Nate standing over the bed, wearing his shorts and T-shirt, his arms crossed. From inside her dreams, it seemed he must have been hovering for some time as she lay sweltering on a sandy beach, fully clothed and blinded by the intense light of the sun, its brightness hiding his contours and not allowing her to know his presence. Suddenly she was lying naked and exposed, the temperature falling into a pleasant warmth and the light receding to bring his outline into view, fully defined, comforting, protective.

"Hello," he said, when she opened her eyes.

"What are you doing?"

"I couldn't sleep. I've been up on the roof."

"What time is it?"

"After three."

"Come to bed." She patted the empty sheets next to her.

"No, you come with me. I want to show you something." She didn't protest. All of a sudden she was wide awake and without any need of sleep. The warm air held a promise of good times to come, a lazy summer stretching out ahead of them.

Wearing her cotton nightshirt, she slipped on her

sandals and took his hand. He led her up the narrow stairway of the apartment building and through the hatch door onto the flat roof, gravelly tar underfoot, over to a single, tattered chaise longue stuck among the pipes and vents. He sat down first and pulled her down to him, positioned her between his legs with her back to his chest. "Look up," he said. "It may take a while."

But it didn't take long at all. She saw the first one, then the second, then four or five in a row. Fireballs appearing out of nowhere, trailing brush strokes of sparks in the dark sky.

They sat in silence for many minutes watching the meteor shower. "It's like my love for you, Lauren, bursting and bright and different every time." He gently pushed her away from his lap to dig in the pocket of his shorts, found what he sought, and dangled it on a string before her eyes. "Here," he said. "This is for you."

Another shooting star. "A crystal?"

He put it around her neck and fastened the clasp.

"Crystals have healing powers," she said.

"I thought so. Actually, the saleslady told me that, but now…"

"I'm healed already."

"I know."

"By you."

"No, by yourself."

She fingered the stone. "Thank you." She settled back down against his chest, feeling the beat of his heart quickening with his thoughts.

"I've been wondering if you would marry me," he said at last. She smiled into the night.

"That just slipped out. I was planning to do this a better way, with a ring."

"I like the way you did it. And my answer is yes."

Clumsily, nearly tipping them over, she twisted around and kissed him full on the mouth. He drew her in, and soon, they were making love on that narrow, rickety chair under the exploding sky.

At last, it was time to return. The next evening, bracing herself for the worst, she went to class.

She arrived at the last minute, after the women had staked out their territories with mats dotting the floor, everyone from the regular group, all the familiar faces. There, in the center, stood Barbara, and next to her, in Lauren's old spot, Risa. The two women were talking, unaware that she stood at the door.

Nikki looked up from the front of the studio, her face open and unknowing. "Well hello, Lauren! Good to see you!" Perhaps Nikki was the only innocent one, for then a stir was felt in the room and all conversations fell quiet and all eyes turned her way, the looks on their faces—all the predictable ones, the women closest to Barbara—saying it all.

Lauren did not waver. She returned Nikki's greeting and walked in. Over there, in a corner on the other side of the room, was an opening for her, a dozen women between her and that spot. *I love these women.* On the way to the corner, she gave many warm greetings, each person responding pleasantly in turn, many happy to see her but many equally curious, some throwing glances Barbara's way. When she reached the center of the room she stopped, not failing to notice Barb's shudder, the small step backward.

"Hello, Risa. Hello, Barbara. How are you?" Gracious, courteous.

"Fine," said Barbara under her breath, looking away.

Risa placed a warm hand on Lauren's arm. "Good to see you back in class!" A very big, blood red smile.

"Thank you," said Lauren. "Good to see you too." She walked on. A whisper behind her?

During class, she summoned her powers of concentration and managed to shed the outside world, to look inward and find peace for fleeting moments. She'd grown to know herself that well. But it was not the same. It was not the dream it had been. And it was sad in a way, but better, knowing she had no need to go back and was strong enough to go on.

Afterward, Lauren was polite with everyone but brief, and she was the first to leave the studio, alone, walking at a brisk pace. Just entering the parking lot, she heard quick footsteps behind her, someone calling her name. She turned and saw Angel running to catch up.

"It's so good to see you again!" she exclaimed. "We've missed you!"

"I've missed everyone too." Lauren hid her surprise. Here was Angel, so quiet, boyish, and awkward, making such an effort to see her off.

"How've you been?" asked Angel.

"Fine. Busy with work. You know how it is."

"Will you be coming back to class again?"

"Well…" Lauren looked at the pixy face with its cap of short hair, the square, tough jaw set solid against pain, hiding the sensitivity. She was captured by the younger woman's expression, its reflection of uncommon depth within. "I don't know," Lauren said. "I'm doing yoga in the mornings at home now, on my own. It's working out better for my schedule."

"I see." Angel looked down, then up again, with hope. "But it's so much better with a group, don't you think? I know another good teacher with morning classes over at Yoga Zone. You could come with me sometime and try it."

"Sure." Fascinated but uneasy, Lauren started to walk toward her car as she spoke. "That would be nice. Next time you go, call me at the store and let me know."

They had arrived at the far edge of the lot, Angel following her into the wedge between Lauren's car and a tall commercial van, parked alongside. Lauren pulled out her keys and hovered near the locked door, wanting to open it, but Angel didn't move, looking as though she meant to say something else, to deliver a message. In her face was an eagerness, a desire to please intensely burning underneath.

The sun had just set, and the sky was shot with orange. It was the last evening in June, lighter than that awful night six weeks before, and here was Lauren, not yet over it, not yet above it completely, waiting to receive the word from a person meant to remind her. The message was coming, she felt it on the way, ready to surface.

"Angel," she said, just to make noise, anything to ease the tension.

Angel nodded.

"That's a lovely name. Unusual." *My messenger.* Risa had been the assigned one, Angel the unwitting.

"It's really Angela."

"Why do people call you Angel?"

She shook her head and gave an embarrassed laugh. "As a kid I was big on sports, played a lot of baseball with the boys on the street. They started calling me Angel after that famous shortstop."

Still, she didn't budge, standing very close. "So pretty," she said, reaching out to touch Lauren's necklace above the scooped neckline of her T-shirt. "It catches the light." She held the crystal between thumb and index finger, resting her hand against bare skin.

"Yes, isn't it? Nate gave it to me."

"Nate?" she asked, still fingering the stone. Their eyes met, Angel's unwavering as her fingers slipped from the stone and descended to the neckline of Lauren's shirt, then gradually, warmth in them, inched lower and lower still, beneath the fabric.

Lauren became rigid. Angel stared into her, would not remove her gaze, would not remove her fingers.

Gently, Lauren took hold of Angel's wrist. "Not this," she began, sending alarm into Angel's features, her eyes darting everywhere on Lauren's face, searching for what she'd thought was there. Angel saw her mistake. Her fingertips recoiled, and Lauren grabbed the balled fist, cradling it.

"I'm sorry," Angel said, lowering her head. "I thought maybe, well… People were talking."

She'd said enough, the message was clear. Lauren closed her eyes hard against the bitterness, willing it away.

She hadn't been deaf and blind. She'd heard it all along in every one of Risa's suggestions, knowing the worst, confirming it today, and still she loved these people. Loved them all.

"Not this," she whispered, shaking her head, dropping Angel's hand. "Come here!"

She stepped forward into Angel's shame and tipped her chin up, saw the hint of a tear, the confusion in her eyes. She took Angel in her arms. "This," she said, squeezing her eyes tight above Angel's shoulder, shutting out the world and its refusal to understand. "*This!*" she pulled Angel closer, squeezed harder, poured love into her, all the love that was too much for one person, for one life.

"*This* is what I want to give you!"

❧ Call Me Back

NONE OF IT was planned, but somehow Joanne fell into the new apartment, the new life, without a second thought or any thought at all. In one big careful hurry she'd packed what she needed, as if she were a soldier in transit, dutifully stuffing a large army duffel with the pieces of herself, only to wake up and find, when she arrived, there'd been movers—men she'd arranged! They'd transported the luggage and several cartons, all neatly packed beforehand by someone else. Herself, apparently, that queen of organization.

Dazed and clueless, she opened the boxes and suitcases one by one, rediscovered their contents and left them unpacked and messy, assigning each of her identities to a corner of her new, tiny living space:

Tucked inside the bedroom closet was her career self, office manager under Manfred Grove at Penn Securities: the gray and navy suits, white blouses, tailored dresses, pumps, and a single maternity dress hidden underneath—proof of her secret certainty that, one day, she'd be taking advantage of Penn's maternity leave plan.

Next to the bed was Rick's tennis partner: a suitcase

of white crew tops and skirts, rackets and balls, the nylon gym bag with health club logo, the cheap tournament trophy from two years back, fall of 1997.

In the kitchen was the suburban hostess: a box of bubble-wrapped china (half of it), stainless and everyday stoneware (half), plastic picnic ware (half) for barbecues on the patio.

Under the coffee table (Taffy's favorite spot) was the cocker spaniel owner: a small box holding the favorite framed photograph (smiling, panting tongue), a brush filled with golden fur, the pink leash, a rubber chew. No Taffy, no pets allowed. She puzzled the longest over this one, wondering what comfort she'd sought in keeping these things, but finding some relief in knowing that her dog wouldn't be neglected. For Rick, animals were easier than humans. He would treat Taffy well enough, feed her, play with her, take her for walks, maybe even love and respect her.

The new landline was also hooked up and fully operational it seemed. She answered on the third ring. "Joan?" said a man.

"Yes," without thinking.

"It's Alec. We still on for Saturday?"

She hesitated, but not for long. "Sure," just in case.

"You'll come here? Let's make it seven thirty."

"Sounds good."

And they said a few more things, the man's voice bordering on sex. Only after hanging up did it occur to her that he'd said "Joan" instead of "Joanne," a common mistake made by strangers, something she'd learned to ignore. She decided to forgive the caller for this small transgression, wondering which piece of her the man had telephoned, which piece of her was the Joan he wanted.

When Rick told her, she hadn't reacted. She'd only said, "I see," as if she'd known all along. In a way she had, because the truth had already carved a notch in her heart, replacing it with an artificial spot capable of pumping the blood without all the unnecessary emotion getting in the way. She kept moving, got up the next morning, went to work, scanned the classifieds and made her plans during lunch break, Manfred and the others oblivious.

Perhaps she always looked like this, attractive and put together but robotic and unanimated, fully functional and useful to others. She accomplished just what was needed without offering more, no threat of a new idea or underlying personality with its own individual needs—ambitions!—none of that.

Within the week she'd found an apartment and moved. Joanne believed that her boss, Manfred, was none the wiser, even though he maintained a faux social relationship with Rick, who worked as a financial analyst at a firm down the street from Penn. Those two would enjoy an occasional lunch at the club, their business interests similar but divergent enough to stimulate animated debate and the sharing of information without SEC implications, no matter what the subject. Certainly no restriction against disclosure of marital troubles. Still, the subject wasn't likely to arise. Joanne imagined that their lunchtime talk about women, the machismo and innuendo, would continue unimpeded, regardless of any change in personal legal attachments.

The second day in her apartment, clarity returned for a brief moment. This time the caller, a different man, asked for "Joan Hyde."

Joanne didn't need to think. She laughed outright and startled the man while wondering at the source of her laugh, a thing that required emotion, a breakdown of the carefully erected containment structure. Joan Hyde. Joanne Hyland. She was struck with the hilarity of it.

"Joan Hyde, please," repeated the caller, civilly impatient, perhaps a salesman. *Those high-top cross-trainers are on back order, did you know, Joan Hyde.*

"She isn't here," said Joanne, catching her breath. "I mean, you've got—"

"Isn't there? Can you just take a message please?" And the man rattled off a name, an affiliation (he was, after all, a salesman) and a toll-free number for Joan to return the call about her pending order. Pretending to comply, Joanne said nothing, her will to protest gone, and soon enough he'd hung up and it was too late. It didn't really matter, the man would call again or not, and Joanne would answer if her arm moved to the phone, if her voice spoke.

She looked down at the little telephone stand, its deep reddish-brown mahogany, the very same piece of furniture that had been in the foyer of their suburban home under the eave of the stairs. "I've been sleeping with her," is how he'd said it, relieving himself right there in the hall, next to that telephone stand which held the instrument he'd used to call that woman, maybe many times, maybe even times when Joanne had been home.

How had this telephone stand arrived at her new

apartment? Another piece of herself taking up residence in a corner. It had arrived somehow, along with other familiar things now in this room: the petite burgundy-rose upholstered loveseat, the cushioned granny rocker, the twelve-inch screen TV that used to sit on their kitchen counter—a very wide and long counter, spacious enough for that little TV for watching the evening news while she washed the lettuce. How had these things gotten here, plugged into the squares on the grid of this ten-by-twelve "living room"?

An electronic noise like screeching jays came up from her hand, and she looked down into the mouth of a shiny black plastic receiver, a stranger, attached to its base with an antiquated, hopelessly tangled cord. She touched the button, stopped the noise, and dangled the receiver at the end of its cord, letting it swirl out of control, a smudge, falling and gone, slow, back the other way and again, testing, coming to a stop. She'd never done this before, not with this phone, this phone, this phone. She had only the vaguest memory of installing it, but perhaps it wasn't a memory at all. Hadn't she always gone cordless? Whose phone was this anyway?

Nights, she couldn't drag herself into that cell of a bedroom. She would fall asleep in front of the TV, folded up into the snug curves of the burgundy-rose loveseat, the little telephone stand nearby. There were many calls for Joan, or if she let it ring, messages to review later.

She wondered what had become of the callers asking for Joanne. Surely, there used to be many, but who were they? A few women at work with whom she shared lunch and office talk, nothing else. Neighbors and suburban couples with young children on the block she'd left behind. High school and college friends, distant by years or miles.

But none of them knew. After all, it had been only a few weeks. Or maybe more. She hadn't said a word to a soul, not even her own mother, someone she couldn't, wouldn't tell, not yet. Give it a little time, just in case …what?

Her seldom-seen brother lived only a short drive away. He was a man reputed to lead an exciting life of freedom and dissipation, everything she'd condemned. She gave in to an impulse and called him, the only person she felt drawn to right now.

"Rick's the one should've moved out," Keith said, blasé.

"He wasn't going to leave, and I just had to get out. I haven't told Mom yet," she warned.

Keith reacted to her news like she was reading the back of a cereal box out loud. She could hear him shrugging his shoulders, lowering his eyelids.

"Nine years down the tubes," she said, fishing for sympathy.

"A waste of time, I could've told you that nine years ago. Men weren't made to be married."

"You're defending him?"

"Not at all. He's a pig. But most of us are."

"That's very reassuring."

"You're living in a dream. Someone had to say it."

"I don't think there's anything wrong with dreaming. Dreams can come true."

"Not for most people. Meanwhile, it's not so bad down here in the pigsty. You ought to try it."

She felt oddly excited and repulsed by this suggestion, a new mixture of emotions that might signal improvement or progress away from the numbness. Her heart raced. But she must have been silent for too long, scared by her pumping heart, because the next thing she heard from Keith was, "Don't act so shocked. I'm not really as bad as all that."

"You're not?"

"Not at all. I loved someone once. I've been dumped before, worse than you. Come over here and stay for a while if you want. Forget everything." An offhand invitation, but she knew it was genuine. She declined, but thanked him anyway before hanging up, always careful to be polite with Keith, a habit sprung from her belief that someday her good manners might rub off. The habit remained, the belief remained, but its importance had dwindled.

The red light caught her eye, a blinking "9," the number of years, number of messages yet unheard, displayed in a little window on the black plastic box attached to the phone, another piece of apparatus she wasn't quite sure of. Every evening after work, Joanne checked it and always found a high number, an "8" or a "5" or a "7." Most of them were men, all for Joan, even though Joanne had left her own outgoing message, not identifying herself by name, of course, but her voice just the same. "We're not able to come to the phone right now," a cautious, single-girl-in-the-city kind of message.

She would sit on the burgundy-rose loveseat next to

the mahogany telephone stand and press the play button, letting this stranger's life unwind. They had something in common. Joan was also a woman on the run, unsure of her destination. She'd left behind men who knew what they wanted but didn't listen. There were new acquaintances trying numbers written on matchbook covers and paper napkins, and there were established friends and lovers talking intimately in code.

She returned none of the messages, except two from a Dr. Greenbaum, OB/GYN: "Joan, the results are back on the urine, the red count is high, we're still waiting on the blood. Fill that prescription I gave you. Any questions, call, 291-5504." A few messages later: "Joan, Dr. Greenbaum again. The white count is high in the blood, not good, but wait! Here's a normal one. [Shuffling papers.] Are there two Hydes? Sorry, Joan, the specimens are mixed up. You'll have to come in to straighten this out. Don't take that medicine!"

She felt compelled to call back, expecting to leave a message with a secretary. The phone rang interminably. She was about to hang up when the receiver was picked up and a male voice came over, from a distance: "...the diaphragm is too high," and then loudly into the receiver: "Dr. Greenbaum."

She hesitated before stuttering into the mouthpiece: "Doctor, you left a message yesterday on my answering machine for Joan Hyde."

"Joan, is that you?" Away: "Slide a little further down, dear."

"No, I'm calling to say you have the wrong number for her. For Joan Hyde. Maybe this was her old number, I don't—"

"Ah, yes, Joan Hyde." The doctor laughed, sounding as though he understood the situation completely. "I do apologize. Thank you so much for calling."

Sunday morning early, she was in a dream, crumpled on the loveseat with the TV still on, holding and being held by the man who'd left a message Saturday afternoon. Of all the callers, he was different: "Joan, it was great last night." A little laugh. "Can't believe my luck. I never meet anyone at those places." [Sweet and boyish, the practiced or true sound of love?] "Call me. Call me back, okay? I want to see you again. This could be the start of something big."

No name, no number, but she remembered him, his eyes the color of shadow, his arms the shape of oblivion, a voice lulling her, beckoning her into the surf. His name was Brad or Tom or Steve—or was it Rick? Ten years ago, his voice had been the same, supplicating and tender with the promise of fairytale.

But then the phone rang, interrupting her dream, awakening her to a stiff neck and a drifting sense of nowhere. "Rick?" she answered, still sleepy.

"Rick is it?" Angry. "Now I know. You can't do this to me anymore, Joan." She knew the voice...whose?

"What are you talking about?" she asked.

"I waited for you last night. Seven thirty, remember? Or did you go to *Rick's* instead?"

Seven thirty. Last night. It was the man who'd called the first day, the man she'd agreed to meet on Saturday, Saturday, Saturday. What day was it anyway? "I haven't seen Rick for days, maybe weeks…"

"You were just hoping for Rick then?"

"Hoping?"

"*Oh, Rick! Is that you, Rick?*" he mocked in a girl's voice.

"But I don't want him at all. We're through. It's over, you know that."

"Good. Then here's another one that's over."

The crash made her jump, the force of his anger traveling the wires between them, pushing the receiver from her ear. In slow motion, she replaced it on the black telephone base, feeling nothing, completely empty and uncaring, thinking of all the others she could call, the ones who wanted her, trying to feel the same way Rick had felt when he told her. *I've been sleeping with her.* A twisted corner of mouth, eyes glazed over and cast down in the direction of that phone, that marital joke of a phone on the little mahogany table. It was white and cordless, not this one. Not Joan's.

As far as she could tell from her general state of timeless, shapeless existence, she'd managed to keep up with her work, to do what was expected, though her eyes felt sunken, her limbs immersed in tar. Still, Manfred had been paying her undue attention for longer periods of time, peering out his office door, which he now liked to keep open as he leaned back in his leather chair while talking on the speaker phone. He made frequent stops at her desk, pushing his face down into hers or touching her shoulder.

On a day when Joanne was alone at her desk and

Manfred was not in his office, Stella came up to her and remarked: "I wouldn't stand for it if I were you."

"It's nothing."

"It's creepy the way he looks at you, Joan. Everyone can see it. He wants something."

"Let him want something. Doesn't mean I have to give it."

"But it's disgusting. A married woman and his employee. I'd call legal if I were you."

"And get fired?"

"It's confidential. There's a federal law, you know. Sexual harassment."

Just then, they noticed Manfred at the other end of the corridor, heading in their direction. Stella turned to go, but Joanne stopped her, placing a hand on her shoulder: "Didn't you just call me Joan?" Their eyes locked and held, Stella's brow falling over a blank, uncomprehending look, but then her eyes darted aside over Joanne's shoulder and she stepped away. Manfred was nearly upon them.

"Would you come with me a minute?" he asked when Stella was thoroughly gone.

"I'm in the middle of something. Can it wait?"

"No. Now. Now, I think is best." A boss's voice. "Come into my office. It's private."

She followed, took a single step inside, and he shut the door behind them, trapping her, sending her pulse racing, a surge of life in her veins saying *this is it, this is it, this is what I want.* But then she remembered the sweet pull of that man's voice, the one who'd sounded different, the one she'd dreamed about, and she was no longer sure.

Call me back.

Manfred pushed a hand into the wood paneling behind her back. "Why didn't you tell me?" he demanded, eyes moving, examining her external parts. "I know all about it. Everything. Rick told me."

"Not everything, I'm sure."

"Enough, the bastard." He touched her shoulder, moved closer, compressing the layer of hot air between them until she didn't know what she was feeling, what she was hearing. "Do you know that girl?" she thought he asked.

"I've seen her."

"Pure slut. Nothing compared to you."

"That's what you all want, isn't it? That's what you think I am."

"You've got me wrong."

"I haven't seen anything else in your eyes."

"I'll prove you wrong. You're more than that, Joan. You're pure class. Let me show you how a man should act. Let me take you to dinner Friday."

She said nothing at first, searching inside for herself and failing, wondering if this was a better way, if the first way had been a trap, starting with a dream and a hope. Maybe she should have started like this, with nothing at all, a man who spoke and acted like Manfred, someone to be turned around and made to buy into the illusion the way she had.

"I can't make it," she answered, finally.

"Why not?"

She pushed out from under his arm, giving in to the pull of her habits, everything she'd learned and believed.

"I already have a date Friday night," she declared, walking out the door, certain she would be calling that sweet-sounding man the minute she found out his name and number.

After that, he left several messages, and she extracted them from a plethora of Bills, Dicks, and Steves, saving them all on the little tape. His name was Lance, he'd said it more than once on her machine, and by the third message he started leaving his number, afraid that she'd lost it—he said so: "afraid you've lost it, Joan."

All she needed to do was call back.

Call me back.

And when she did, he answered in half a ring, as if he'd been sitting by the phone, just waiting.

She said his name, no more.

"Joan!" he cried out.

The next few days, Manfred was not happy, but Joanne couldn't be sure of anything. Stella behaved as she always had, no sign of their special, shared knowledge, a conversation that may have never happened.

Joanne wondered if the episode in Manfred's office had been real, if he'd called her "Joan," if he wanted her the way she'd imagined. She caught him looking at her again and felt responsible for his attention, wanting to know if he'd initiated it without her complicity, without her resignation to the inevitability of sex. She was almost willing to give herself up, not caring much one way or the other, envisioning it quick and grabbing, the skin of her thighs sweating and stuck to the leather couch in his office, the door open a crack, Stella, the others, circling outside.

But by then she'd made the call to Lance—hadn't she?—and Friday night was fast approaching with another chance to test the dream, to disprove her new suspicion that Lance could be no different than the rest of them despite that small bit of deceptive something in his voice passing for genuine, a part of the illusion.

As it was, the dream endured, the way Lance stood when she entered the restaurant, held the chair for her, respectful, alert, and sincere, bestowing his manly gifts. There was a time of drifting, minutes or hours, an eternal universe of shadow and light, hot and cold, a rushing outward toward him through a vast distance, falling into the oblivion of him. She'd seen him once or a million times, been with him intimately in this life or another, and now, here he was, a warm hand on hers, the crisp softness of white linen underneath.

"I'm sorry to be asking this," she said, emerging, "but where did we meet?"

He looked confused, not offended. "You don't remember?"

"No."

"It may have meant more to me than it did to you."

"I remember the feelings, not the place."

He smiled. "Those are the important things. It was the Indigo Club, do you remember now?"

"Not exactly."

"You asked me to dance."

"I did. And later?"

"And later…so beautiful." The look in his eyes made her know what had happened.

She bore into him harder then, working against the dream, trying to shock him out of mist and air back to concrete and clay. "I have to tell you, I may have given you something."

His eyes, still the color of shadow, opened wider, pulling her in. "That doesn't matter to me."

"The tests aren't conclusive yet. I have to see the doctor again."

"It's okay, we'll deal with it." His voice, still sweet, had a vacant, chanting quality. His fingers caressed the secret cup of her palm, making her frantic until she found another way to shoot him down.

"I also have to tell you, I just left my husband. I'm confused, I could end up hurting you."

"I'll take that chance."

She shook her head, rattling the world into focus, but his eyes wouldn't let her go. "You're too good to be true, so you aren't here. You can't be true."

"What is truth? We're here together."

"But are we? I don't know who I am."

"Neither do I."

"This couldn't last."

"Nothing does."

"But we're supposed to pretend that it will."

"Then let's pretend."

A movement somewhere, and she turned away in relief. The waiter was coming toward them, snaking through the tables, yanking at a long black electric cord, stepping over it, readjusting it, threading it around the patrons' feet until he arrived at their table, holding a black telephone not unlike her new one, a curlicue, twisted cord dangling from the receiver, a black box attached, flashing "9."

"Joan Hyde?"

"Yes."

"A call for you."

He lifted and held out the receiver. She took it from him while he remained at attention tableside, a stiff, functional telephone stand.

"Hello," she said with Lance watching, the waiter watching, a sea of faces turned toward her, mouths open, forks lifted and frozen, midair.

"Joanne?"

A call for Joanne. She wasn't entirely sure now, but the voice was familiar. A woman's voice that didn't wait for her reply but kept talking. "This isn't you," said the woman's voice. "Don't go with this man. Don't do it. It's too early yet for you to know. I'm telling you, don't do it."

"But you've got the wrong number."

"Don't play games with me. I know it's you. Of course it's you." A pause. "Joanne? Are you there?"

She said nothing, unsure, but then the room changed, the faces disappeared. No one. She was truly alone, had no one at all except this woman, a woman making a call to Joanne. Textures came up through her fingertips, the smooth feel of plastic in her left hand, the raised ridges of borders and patterns of flowers on the woven upholstery under her right hand, pushing her up to sitting on the burgundy-rose loveseat. She lifted that hand, felt the tangle of hair on her head.

"Answer me, Joanne. Are you there?"

Colors and shapes cut the space around her in sharp lines and curves, circles and patterns defining their niches, boxes and suitcases overflowing, spilling and scattering bits of her everywhere, over there, under her feet, by the door.

"Joanne? Answer me! We're worried about you. Are you there?"

"Yes, yes I am, but there's nothing…" *Nothing to worry about, nothing, nothing at all, nothing, just everything…*

"Keith called and told me about it. We're worried about you. Do you hear me? We're worried about you, Joanne…"

℘ Cactus Flower

ROY SAT ON his haunches squinting up at the clouds, thick and white as whipped cream piled high on a glass plate. His nostrils sucked dust and the air pulled moisture from his eyes before it could surface.

He had been to other, damper places, but belonged here. Red-brown like the earth, he felt like another, larger morsel of it. He lived inside it, erecting no structures, no barriers, carrying his possessions on his back: a bedroll, canteen, knife, revolver, tin pan, a few other things. Everything he needed, and his wits besides.

His eyes followed the path of the sun, leveling on distant peaks at the horizon. Around him spread an extraterrestrial canvas: miles of pock-marked dust sprouting pockets of Indian paintbrush, century plants, and the vivid blooms of beavertail cactus. A few outcroppings of layered rock—shelter from the sun. Home to Roy, snakes, and lizards.

A dot moved, grew larger, became a human figure shimmering in the heat. Roy stood and tried to swallow, finding nothing in his mouth but a thick coat of dusty phlegm. He spat and tugged at the spines on his chin where he'd hacked at his whiskers with a knife to keep the heat away.

Minutes passed.

The figure slowed then stopped, dead still, not ten feet away.

Roy stared. The newcomer stared back then moved slightly, hand touching rifle slung over back, body shifting under denim shirt. It was then he could see she was a woman.

Her gesture toward the rifle was a matter of habit, not of threat. But his heart, instead of slowing, galloped a few paces as he looked into her milky blue eyes, light as opal. Tumbleweed for hair, front teeth poking out long and brown like a prairie dog's. Skin thick and tough as rawhide, covered with bristly fuzz like thistledown.

She removed her hand from the rifle and hitched up her silver buckle, shaking the inhabitants of her belt: a dozen or more rattler tails, some near dust, others fresh kill. Roy's head chased words, finding none; he didn't have much use for them.

She was the first to speak. "Goin' east?" Not an invitation, but a warning.

"Nah," he choked, then turned his head and spat to clear room for more. "Goin' west."

That night, bedrolls laid together under the stars, they tussled a mite, but nothing came of it. She was dry as the air and tight as a rusty pocketknife.

"Move y'r paws," she said, pushing him away.

He rolled over onto his back, hands behind head, gazing at the moon. He lay that way a long time, and when he turned to look, she was five arm lengths away, asleep with her hand on the butt of her rifle.

At dawn, he opened his eyes without her knowing. She sat with her back to him, licking her knuckles like a bobcat and stroking her tangled head, smoothing and matting the fur as best she could. He closed his eyes again when she turned around.

Pure east or west didn't work, neither one of them willing to give in. For an hour or more he trudged southwest, two paces in front, until she began her determined, steady drift to the southeast. The distance between them grew while his heart loped along just fine to a point, then froze up the way it always did when he stepped near a rattler, coiled up for the strike. To find his breath again he closed the gap, staying back a ways as if she couldn't see, until he was no more than two steps behind, getting hot under his collar, feeling his blood boil worse than being stranded in a 110 degree sun without a rock for cover. To cool off, he broke away and found his own path again, increasing their distance, plodding along toward the southwest.

Who needs a woman anyhow? Roy's head told him.

A while later he heard her muttering, close behind.

Three days of zigzagging and they were twenty miles due south of where they'd first met. Good and sick of agave and jerky. Running low on water. And here he was, letting her take him south.

But Roy knew of a stream ten miles off, southwest. He wouldn't allow himself to stray. He wouldn't be led to die of thirst.

Plodding along, he drifted off when it wasn't his turn, half wondering if she would follow. The distance between them grew the longest yet, but he kept his eyes forward, refusing to see her.

A rifle shot turned his head. He froze, watching her in the distance. She stooped, pulled her knife and hacked off the tail, found a place for it on her belt, then hacked off the head, leaving it in the dust. She stood, winding the thick body around her hand like a coil of rope.

She looked at Roy but didn't budge. He looked at her, motionless.

Then she took a step toward him and called out. "I ain't goin' west, but I need the water." Roy's eyes popped wide in awe. She walked to him and he waited until he could see the raw end of the snake, dense and meaty, before he started walking again. She followed.

A strange excitement crept over him like the way he felt sometimes looking at the deepening orange-purple of a sunset. He wanted to talk. He thought of some words, then spoke while they walked. "Ya got a name?" he asked.

"S'pose so," she said.

They walked another ten yards, dust billowing.

"Well, what is it anyhow?"

She cocked her head to the side. "Don't rightly 'member."

Roy searched for more words, tugging at the straps of his pack. In another dozen steps his excitement slowly vanished, replaced with lonesomeness, his sunset darkening into night.

"You c'n come, I guess," he said, finally. "But you

hafta give me some of that." He nodded in the direction of the snake.

Later, they had a tasty meal.

On the fifth night, their canteens full, he decided to try her again. She didn't push him away right off, but she didn't like it either. Nothing seemed to fit or work right, so he gave up.

"Don't have no use f'r it," she muttered.

"Well, ya ain't hardly tried."

She moved away to where he couldn't touch her. "Once, a baby come outta me backward," she said. "Ain't worked right since then. That's all." She moved another couple yards away and settled down, turning her back to him. When she spoke again, her voice was fuzzy and muffled. "Had a coyote face, so I left it f'r the coyotes."

He rolled onto his back, hands under head, thinking of the coyote-baby. She won't want to stay after this, he thought.

At first he couldn't sleep, and then, as soon as sleep tugged at his eyelids, he became determined to stay awake. He looked over at her, sleeping on her side, hand on the butt of her rifle.

He gazed at the stars again until they were a blurry mass.

A second or an hour passed. He awoke and turned his head. She was still there, in the same position.

He rubbed his eyes, set his eyelids hard in their sockets, but they lowered in spite of himself, sending him into a deep sleep.

His eyes opened again in the first gray light of dawn.

He sat up and looked to the left, to the right, and all around. She was gone.

No more south or southwest. Pure west, following the path of the sun. The pink ball drew him on, and he watched it turn white as he headed toward it. The coyote-baby shimmered before his eyes. He spat and it was gone.

His feet moved one in front of the other, but his body stood still and unsure at the edge of a canyon, too deep to go down, too wide to go around.

The sun rose directly in front of him from his chest to his crown, reaching straight overhead as he came up beside a prickly pear with a lone flower, fire orange.

He stopped, looked again. Not one, but two, blossoms merged.

His heart beat hard up in his throat. He turned around on his heels and shook his head. The sun should've come up from behind. He'd been going the wrong way all along and just now saw it.

He turned back, facing east again.

She was there, a good ways off, quivering within a transparent wave of heat. He squinted hard. She had stopped, her head tilted slightly sideways and back as if sensing his approach.

The sides of the canyon clapped together. His footing was sure. He walked on, and she waited for him.

❧ Thirty Dollars a Bag

TWO HOURS BEFORE departure, Reed is circling long-term parking at LaGuardia. He sticks to the aisles closest to the terminal, thinking of Blaire in her high-heeled boots. So far, he's seen only that skinny spot, straddled by the two oversized SUVs, both rudely on the line. He circles yet again, and seeing nothing else, he's determined to grab it.

In this, and everything, he's thinking of her. It's the first day of February, a biting chill, and he wants to shorten her pain. Like a trooper, Blaire declined his offer to drop her at the terminal while he parked the car. She remains by his side with that bright smile and a little undercurrent of shared intent—their internal vision of things to come. He feels her mood as an affirmation of his hopes. No matter the obstacle, they will clear the path together.

In a clean, well-measured turn, Reed slots the Camry neatly between the two monsters, lining up a little closer on the driver's side to give Blaire a few extra inches.

"Perfect!" she exclaims. Blaire has no difficulty expressing her appreciation for small proficiencies—in this case, Reed's driving skill.

Their near imperfect fit fades into nothing, like the others which nearly sabotaged their plans. The weather has been a concern, two feet of snow predicted by inevitable extension of the Doppler track. But at midnight, the Nor'easter took an unpredicted westward drift over central Pennsylvania, away from the airport. No flight delays. The roads are nearly empty as a result of the faulty mass hysteria, and they're able to make up the time they lost on Blaire's last-minute crisis over her three-ounce liquids. It was time to leave for the airport when Reed politely remarked, "That one-gallon bag is against TSA regulations. Too big." Blaire flew into a paroxysm of activity, dumping her little bottles onto the bed and communing intimately with them for several tense minutes, considering, sorting, tossing. Finally, the bare essentials were puzzle-pieced together, zipped into a stressed one-quart bag, and out the door they went.

All these little shared experiences are still new and therefore exciting. They've known each other almost a year, and they're all but living together now, but they've never flown together and they've never been to the Caribbean. Reed wants this trip to be picture perfect, something to fill their permanent, internal scrapbook. He's an unremitting romantic and only fractionally aware of the trouble this causes him. As a boy, he hardly noticed when his thoughtful gestures brought glee to the faces of old ladies, but as a young man, he started to see that many of the women he dated adored this quality in him. So refreshing, considerate, chivalrous.

Blaire has expressed the same sentiments, albeit in

her unique manner, somewhat less saccharine. He likes this about her. She displays admiration with her characteristic touch of irony, the raised brow and slightly pursed and puckered lips as her nose descends to the fragrance of a dozen red roses. Who, really, can quarrel with good manners and thoughtfulness?

Day 362. He turns to face her before they alight from the car. She snugs her hat down over her ears. Fur-framed, the heart-shaped face is poignantly pure and wintery with smoothly sculpted lines and cranberry lips. She smiles at him while sending a gloved hand to the door handle. Popping the door open a sliver, she laughs. "Aren't these clothes ridiculous?" She balloons her cheeks to mock the puffy jacket she wears. The color is charcoal, and the fur-lined collar and cuffs match her hat. She looks incredible.

He understands her meaning. "We'll be in bathing suits before you know it."

She presses the door open a little wider, slides her leather-booted calf into the crack, and evaluates. "Doesn't help at all that we're thin! Not with all these clothes on."

She will fit, but will he? Reed opens the door on his side. And will the ring? Against his left pectoral he feels the hard little box which cradles the two carat diamond, carefully tucked into the inner pocket of his jacket, a safety pocket with a Velcro closure. There the ring awaits its carefully planned entrance on day 365.

He has no idea if it will fit her ring finger. "Size?" the salesman had asked. Reed was mortified, unprepared for this detail. "Sorry, I...," he stalled. The salesman wiped all judgment from his countenance and smiled warmly, for he'd seen the same lost look on the faces of many men, the clueless, nervous, smitten, financially-strained bridegrooms to be, all hoping for a "yes." "It really doesn't matter so much," he assured Reed. "We can always adjust the ring to fit later."

But the dream, as everyone knows, is the perfect fit. On a balmy, tropical moonlit night, the question is asked with the help of a little wine and candlelight, there's a glistening-eyed "yes," and the ring slides effortlessly onto the finger.

Reed does not presume to know what her answer will be. He is not overly confident. Nor is he overly insecure. He doesn't slight himself. He has a bright future ahead of him, even if his bank account doesn't exhibit current wealth. He's still paying for law school. But the era of youth and idealism officially came to a close with the end of his three-year commitment to the Legal Aid Society and his new position in the consumer class action litigation division of Brigland Stroh & Fitzgerald, PC. Triple the salary. Triple the boredom, but he's giving it some time and sprinkling in a little *pro bono* work in the area of employment discrimination.

Not coincidentally, in the same week of his career change nearly a year ago, he met the beautiful Blaire, a mid-management executive with a hotels corporation. They're both thirty, and nothing is more fitting for them than the life he imagines. Nevertheless, today they are traveling together Dutch treat, as she wishes.

"The new flight reality is thirty dollars a bag," Reed muses in response to something she said. He's not fully concentrating, off in a dream about his perfect passage through security an hour ago. The conveyor belt carried his jacket along, pausing in the tunnel to display its skeletal contents on the security monitor, that telltale ring shape. In the nick of time, he averted Blaire's attention! No questions from the TSA officials, no pat down, no exposure.

"I get that," she says. "But a shopping bag! That was never thirty dollars. It goes under a seat. It *always* goes under a seat. No big mystery."

Row 33. Reed sits in the middle between Blaire on the aisle and a man in business attire to his left at the window. Boarding is ongoing, and a commotion jams the aisle at row 29. Reed takes a look but his eye misses. The ring is still in the back of his mind. He tells himself it's safe in the compartment above them, still tucked in its box, Velcroed into his jacket, balled up and shoved under Blaire's furry puffer in the space between their two carry-on bags. He tells himself it's better there than in his shirt or pants pocket, although perhaps not as safe as it might be inside his travel bag. Couldn't be helped. En route to the airport, he felt more secure with it next to his chest, and later, there was no opportunity to transfer it to the bag without her seeing.

A middle-aged woman, short and plump and disheveled, blocks an entire aisle of passengers while attempting to stuff a crumpled paper shopping bag into an overhead bin already dominated by two mini suitcases of regulation-compliant dimensions. Reed sees her now. A balding woman. Her high forehead glistens with sweat, and a white dumpling of midsection pops forth from the upraised lower edge of her shirt. Color of the shopping bag, aqua blue. Contents of the bag, unknown. Something large, rectangular, heavy, and hard. Something that would completely fill an under-the-seat space and cramp the toes seeking comfort there. Reed likes to take his shoes off while in flight.

"If everyone didn't bring their luggage on board there would be plenty of room for it," he reasons. "No one wants to pay thirty dollars a bag." He immediately regrets this comment because it makes him sound cheap, and he is anything but cheap. What's mine is yours, he will say to Blaire—when the time comes. His suggestion that they limit themselves to carry-on bags was occasioned by her suggestion—no, her insistence—that they go Dutch treat. Thinking of her. And of course, it's comforting to know that their bags will be attached to their bodies when they board their connecting flight in Miami for Turks and Caicos.

He feels a twang of empathy for the strangers in the aisle, this dumpy woman and her companion (husband?), a confused, mousy fellow, now trying to help her shove the ill-fitting article into the unyielding spot. The aqua blue bag is obviously very important to them, particularly to her. A Slavic-looking couple.

"Oh Reed!" Blaire hisses, head low, inclined toward him. The way she says it, the name squeezes him—no longer fits. Her voice is partially distorted by the sucking sound of the air nozzle under adjustment by the upstretched arm of his overheated, suit-jacketed neighbor. "You have such a thing about making excuses for everyone!" she scolds, causing Reed to draw in a protective breath. It reminds him of their first day, 362 days ago, the day she named him: *Devin? Isn't that a girl's name?* Like she did then, she now throws him an oblique look, catching his eye with a twinkle of fun in hers along with that devilish grin, tart cranberry.

The sting recedes. Blaire's looks still astonish him, especially the plump pucker of her mouth, just made for sucking a chocolate ice cream scoop into a peak or planting a wet kiss on his bare collarbone. *A cute name for a five-year-old, but not for a man built like you!* With Blaire, it's her reasoning he buys, if not always the conclusion. From that day on he's been "Reed," fully summed up by his last name, the final incarnation of his ancestry.

He reaches over the armrest and gives her hand a warm press, letting her feel the strength, those muscles of his, but her eyes are on the couple in the aisle. "Who *are* these people?" she says under her breath. Whenever Blaire decides to focus, well, granite is chiseled under the laser beam. Her single-mindedness and intensity have been assets in her career and will carry her even farther. But he likes this quality best when her eyes are locked on his during love-making, or when she can't stop staring at the two dimples in his lower back, visible above his low-riding briefs. Those moments linger in his subconscious and ground him whenever she directs her focus on a less desirable subject, like a frumpy couple in the aisle of an airplane, where a falsely-smiling flight attendant has joined them with an air of firm insistence.

"What, on earth, is in that bag?"

Her question presents a choice. He can retreat into reverie, or he can seize the opportunity and engage.

"Her knives," he says. "For a culinary competition. It's a case of razor-sharp knives. She has a special permit."

Blaire scoots an eye up to his and grins. She's on. "Sorry, Reed. Don't think so!" Judging the prey. "Unless you call borscht a culinary delight. No, I'd say she has a steel lock box in that bag—stuffed with rubles. Their life savings."

Ha ha! But he can go one better.

"Plausible, but I don't think so. Hmm. Where have I seen those two before? I know! In the sports section of the newspaper. The Belarus tennis doubles champs! They have a trophy in that bag!"

She's laughing now. And the flight attendant has custody of the aqua blue shopping bag, off to look for a fitting spot. The tennis champs take their seats.

A garrulous island man taxis them in a dusty station wagon from the pocket-sized airport to the hotel, where they arrive late in the afternoon. The first day is really the first late afternoon, with the sun nearly setting, followed by the first evening, with the anticipation of dressing for dinner and maybe something beforehand. Funny how any hotel that has been thoroughly investigated on the Internet, as Reed has investigated, always looks ten percent less than depicted but cannot be accused of fraud.

They hardly notice because they're wrapped in the moist, warm air, and they glimpse the distinct turquoise blueness of the water from the patio window. Immediately they strip for their before-dinner appetizer which also, strangely, turns out to be ten percent less than imagined. Afterward, Reed makes the mistake of falling asleep, if ever so briefly, comfortably spooning Blaire with his knees notched into her knee backs, crotch cradling round rear, a bit of dusky light still filtering into the room. In his dream, the Belarus tennis champs perform an ill-fitting coupling, the female partner straddling her male counterpart, nearly crushing him. She suddenly dismounts. A squirming resistance, and Reed's front side grows cool. He clutches, draws his knees up, and everything is wrong, his knees in the small of her back, her hand reaching behind to push him away. His eyes shoot open into the pitch. Water is running in the bathroom.

The water stops. Still confused, he rolls over onto his back. "Let's get out of here!" Blaire calls from the bathroom. A swimming idea. He bolts upright. The ring! Where is it?

His eyes adjust, and he sees enough to fumble for a light switch. The jacket is gone, nowhere to be seen! He stumbles over clothing and into corners until he finds it, precisely where he placed it before the stripping, carefully shouldered on a non-removable hanger in the closet. Directly behind it in the wall is the little safe for valuables. Thinking quickly, he extracts the ring box from his jacket pocket—she's still in the bathroom—reads the directions on the safe, comes up with a code, inserts the box all the way in the back, and shuts the door, entering the numbers. There. He jiggles the locked door to be sure.

Blaire orders the mahi-mahi, while Reed chooses surf and turf, the closest he ever comes to seafood. Everything on the menu is exceedingly expensive, but he has steeled himself for this eventuality and is prepared to meet it. Blaire doesn't seem worried about the prices. Reed is sure he won't be allowed to treat, and two credit cards will be laid on the tray at the end of the meal.

"Delicious," she says. "Have a bite?" She doesn't wait for an answer. The fork, with a compact morsel balanced atop, hovers near his mouth. One false move and it will fall. He opens to accommodate. "Very good."

"Delicious," she corrects.

"Care for a bite of lobster?" He will not presume and doesn't make a move. "Or steak?"

"No thanks. You have butter on your chin."

He wipes with a linen napkin, and the affable waiter is back at their table, asking, with his lilting accent, how everything is. "Just delicious," says Blaire in a sparkling tone, bestowing the smile she reserves for wait staff. Reed takes another large swallow of pinot noir and eyes her proudly. She's wearing a thin-strapped, sunny-colored dress, her dark hair pulled up to expose neck, shoulders, and clavicle. Her skin has the softness of an air-brushed photo under the influence of the candlelight.

The waiter glides away and Reed takes a look around the restaurant to see who else might be admiring her, might be jealous of him. A realization has been brewing slowly since they boarded the small aircraft in Miami, bound for Providenciales, and now it comes to a head. The travelers on the plane and in the airport, the hotel guests in the hallways, the diners in this restaurant—all of them look like Reed and Blaire. Not exactly, of course, but certainly no different. The porters and the taxi drivers at the airport, the hotel lobby clerks, the landscaper in the hotel courtyard, the bartender and waiters and busboys—all are people of color.

Reed is suddenly embarrassed.

"What is it?" Blaire asks. Her focus, inexplicably, has shifted from the mahi-mahi to his face. Her liquid eyes, a candle flickering in each, inspect him fiercely. "Are you sick? Are you choking?" She almost gets up, but he shakes his head vigorously, raising a palm and uttering a single-syllable laugh that sounds more like a cough.

Reed is not known to blush. In the dim lighting, maybe Blaire can't see the blood pumping into his cheeks. He would like to confess his embarrassment, lay bare the reasons, but it's impossible. He fears her response. Doesn't fear it exactly. Simply knows that it won't match his.

She's still examining him. "You looked like you were choking on a bone!"

"Don't worry. It's nothing! No bones in lobster tail."

"A piece of shell then." She laughs lightly, and without needing further explanation, dives into her food, the crisis over. But, after the next mouthful, she says something that can't be pure coincidence. "On the way from the airport, the driver was talking, and I was looking out the window, and I was thinking…"

He remembers seeing, along the roadway, the modest bungalows, the aging cars.

"…people here seem to have enough. You should see how it is in Jamaica. So much poverty only a block from the resorts."

He's amazed at this subtle offer of comfort, proof

that her eyes can penetrate his soul! He accepts the offer. "You're right, the people here *do* look happy," he says weakly. But in the next instant, he suspects her fib. "You mean, you've been there? To Jamaica? But didn't you say…"

She flaps a hand down through the air. "It was before I met you."

"…you'd never been to the islands?"

"I've never *vacationed* in the islands. It was a business trip. We own a hotel down there." *We* meaning her corporate employer.

Just another one of their semantic miscues, he supposes. Been there? Vacationed? There've been others. He wants to resurrect the mood and reaches across the table to touch her forearm. "I'm just glad we could get out of New York. Get away together. Our first island vacation!"

"You're right, it's so much nicer mixing pleasure with business. The meeting will take only a couple of hours, and the rest of the time is for us."

His heart makes a little thud. He looks at her blankly.

She scrunches her brow. "Hello! Now you're going to say you don't remember?"

"No, no, of course I do." There's a vague memory, more of a feeling really of what might have been said while his mind was off somewhere imagining the beach and plotting day 365. "Remind me, when is the meeting?" He doesn't want to admit his ignorance of the subject matter and persons involved.

"Tomorrow morning. You can sleep in, and I'll be back before you know it."

He stutters a happy response and raises his glass. Not immediately, she reciprocates. "Here's to a successful meeting!" he says. Her mouth is puckered and twisted with attitude. A smugness he's seen before. Glasses clink. Maybe he doesn't look too ridiculous.

It's nearly midnight by the time they finish desert and coffee and snifters of cognac. They confer over the appropriate tip and sign their respective credit card slips. From inside the cobwebs, Reed perks up. "Here's an idea. Let's walk back to the hotel on the beach!" He recalls now that the midnight walk on the beach is a prominent image in his dream.

She seems game, if not completely enthusiastic. The taxi ride to the restaurant took all of two minutes, and the walk back will be easy, a distance comprised of three resort hotels. They set out.

Immediately, problems arise. Reed has failed to consult a lunar chart and the moon is only a sliver. The beach is dark, and the sand, when they remove their sandals, is much cooler than expected. Reed hooks his sandal backs with two fingers, and Blaire struggles with a wayward lock of hair, wind-whipped into her mouth. He circles her bare shoulder with his left arm as they walk. She trembles. No one is around. To his right, the hoped-for moonlit shimmer of tropical ocean is a limitless, inky omen of nothingness. He turns his head diagonally left along Blaire's profile, keeping his bearings by following the lights on solid land. Behind them, a jangle of glasses and silver and plates and voices recedes into a memory of their first dinner on the island. Gone. He drank too much. Her shivering can be blamed on the sharp breeze, not fear.

At once he thinks—no, he knows—she is fearless. Must life partners match in every respect? The projections of one may fill the hollows of the other in a perfect fit. Right now, slightly drunk, Reed is just as fearless as she is. There's nothing, really, to worry about. The ring is locked inside a tiny safe, three hotels up the beach.

He stops and draws her near. "You're cold!" He kisses the cool tip of her delicate nose, almost a child's nose. He kisses her lips. Warmer, but not receptive. Wanting to talk instead.

"Great idea!" she says.

"Come on. This is fun!" He's about to suggest a skinny dip—a small joke—but holds his tongue.

"Let's just get back."

They pass a hotel with a deck that juts onto the beach, displaying paddle craft of various shapes and sizes. They pass the next hotel with a large courtyard and grounded spotlights aimed up into a magnificent fountain, its geysers and jets spouting colorfully, playfully, wetly, making a happy, lonely sound, unheard by anyone. Except themselves. Reed would like to stop and enjoy it, but they continue walking, and when the fountain is at their backs, it suddenly shuts down, the airborne water descending in a tremendous, final splat. They turn to look. Silence. Why now? Why them? Five seconds later, the spotlights click off, replaced by a negative image of their upward beams, in black.

The room is on fire, flames dancing toward the closet and

the safe within. Reed opens his eyes. He's bathed in a rectangle of intense sunlight pouring in from the glass patio door. Naked on the bed, he's drenched in sweat, the sheets ripped off. Without question, half the day is gone. Sitting up quickly, he slams into a helmet of steel. Stupid to drink so much.

She's not in the room or in the bathroom and it takes him a moment to remember.

First thing, he goes to the safe and enters the code, but the door will not open. The code is the same sequence of six digits he uses for everything, the PIN for his bank card, the password to his computer, the lock on his briefcase (shortened to the first four of the six). He knows he shouldn't use the same password for everything, but he must, otherwise he won't remember it. Maybe his concern for safety spurred him to create a new code last night. He enters the usual six digits again. Locked.

Take a shower. Try to remember. This morning he notices the inconvenience of this bathroom, how nothing seems to fit. A third of his shaving kit teeters off the edge of the counter, the tray in the shower holds only the soap or the shampoo but not both, the rack under the shelf of stacked towels is too narrow to hang more than one— Blaire's. He considers throwing it, now dry, onto the floor, freeing the rack for his wet towel, but he throws his own on the floor instead.

Three tries to open the child-proof, travel-size aspirin bottle, followed by a silent debate whether to drink the tap water. Finally medicated, he walks out of the bathroom naked and she's standing there in the middle of the room. Seeing her so well put together, he feels he's been caught in something naughty. Stiffening, he says "Hi!" and moves toward his open bag to grab his swim trunks.

"Just getting up?" she asks. "Not just," he denies and sits on the bed to pull them on. Jesus God, that outfit she's wearing—did it really arrive here in that little carry-on bag? Unwrinkled, she is at once casual and professional, island trendy comfortable and corporate. Dress sandals with a little heel.

Decent again, he stands and reclaims his steady voice. "How'd it go?"

"Great!" She's clearly pleased with herself. "I'll tell you everything when we're on the beach! We've got to get out there! It's gorgeous!"

She rips off the island corporate look, granting Reed a lovely glimpse of flesh before wiggling into her bikini and cover up.

Fifteen minutes later the aspirin kick in, helped by a cup of coffee picked up on the way to the beach. The day is glorious, crystal blue, 84 degrees. Day 363. Beach, swim, sun, fun, laze, talk. She talks and he listens, because listening is easier here. They're sucked into a bright vacuum away from everyday life with its defensive energies. A beautiful panorama spreads out before them, marred only by the occasional toddling pairs of winter-white tourists. While she talks, it's possible to ignore the frightening oblivion in this expanse of fine, white sand pushing into the transparent water dropping off a mile from shore into murky, unknowable depths.

The meeting was, as Reed knew all along, actually an

interview of a prospective manager, a local, for Blaire's new hotel, under construction in Grace Bay. Blaire's, because she *is* her corporation when she gets to talking like this. Back in New York, she will push through the approval to hire this very impressive local person.

"Good work! That's exciting," he says, and she puts on a face meant to hide how important it is to her to be important. But he can see. And he doesn't slight her this; she deserves her due, but he's feeling a bit anxious, so he jumps up from his lounge chair and says, "You're starting to get pink." She rolls over onto her tummy, unties her top, and he takes his sweet time rubbing the sunscreen over the length of her body, running his fingers up under the edges of her bikini bottoms. When it's obvious he's repeating the same territory, he sits back down in his chair, rubs a little onto himself, and stares out to sea.

They completely enjoy that marvelous afternoon of day 363, and at the end of it, the internal scrapbook is full. There's absolutely no more room, the rest of it better forgotten. The evening is much like the previous one, without the pre-dinner snack because it's too painful. Reed's nap on the beach, lying on his stomach with head turned to one side, has resulted in a sunburn to half his face and a large round circle in the middle of his back where his hands could not reach. While Blaire is showering, he tries the safe again, without success. They go to another five-star restaurant where the alcohol and food are just as enticing, the resulting headache just as hammering.

Day 364 is much the same.

And so, when day 365 dawns in a dark, torrential

downpour, Reed is almost relieved. Their last, full day on the island will have a different, cozy start. The rain cannot last long. The advertised climate is 350 days of sun every year. So they will make love, followed by snuggling in bed, coffee and breakfast in the room. They will read their novels. And by afternoon, surely it will clear. And when it doesn't, Blaire will be restless and Reed will seize the opportunity to convince her to get out of the room and try the hotel gym. While she's gone, he will call the front desk, and the security manager will come, and Reed will very convincingly explain that the safe just doesn't work, and he will prove this by punching in his six-digit code, and magically, the safe will open. Reed will be very embarrassed. When the man is gone, Reed will shower and shave, and Blaire will be back, and it will be late afternoon, still dark and wet.

And when every will is done, they get into a taxi like the back of a squad car and find the next five-star restaurant. Reed carries the little hard box in his right pants pocket.

On the way, they are silent as the rain pummels the roof.

Reed searches for the fairy tale. If he were making a movie, he would try ten different endings, looking for plausibility and mood. Only one will fit.

They are seated across from one another, all the ingredients in place. Wine and candlelight and soft music. Yet Reed hesitates.

Blaire jumps into the opening. "There's something I've been wanting to tell you," she announces with shining eyes.

And I, you. But he says nothing.

"I was going to wait until we got back to New York, but…"

But? There is nothing else to talk about. He remains silent.

"My boss offered me a promotion."

He smiles, even knowing that more is coming. Rain on the roof.

"There's a transfer involved. He needs me in Miami."

She holds his eyes with appropriate theatrical emotion. A pregnant pause. "Oh, Reed!" she blurts.

A makeup artist runs in with a dropper of saline.

"You're such a great guy, so much fun!"

He closes his eyes.

"This year has been so…!"

He doesn't hear the rest. *Has been* rings in his ears.

℘ The Walking Club

SO LITERAL, GLIDING on the surface, Christine was
always the last to "know" things about people, those little
gray secrets she should have suspected. Wearing her own
thoughts on her face, she missed the clues in others, some
subtle, some obvious when examined after the fact. She
would smile and contentedly lead her naïve little life until
she was hit with the shock of discovery—or
disappointment.

By forty, the lesson should have been well learned
and a new intuitiveness attempted. At least she was
conscious of this need, but still, she was caught unawares
by Margot and the Walking Club.

The invitation came on a fiery autumn morning.
With the boys in school and work under control,
Christine made good on her resolution to get in shape
and went up to the nature preserve. Brisk walking three
times a week was the prescription for those starting up
from the couch. Following the blazes painted on tree
trunks, she took the "red" trail, saving the yellow, green,
white, or blue for another day.

The red might have been the roughest or easiest, she

didn't know, hilly for sure. Crimson and gold leaves twirled, brushing against hair and skin. Wonderfully crisp air pulled in cool and expelled hot, inflating her lungs taut against a stubborn ribcage. It burned but felt good—for a while. After ten minutes up the path, she turned back.

Near the trailhead, coming toward her up the path, were three women, Margot in the lead. Christine knew Margot the way one knows a person in a small community, not a friend or acquaintance but someone to bump into and acknowledge with a smile of recognition and pleasant greeting. Christine's smile always held something more, what she hoped was a secret—the excitement of her admiration for Margot. Their children attended the same elementary, where the two women brushed shoulders at school functions. Christine would steal glances: Margot alone, Margot holding the hand of her look-alike daughter, Margot lengthwise against the backdrop of her husband. Christine had admired her from afar, had spoken a few words to her once or twice, and had received her smile.

What was the source of this fascination? An instantaneous impression packaged in Margot's upright carriage, her hair and clear skin, the dab of makeup and lipstick, never too much, her confident voice, well below strident, filling the auditorium during a school board meeting. And the way Margot touched her husband's arm in public, not out of need or dependence, but from the naturalness of their union, it seemed. Her husband was a marble sculpture of a man, well up to his wife's standard of finesse.

On the trail, as the three women neared, Christine

perceived only Margot, the other two mere appendages. Margot was bringing them up fast, defining their destination with every tender yet deliberate step of her hiking boots, a feminine sort of non-clunky kind. Christine dug for a tissue, blotted her glistening forehead, and stuffed the tissue back into a pocket. She wiped at her face again, worried that her moist skin had snagged and glued a shred of the tissue. She was suddenly aware of her worn clothes and tennis shoes, the dampness under her arms.

The appendages came into focus. She recognized them. First, there was Paula. Four years ago, their sons had briefly experimented with friendship. Second, a nameless familiar face. Another woman seen at the school and in the supermarket.

Christine raised her hand and smiled. No immediate acknowledgment from Margot, who was intent on her course until the last possible moment when she suddenly fixed her eyes on Christine at the cusp of a decision. Would it be a brief "hello" as they squeezed past, or a more lengthy conversation? Margot halted, the ranks pulling up behind, and she relaxed her intensity, a winning smile settling into her features. The choice seemed considered, the motivation behind it unclear, but not something Christine could have discerned or even pondered in her present state with racing heart, sweaty armpits, and a drip of watery mucus threatening to dribble past the tip of her nose.

"I know you!" exclaimed Margot, her lips and cheeks full and bright. Face made up for a walk? Hard to tell, so natural yet unreal.

"Yes. I'm...your name is Margot, right? I'm Christine Henley. My sons go to Cooper."

Margot just smiled at this factual declaration, showing no surprise at Christine's implicit admission. "These are my friends, Paula and Eileen," said Margot with a casual backward extension of her hand. The women gave polite greetings, Paula and Christine exchanging special looks of recognition.

"Beautiful day!" said Christine.

"Any day is great for a walk," said Margot. "You do these trails often?"

"Well," Christine laughed, "not for a while. I thought I'd get out more often and try to lose a few pounds." Behind their leader, Eileen and Paula had started a conversation, most likely about walking shoes, judging from their downward glances at upturned soles.

"Then you should join us!" declared Margot brightly. "The Walking Club." Said with capital letters.

"I'm on my way home now..."

"Next week then. Every Tuesday at ten." Margot sidled past, her troops taking the cue to follow. "We meet in the parking lot," she called out over her shoulder. Smiles and waves.

Simultaneous excitement and trepidation. Christine stopped in her tracks and dared to glance back. Already they were out of view, around a bend in the trail, lost behind an outcropping of rock. Maybe even further up the trail than that, racing ahead at a fast clip, faster than Christine could handle. Or could she?

The next Tuesday, Christine arrived at a quarter to ten

dressed in her newest sweats, jacket atop, still the old tennis shoes. A gray morning, the threat of a shower, the parking lot deserted, wind slicing like the icy blade of a skate. The height of color was already gone, last week's event. She pulled up the collar of her windbreaker and waited.

The Walking Club, women she scarcely knew. As a prospective member, she'd gotten herself into "condition" for the adventure with just two walks, last Tuesday's and another one last Friday, plaguing her body with a constant, stunned torment, random jabs of sore muscles floating under the soft surface. The whole week she'd been thinking of the Club, sure she would join them, sure that she *had* to, while beset with near-incapacitating terror. She belittled her insecurities. She was, after all, only meeting a few women for a walk and could turn back at any time, even halfway up the trail if need be. Dignity could be maintained without excuses. Sorry, this is as far as I can make it. Maybe next week.

The lure of company had been the thing. Margot's allure. Neither a loner, nor a social butterfly, Christine could not claim any close relationships with women. She vacillated between fretting over this lack and resolving that it really didn't matter. She had the people she needed and enjoyed. Two sons to raise, a shared life with Jack, relatives nearby, her part-time identity as a CPA, clients for chatting. The family relationships were close, nurtured and treasured. Acquaintances were less important to her, less comfortable, than the hours she spent in her cramped home office with calculator and numbers on a tax form, solid black against crisp white.

Opportunities with other women abounded, yet she purposefully shunned them: the coffee hours, Tupperware parties, bake sale committees. Liaisons that merely skated the surface. Not interesting, and besides, no time for them. Of course, these events provided opportunities to meet new people, holding the promise of something more meaningful to come. But her few attempts had never yielded a deeper connection, so she'd closed the avenues altogether and grew accustomed to her lack.

Most days she counted her blessings. On this teeming planet, there could be only a few ideal companions of either sex, recognized immediately by the certainty they inspired. She'd found the one man in that category, Jack, her designated mate, her finely-molded complement. Was it pure luck or fate that she'd found him? In the early days, her discoveries of their commonality had been easy, and after that, all his surprises, once she'd gone deeper, had turned out to be joys, not disappointments.

Chilled to the bone, Christine waited in the parking lot, remembering Margot's look and invitation: *You should join us! The Walking Club.* A new feeling. Was it the kind of certainty she believed to exist? But then, just asking that question showed her need for confirmation.

At seven minutes to ten, Paula drove up and parked alongside. She stepped from her station wagon, outfitted in a brand-new jogging suit with turtleneck underneath, perhaps the same outfit she'd worn last week, Christine couldn't remember. Hadn't noticed.

"Hello!" said Paula, walking up to her. "You decided

to come along? That's great!" She leaned up against Christine's minivan, her face jumping out iridescent against surrounding grays and browns of sky and trees.

"Thought I'd give it a try anyway."

Paula responded with words of encouragement tempered with a warning that she'd been a little sore at first—Margot liked a fast clip—but on the whole she didn't regret it and now felt up to the challenge, this, her third time. Christine was taken aback. Just her third time? Well, yes, Paula said, she'd just joined, but Margot and Eileen must have been going out for quite some time now. She wasn't entirely sure when the Club started, and there may have been other members throughout its history.

"How are the boys doing?" Paula asked. They lapsed into small talk about their children, Christine remarking qualities she'd noticed about Paula long ago, her easy way, the melody in her voice, her attentiveness. Paula remembered names and details about Christine's work and her two boys. The same could not be said for Christine's memory.

All too soon Margot turned into the lot, slashing the landscape with her quick, cherry-red sedan, parking it a few slots away. Christine raised her wrist. Ten straight up. Margot emerged. The same hiking boots but the rest different (Christine *did* remember), now wearing tight-fitting, manufacturer-faded blue jeans tucked into boots, western pullover sweater in a drab color, royal blue bandanna at her neck. A wide, soft band of the same royal blue covered her ears, its border graced with tips of shiny pecan curls, handfuls of thick hair circling her nape.

Every lock in place, and yet the wind whipped, carving caves and slicing crevices, the shapes temporary, the hair always returning by magic to its original mold. One of those sculpted cuts that can only be achieved on hair of the perfect consistency and bounce.

Margot paused at the side of her car looking at her cell phone while absently putting her car key into a fanny pack. She looked up and smiled but didn't move. Not a step. Christine and Paula walked over.

"Hello, Ladies. Chrissy! How good to see you!" Christine smiled, hesitant to correct the name it was Margot's right to bestow. "Chris" was allowed some people but never "Chrissy." Until now.

Margot turned to Paula. "Nice color on you," she said, tugging gently at the front of her own bandanna while eyeing Paula's turtleneck. "It does something for that sweat suit. Well, everyone set? We have a good day for it."

"Brisk," came from Christine's mouth as she shrugged her shoulders against a blast of wind.

"I love a crisp autumn day," said Margot, not looking at Christine. "Shall we?" She took a step toward the trailhead.

"Maybe we should wait...?" But Paula let the suggestion fade as Margot glanced impatiently at the face of her cell phone and declared, "Five after." She inserted the phone into her fanny pack as Christine glanced at her wristwatch. Three after. "Eileen wouldn't be late," Margot said. "She isn't coming." This assertion bespoke omniscience, and Margot's forward step embraced absolute justice. Paula and Christine bobbed their heads in agreement. They followed.

"Why don't we take yellow today?" decided Margot.

"Okay," said Christine, not sure what she was getting into.

"Sounds good," said Paula.

Margot strode toward the right fork, marked with a yellow circle on a tree trunk. "This one's my favorite," said Margot. "The complete loop is just two miles, half of that around Sandler Lake."

Two miles, said Christine inside her head. Two miles. But apprehension was not allowed. They were walking in a single-file unit, not mere individuals. Christine would not permit herself to lag far behind and didn't have time to anticipate the pain, her thoughts cut off a moment later by Margot's exclamation, "Well, look at that!" while pointing at a treetop ahead, rushing toward it. Christine saw a flash of red color. "A scarlet tanager?" guessed Margot. "At this time of year? Darn, I wish I'd brought my field glasses. Paula, did you get a pair yet?"

"No, sorry," reported Paula, her breath short. She flashed Christine a look, an admission of some kind. Something about the field glasses?

"Must be a cardinal," reported Margot, straining to find it again. "But we're too far away to see." She pulled her gaze from the treetops and looked over her shoulder at Christine, transmitting warmth and encouragement in her smile. That feeling grabbed Christine again. Incipient certainty. "How you doing back there?" Margot didn't pause for an answer. The question was enough. She turned to face forward again and kept walking. "One of those mornings!" she said loudly so her followers could hear. "We got up late, Dabney missed the bus so I drove her to school. Ran out of the house without my field glasses." She laughed in a musing way.

So, Margot had "those mornings" too. Got up late occasionally. Forgot things. Christine thought of her own oversight this morning, letting Jack go off to the station with her wallet in his car. His little compact was easier sometimes than her minivan, and she'd used it the night before on a run to the store, left her wallet inside, and didn't realize it until too late. Ah, well, we all do these things, even Margot, human just like the rest of us.

Christine attempted an appropriate, witty response but emitted only a burst of sound as the words caught in her throat, impossible to utter between gasping breaths and the rising blood of exertion showing in her pink, wind-stained cheeks. She worked on deepening her inhale and exhale, regulating them and hoping to reach an automatic stride, even if painful. But the rocks and roots jutted from their hiding spots under slippery, fallen leaves. She jerked, stumbled and slid, concentrating hard on slowing and deepening her breathing. Margot and Paula shared an exchange about past bird sightings, Paula's words coming out in quick, panting bursts, but coming out nonetheless. Christine aspired to the same level of communication, visualizing the day when she would possess it. Hopefully, like Paula, by the third week.

"You all right?" Jack inquired absently, peering up at her over the edge of his trade journal. It was nine o'clock, the kids were in bed, and he'd been intently reading for the past fifteen minutes. As far as she could tell, he hadn't looked up when she rose from the easy chair to reach for her copy of the new tax regs. Still, she'd deliberately woven casualness into her movements, hiding the stiffness and soreness—or so she thought. Jack had noticed. It was that way he had, the way they had with each other, just knowing things. Such a comfort to attain that level of unity, but there was no turning back once it had been achieved. A distinct disadvantage in moments when privacy would be nice.

He might have noticed the way she moved, but he couldn't have read her thoughts, now could he? Her mind had gone back to that moment of thrilling discovery, a sign of commonality—hers and Margot's—minutes after the scarlet tanager sighting. Stamped in memory were Margot's words: "I'm not interested in sharing fudge cake recipes over coffee. I have to get out and *do* things." Now, wasn't that *exactly* the way Christine felt?

"I'm fine," she answered, feeling dishonest.

Jack lowered the journal to his lap and eyed her curiously as she sank back into her chair. "You hurt yourself?"

"No, no, I'm fine. A little sore though. I've been exercising."

"Good for you."

"Walking. Hiking really. I did two miles today."

Jack raised his eyebrows in amazement, a single coarse gray hair drooping down and catching on one of his lashes. Said nothing.

"All the way to Sandler Lake and back. With some friends."

"I'm impressed. Keep it up. I oughta do more of

that." He squeezed a love handle above his belt and laughed. Apparently satisfied with her explanation, he picked up his journal again, leaving Christine with the guilt of incompleteness. She'd told the truth while omitting its significance. Jack may have sensed more and was deferring to her need for privacy. He could afford to step back as long as he perceived no threat.

There it was, the proof. Jack's retreat confirmed that her mission wasn't dangerous to them. Important, but not dangerous. Like everything else of significance to her, it would all emerge in the end, assembled and amplified in a verbal package. He would listen and respond with words of understanding and support, avoiding any suggestion that he'd seen the surprise gift in the closet before he'd unwrapped it.

Christine flipped the pages of her tax book and scanned the fine print, not seeing or reading. She was at the commuter train station again, one o'clock this afternoon, less than two hours after the walk. Finally, she couldn't do without her wallet and had to go fetch it. A lonely feeling amidst the sea of cars in the dead of midday, the white collars absent, toiling away in the city.

After a brief search, she found Jack's car in the usual row and opened the door with her extra key. She found the wallet right where she'd left it, inside the console between the seats. Then, driving away in her minivan, snaking through the rows of cars, she passed an outlying corner and—something odd. The red sedan. Margot's.

Christine couldn't have been mistaken. She replayed the image now, just to be sure. Margot sat in her front passenger seat, the door open, her legs swung out with feet on the pavement. A man, no one Christine recognized, stood near the opening, an arm on the roof of the car, leaning toward Margot, talking to her. Smiles on their faces.

Christine drove by, her window allowing a view from just five feet away. Margot's face turned toward the minivan for an instant, then back toward the man. Flushed? But Christine had never seen a rise of color in Margot's cheeks, whether from embarrassment or exertion. Margot continued her conversation without a change of expression, nothing on her face to suggest that she recognized Christine. But she must have seen her. It was impossible not to.

So strange, after that little epiphanic moment she'd felt with Margot just a few hours earlier. And afterward, there'd been more of those moments on the trail.

A mile into the loop, coming up to the edge of the lake, the trio paused. Overheated and damp, Christine was completely out of breath and grateful for the break. Margot's dry glowing face turned to her in animated chatter. Christine dabbed her forehead and neck with a hanky—she'd brought cloth this time—longing for communication, a way out of her gasping silence. Paula was a short distance off, crouching to search for flat skippers in the pebbles and stones at lakeside.

"Thank God Dabney has Mrs. Hart. All those horror stories about Carlisle. I'm sending a petition to the district to have her fired. You want to sign it, Chrissy? But wait a minute. Doesn't one of your kids have her?" A plunk. The sound of Paula's ill-fated skipping attempt.

"No," Christine sputtered. She pulled in more air and

added: "Last year...Mrs. Hart." The words made no sense, but she couldn't manage a complete sentence.

Margot discerned the meaning. "You have a fourth grader? How about the other two?"

Two? One plus two makes three. Christine was stunned to think that Margot believed her to be a mother of three. "Just two," she replied, still raspy. "Second and fourth."

"Are they in Girl Scouts? Maybe I've seen them at the meetings. What are their names?"

"Boys. Derrick and Glenn."

Margot threw her head up to the gray-sheathed heavens and laughed unashamedly, drawing Christine upward to the private niche she'd carved for the two of them with her resonance. "And a pet dinosaur, right?" She laughed and laughed, Christine joining in, feeling chosen in a new way, included and excluded at the same time. "Forgive me, Chrissy. I'm a little off today. It was one of those mornings, you know!"

After that, Margot led them back out to the trail. Taking up the rear, Christine concentrated on overcoming physical pain. She was not positioned for easy conversation, even if she'd been able to talk. Occasional passing comments, small exchanges between Margot and Paula. At the end, after Margot had left for home, Christine and Paula had a pleasant conversation.

Snapping back from her reverie, Christine glanced up at Jack, still absorbed in his journal. Perhaps he sensed the significance she placed on these new events and believed it to be illusory. Perhaps her disappointment would be a cure, the feelings would pass, and everything would remain the same, their lives unchanged. But she wasn't ready to think so. Not yet. It had been a slow start to something greater, perhaps nothing worse than that.

The following Tuesday was very much like the previous one. The same kind of day, all the cheerful, sunny days in between forgotten, their existence doubted under a permanent gray sky.

The timing much the same: Christine, then Paula. Before Margot arrived, a chat. It was an easy conversation, Christine not worried about her own words (for it was Margot who raised the butterflies). She was free to talk without thinking, her mind available for listening. And—who would've thought?—Paula was currently showing her oil paintings in a gallery downtown. Christine had only vaguely remembered something like that. Paula, an artist.

Ten o'clock. Margot. Plum stirrup pants inside boots, ivory cowl-neck sweater to hips, ivory headband. Field glasses on a leather cord around her neck. They should start right up, Margot informed them. Eileen wasn't coming. Had called a few days ago, said she wouldn't be coming for a while.

"Why? Did something happen?" asked Paula. Christine thought of last week, when they started up at three minutes after ten without waiting.

"This and that. You know. Busy." Margot looked at Paula and raised her eyebrows, but the look was gone before Christine could apply her modest powers of intuition. Nothing like disgust or annoyance could ever be pinned on Margot. Just a fleeting, almost mocking, disdain in that quick lift of the eyebrows. In the next instant, she was smiling and vibrant and ready to go.

Margot strode out immediately, choosing for them the white trail with a declaration of "white is right"—a crusade? but with a little laugh—her energy twice that of the week before, almost frantic in its intensity. Single file up the path in order of strength, Christine bringing up the rear with nose into Paula's scapula, digging in with each step and pushing on, wanting more.

Christine, wanting more? Margot's urgency massaged Christine's sore muscles and punched them into walking shape. A madness was it? *Eileen, you don't know what you're missing! We're the absolute finest, Margot making us so!* Step by step, she was building strength and agility against hidden perils underfoot, the slip of damp fallen leaves and an unpredictable path, level then climbing.

Now came a small hill, *steep* actually, requiring the use of hands. Margot tackled it first without slacking her pace, stretching a leg up to the next foothold. She, their example, delicately placed one hand (manicured nails, clear polish) on a jutting bare branch for balance and was up in one easy swing. Next came Paula, stretching for the spot, reaching for the branch, Christine in the rear, concentrating hard on making the foothold when, *Oh!* A cry. Christine clutched at her throat, feeling no vibration. Not her own cry, though it should have been. Paula was down at the top, holding her foot.

"Are you all right?" Christine made the hill and crouched near. Margot, twenty feet ahead, looked back at them. She stood like another bare trunk against the sky, one leg straight, the other bent at the knee, foot on a rock.

"I can't believe I did that!" Paula held her ankle, rotating it slowly, cringing.

"Twisted it?" asked Christine.

"Okay back there?" Margot said in a school-teacher voice, looking down at them over her left shoulder. Not waiting for an answer, she turned her head right to look up the trail ahead.

"Came down on it funny. I can't believe this!"

"Is it bad? Can you stand?" Christine held out an arm to steady Paula as she hopped up onto the good foot.

Margot regarded them once more. "Can you go on?" she asked and turned away. Head left and right again.

Paula shifted her weight, hobbled a bit. "I'd better rest it. You two go on—"

"No. We'll rest a while and take you back," said Christine. "You might need help."

"You need help?" asked Margot with a big smile. One more turn of the head and the smile was gone.

"No, you two go ahead." Paula was hobbling back and forth, testing it. "We haven't gone very far. I can make it back on my own. I don't want to spoil your walk. You go ahead."

"Maybe we should call for help? Someone to meet you in the parking lot?" suggested Christine, looking at their leader.

"No signal up here in the woods," said Margot without checking her phone.

"Please. Go on. I'll be fine."

"You sure now?" said Margot, big smile.

Christine smiled in sympathy at Paula and turned

again to Margot, catching her gaze. A slight nod, a slow blink over cobalt eyes. Christine noticed that color for the first time, or maybe it just seemed different. A solid color, lending density and substance to Margot's silent message. Christine felt reassurance, her momentary guilt overcome with exhilaration. They two would go on together, alone, and Paula would be fine. Just fine.

"Let me at least help you down this hill," said Christine, offering her arm. Paula accepted while Margot waited, calling back, "Go slow now!" After Paula was safely down the hill, Christine came up to Margot's side and took a final look back, one last look at Paula, limping. "Don't worry," said Paula with a wave of her hand, pushing back the air of Christine's ghost. "I'll be fine."

"I'll call you later and see how you're doing," said Christine. Final words to quell the last touch of guilt. Bye-byes.

Margot uttered, "A shame," and started up at her fast clip, Christine diagonally behind. "But I don't think it was a bad sprain. She'll make it back all right. Too bad though. I've told her before, good ankle support really helps on these trails."

Christine looked down at her own tennis shoes and compared them to Margot's boots. "I guess I should get some better shoes."

"It's the best investment if you're committed to walking." Conversation at an end, both looking ahead, the woods felt suddenly empty, the sounds of a third body now gone. Christine's heavy breathing returned, and with it the realization of Paula's unintended camouflage—the light rush of Paula's breath, her occasional comments, the crunch of twigs under extra footsteps, composing a natural mask for Christine's panting inability to communicate.

But Margot didn't seem anxious to talk, not for ten minutes that seemed like forty. Their pace continued the same as before, drained of the desire and push that had marked the early moments of the day's adventure. Finally, at a high point overlooking a small meadow, the trickle of a stream cutting through, Margot stopped to admire the view. Christine pulled up alongside, making efforts to slow and deepen her breathing, quiet her chest.

"So beautiful," managed Christine, looking out.

Margot lifted her field glasses. "Usually you can see something interesting in this clearing. There. A cedar waxwing. Pretty." She scanned slowly. "Just a couple of sparrows. Poor sparrows, so plain. This isn't really the best time of year. Spring and summer. Now, *that's* pretty! A red-winged blackbird." She lowered the glasses, keeping an eye out on the field.

Christine thought of asking for a look through the glasses but changed her mind and decided to speak, realizing she was now able, the rest having restored her to normal breathing. "I should take the boys up here for a hike," she said. "They'd love it. Jack too. He doesn't exercise much, but if I just got him out here, I bet—"

"Don't count on it. You know how men are. Not interested in *anything* we suggest. They all seem to have their own agendas." Margot shook her head and rolled her eyes before leveling a hard gaze. "Am I right, Chrissy?" A female-to-female look and a laugh that demanded agreement.

"Right," said Christine with a smile. Inside, she wondered why.

"Oh, Dabney and I have been up here a number of times. She can do three miles, no sweat. Just eight years old. I'm teaching her to be strong, and she's learning. Go out and *do*."

"That's great—"

"Be independent. Don't rely on *any* man. But she adores her daddy, of course. I think all girls do, don't they?"

Christine thought of the formal, distant relationship she had with her own father. "Many do, I suppose."

"I *adored* mine," said Margot, gazing out into the clearing. "That's all a big part of it, really. Daddy is always Superman. Flying out of the phone booth at the last minute to prove his existence. Meanwhile, all that mystique builds up around his absence."

"Oh, I don't know about that," said Christine. Margot turned an eye on her, making her regret the limp, disagreeing remark.

"Of course, every relationship has its own unique problems." Margot raised her eyebrows. "Yours might be something else."

"Sure, there's always something…"

"Something you need that he can't provide. So maybe you have to find someone or something else to provide it. No matter what your problem, Chrissy, you just try to work around it, don't you? But you don't rub his face in it, you don't remind him of everything he lacks. You have to keep your mouth shut about some things to control the damage. Don't you?" Margot paused, now gazing out over the clearing. Christine shifted her weight uncomfortably and inched slightly away to the right.

"After all, you have to stick together," continued Margot, not seeming to notice. "And you do it for them, don't you? The children. A little girl who needs a daddy." Margot turned and stared hard, demanding agreement.

"Yes, of course." Christine nodded, wondering at her facile agreement and slightly ashamed of it without knowing why. An icy breeze encrusted the moisture on her neck. She shuddered and pulled up the collar of her windbreaker.

Groping, finding nothing direct or wise to say, Christine ran from it. Easier to change the subject. "Oh, I meant to tell you last time. I'd be glad to come by and sign that petition."

"Petition?" asked Margot. "Oh, that." She turned away and took a step up the trail, expecting Christine to follow. "I already sent it to the school board," she said, her back to Christine. "I didn't think you were interested."

Back home later that morning, Christine fought a sick disappointment. She'd gotten what she'd asked for, hadn't she? To be the chosen recipient of profound confidences, Margot's thinly-veiled confession. It was the kind of choice made by a close friend. Or no choice at all. A need occasioned by unwanted circumstance. *Damage control.*

Christine pushed her mind away from it. She remembered her promise to call Paula and searched her address book for the number, finding the smudged and aging entry. Hesitating at the kitchen phone, the sickness welled up again. What could she possibly say to excuse her behavior? So sorry to have left you alone and struggling, but Margot and I simply *knew* you would come out of it fine. Just fine.

She left the kitchen and went to her office looking for the solace of familiar equations, formulas that worked. But she couldn't concentrate and found herself grabbing for a coat, out the door again.

Without thought, she headed downtown to the place Paula had mentioned, a small gallery tucked humbly between a large department store and a bank. A funny little place Christine had passed a hundred times, always afraid to venture inside and risk the scrutiny of the proprietor, someone who would surely detect a fraudulent interest, a poor disguise for ignorance. But when she entered and saw the wealth of color and texture, she felt suddenly true and worldly. It was her right to be there, to enjoy the art in her own way.

The woman behind the desk seemed to agree. She looked up, smiled a "welcome," and buried her head in a book, allowing Christine to meander through the gallery without distraction or pressure. She took her time. Nearly every style and medium was on display, the paintings crammed together helter-skelter. She paused before each one and considered it, her lips silently forming the word "no" before she confirmed her impression with a look at the nametag underneath. A wild contemporary collage of reds splashed on canvas. No. A drizzly, indistinct watercolor of weeping willows. No. A metropolitan skyline with stabbing shadows, all blacks, whites, and grays. No. These were not Paula's, she knew, although she hadn't a notion beforehand of Paula's style and subject matter.

Finally, she came to them. Two oil paintings, companion pieces, scenes of full-rounded, domestic contentment. Detailed and realistic, yet dreamy. The soft colors placed Christine in a corner of a spacious backyard on a warm June afternoon. Endless light and leafy shade, a day stretching on forever. At a wrought iron table, a man and a woman sat with frosty glasses of iced tea close at hand. In the first painting their son, about six or seven, held a soccer ball while standing at the table, father's hand on his shoulder, both parents gazing into the boy's eyes, expressions earnest and interested. In the next, the boy was at a distance on the lawn, in motion with one foot in the air, the ball up high competing with the sun, the mother and father leaning back with quiet smiles of pride and amusement. The circle complete. Nothing lacking.

"Are these for sale?" asked Christine of the woman behind the desk.

"Yes. As a pair they are."

"How much?"

"Let's see." She looked at a list. "Five hundred dollars."

"Too little," said Christine as she considered them, her eyes moving from one to the other and back again. "They're worth much more. I don't have the kind of money they're worth."

Suddenly anxious to return home, she thanked the proprietor and scurried out. Went much too fast in her minivan. Burst in the front door. Found her address book still open to Paula's number. Punched the number in, waited breathless, praying to hear a real voice instead of a machine. Her heart jumped when Paula said "hello."

"Your paintings!" spilled from Christine's throat, the next words following in a jumble, too fast for her tongue. Ideas tripped into each other. "I just saw them. They're marvelous. They say so much! How can you possibly part with them? It must be so difficult to sell your art to a stranger."

Paula laughed, delighted. "It *is* difficult."

"I imagine it would be nice to share them with the world while keeping them for yourself."

"Yes, well, several people have seen them at the gallery, and the person who buys them will be someone who understands them. That little bit of communication makes it worth everything."

Christine paused to think and wonder. Suddenly she remembered the other reason for her call. "How's your ankle?"

"It's not too bad. A little swollen."

Christine felt the sudden rush of shame. "Paula! What can I say? I'm so sorry I left you behind on the trail. There was no excuse for it. Please forgive me!"

The next Tuesday, partly out of curiosity, mostly desirous of a walk, Christine returned to the nature preserve. A bright day, cold, but no wind.

She waited longer than Margot would have. Five after, ten after. *She wouldn't be late. She's not coming.* Christine started up the white path, alone.

Perhaps when Paula's ankle healed she would join

Christine for a walk. In the meantime, there were other possibilities. Paula had mentioned an exhibit she'd like to see and asked if Christine would come along. Yes, decidedly yes. The invitation was accepted with certainty, no guilt attached. And now, fully committed to her fitness plan, Christine would keep up the exercise, Walking Club or no. After all, a few good things had come of her brief membership.

She paused at the clearing where she'd stood with Margot the week before. Beautiful, even more so with the sun shining. Jack would love it here. He'd agreed to make a family outing of it this coming weekend. They would set out together, the boys tagging along or racing ahead, Christine and Jack at a comfortable pace without competition. Their stride would be open and free in their complete knowledge of one another. Her omissions had been recently confessed and clarified, nothing remotely dark enough to classify as a secret, nothing tragic enough to be considered a lack.

↶ Everyone But Us

THERE WAS THAT time, summer of '72, when they found themselves stranded somewhere in Arizona, one of those dumb narrow escapes of youth. Gaylie couldn't think of it now without a shudder and a smile, her nostrils filling with a mixture of desert sagebrush and cracked vinyl upholstery.

Being poor students insensible to material needs, and in love besides, they'd learned to get around Santa Cruz in Robert's used station wagon, a monstrous clunker with fake wood paneling on the sides, over a decade old and a deal at three hundred dollars. Their fond nickname: "The Tank." The engine hummed well enough, and Robert, an English major with a history minor, seemed proficient in all the necessary maintenance, oil changes, and flat tires.

Not until junior year did Robert experience a poignant episode of homesickness. Part of it had to do with their love, Gaylie believed, and his desire to show her off to his family. He was proud of her and proud of loving her and rightly so. She was smart and beautiful, her mysterious face mimicking the California coastline: foggy, rugged, unpredictable. She inspired his many spontaneous, metaphoric communications of love, a few of them rendered permanent in his spiral notebook:

Marie Gayland fog and wind
my heart the sun
burning into jagged cliffs
coastline of love

Robert had so truly captured Gaylie's native California spirit that she felt driven to learn the source of his wisdom and vision. Easily, she agreed to accompany him on the cross-country trek, her only anxiety arising from her ignorance about New York, a vague and ominous impression gleaned from popular culture.

Robert assured her that the remote suburb of his early youth was nothing worse than drab and tame. "I had that advantage," he told her, a revelatory look on his face. His two-year distance from home had allowed him to understand so much. "The museums, the theater, all the best things the city had to offer were close enough to see when we wanted. All the worst things we could avoid." He laughed then, Gaylie detecting an emotion behind it. Guilt?

"I wonder how they see it," he said. "The poorest people in the city, surrounded by the finest things, unable ever to enjoy them."

Gaylie pretended to understand, but her knowledge of class struggle was limited to a concept she'd learned in Sociology 1A. People, their psychological needs and drives—the consequences—all confused her and failed to penetrate her scientific mind. In matters of human intercourse, she was left with her instincts, often very good and more than adequate but still less satisfying than hard scientific data. Her choice of major, marine biology, said much about her nature, a comfort with tangible reality and the psychological simplicity of nonhuman living things.

Robert had his own way of describing her nature: "Marie Gayland, majestic orca rising, graceful arc, splash and entry..." She accepted his poetry with awe and confusion, admiring his manner, so unscientific and full of heart that it felt easy to her, like the wordless chatter of dolphins.

Days before the trip, Robert put serious time and effort into the car. What was another three thousand miles compared to the hundred-fifty the Tank had already seen? He replaced the bald tires with new retreads, tugged at and adjusted hoses around the engine, tightened screws underneath as he lay on his back. "Splatter and dark smudge, the oil of motion, man's destiny..." Robert's mechanical ability was based on instinctual kinetic poetry, an impractical ignorance he would, one day, understand and confess.

Back then, blinded by love, Gaylie's faith in him was so complete that the thought of road trouble never crossed her mind. "We can do it in six days and still see some of the sights along the way," he declared. They planned to take a southern route with a quick detour to see the Grand Canyon. An adventure, all pleasure. Robert even found a used eight-track tape player and bolted it under the dash. Gaylie supplied the tapes: Mamas and Papas; Crosby, Stills, Nash.

They started out early one June morning, fog still blanketing the town. A stop for coffee and doughnuts.

They were cheerful, ebullient even. "Imagine their faces when I pull into the driveway!" said Robert.

"What did they say when you told them I was coming?"

"Nothing." He laughed. "Shrouded in mystery, a stranger arrives, the errant son returns…"

"Nothing?"

"I didn't tell them." Behind the steering wheel, cardboard coffee cup between knees, he was smiling broadly. He took his eyes off the road, glanced at her, and noticed her crestfallen face, making his brow pinch into a frown. "No, Gaylie, you don't understand. I didn't tell them *anything*. I didn't tell them we're coming. I didn't even call them. This is a surprise. I thought you knew."

"No. You didn't say!" But she laughed through her displeasure, which really amounted to nothing more than confusion. She wondered about his parents and what had made him run so far away and what now made him so eager to return, to evoke their delight and approval. For he didn't anticipate disapproval, she could see that in his face. No, this would be a surprise visit of a pleasant sort.

Just two hours into the trip, entering the San Joaquin Valley miles from cool, coastal air, they discovered a significant oversight: The Tank lacked air conditioning. As the afternoon wore on and the heat intensified, Gaylie's internal tides missed the sound, smell, and rhythm of ocean surf. She braided her long, sandy hair and pinned it on top of her head. They pulled over to change into shorts. Gaylie stripped to a cotton tank top and Robert removed his shirt completely, exposing a hairless chest the texture and color of caramel.

Back on the road, he made the best of it, his dark eyes happy. "You're so lovely, flushed and wet." Gaylie smiled at his words but pulled away from the hand he laid on her bare knee. "Sorry," she said. "I'm just getting tired of Mama Cass. Let's turn this off." She reached forward and ejected. Better. The singers' voices had been keeping uneven time to shimmering heat waves on the asphalt, melting into distortion.

Between Barstow and Needles, the desert became unrelenting. Like a beached marine mammal, Gaylie yearned for water. She perched on one knee and leaned over the seat to reach the cooler on the floor in back. The slosh had told her, even before opening it, that the ice was fast going. She dipped a couple of bandannas in the ice water, removed them dripping, put the blue one flat on Robert's upper back and the red one on her neck and chest. "Oooo!" he exclaimed. "Icy trickle, splash and sizzle. 'Now entering Arizona!' A whole new state, Gaylie! What progress!"

Gaylie smiled and draped the wet bandanna on her forehead, the edge coming to rest on the top rim of her sunglasses. Progress. One out of fifty; how many to go? Of course, they wouldn't be passing through all the states. She was having difficulty thinking in this heat, the open window an oven door, white light penetrating her dark glasses and spilling in the sides. She squinted against the pain, light stabbing and dust brushing her dry eyes. A flat, dusty, empty expanse surrounded the highway, melting into silver water a mile ahead.

No one is on this road, she thought. *No one but us. Everyone knows this isn't the place to be at three o'clock on a summer afternoon. Everyone but us.*

And then she saw the steam rising from the hood. Robert didn't seem to notice because it was, at first, not quite noticeable, almost indistinguishable from the undulating heat hovering over a watery mirage. But the steam kept coming until Gaylie saw the change in his eyes, incipient speech stopping dead on his tongue. Even Robert hadn't a verse to combat this new threat.

"I think we have a problem," he said and pulled over onto the shoulder.

The task of opening the hood took several minutes, Robert attempting to protect his hands and body from escaping steam. "All we need to do is wait, Gaylie. Just a little while until it cools down and then I'll fill the radiator. I brought plenty of water." He smiled. "Water, fluid of life."

Gaylie returned the smile but suddenly felt faint and went to crouch by the side of the car in the narrow rectangle of shade it provided.

"You all right?" from behind the hood.

"Fine. I'll be fine." She dropped into a sit on the dust.

Time passed, how long she couldn't say. She remained on the ground, their hulking metal chariot separating her from the roadway. She heard but didn't see the cars that passed, one at a time, with long distances in between. Engines whirred without concern, no sounds of slowing. Robert was talking to himself and finally unscrewed the radiator cap with an "Ouch!" and hissing sounds as he poured the water in. "I'm gonna start it up, Gaylie." She stood and saw him get in behind the wheel, turn the key and pump the gas pedal, over and over again, the engine failing.

"You're flooding it," she told him, leaning into the passenger-side window.

"I'll just give it a rest and try again."

Gaylie pulled her head out of the window and went to lean up against the back of the Tank. She was still hopeful despite every sign pointing to hopeless, maybe because it was just a bit cooler, the sun lower to the horizon but high enough to give them time, at least three or four hours until dark.

She heard a low, distant rumble before noticing a speck miles back from the direction they'd come, growing larger in sound and shape until it was a towering big-nosed semi bearing down on them. The truck stayed well within the boundaries of its lane, but the sight of it made her nervous and she scooted sideways along the back of the car away from the road. Dust stirred and billowed as the rig passed, the sound of its engine lowering, gears changing. Slowing? Robert stepped out of the wagon and they both stood, looking ahead, watching. Size and mass worked against the hydraulic brakes. Half a mile down the highway, it finally came to a halt.

"He's stopping for us?"

Robert made a visor with his hands. "Metal monster, desert angel. Here he comes."

To Gaylie's amazement, the semi was thrown into reverse and came barreling toward them. She had no idea something that large could be wheeled backward at such a rate. The back end of the tractor-trailer was soon upon them, making her nervous all over again. Ten feet from the hood of their wagon, the truck stopped with a metal screech and whooshing release of air pressure.

The driver left the engine running, jumped down in two steps, and walked toward them. He was lean as a jackknife in a stained undershirt and thin tubes of blue jeans, bottoms tucked into cowboy boots. "Little trouble here?" he said, coming up to the open hood.

"Just have to cool it down, I think," said Robert. Gaylie saw the concern in Robert's eyes behind the casual lilt of his voice. He was glad someone had stopped.

"Lemme take a look." The man put his hands on the top of the grille and leaned inside while Robert looked over his shoulder. Gaylie came closer, still keeping some distance. The trucker's left forearm was three shades darker than the right forearm and the top of his hair seemed funny, old and dusty with the two sides meshed closely around the part. A toupee? The man pulled himself upright and then she could see; the hairpiece dipped slightly to the side.

"The block is cracked."

"The block is cracked," echoed Robert.

"Yeah. Cracked. You won't be goin' anywhere in this thing."

"The block." Robert scratched his black curls, full of life next to the trucker's dry mat. Yet the man's face was smooth and youthful. He wasn't much older than Robert, maybe twenty-six or twenty-seven.

The trucker folded his arms across his chest and Robert followed suit. Gaylie put her hands on hips and shifted from left foot to right. In her left fist she still gripped the red bandanna, now bone dry.

Several seconds passed, the trucker eyeing them one at a time while Robert gazed down into the engine and Gaylie worked on averting her eyes. Finally the man said, "You're from California?"

"Yes" and "no" said Gaylie and Robert simultaneously. Robert followed up: "That's where we go to school."

The man, still inspecting them, nodded as if they'd explained everything. "You'd better come with me. You're not goin' anywhere in this thing."

"You could get us to a service station?" asked Robert.

"Sure." The man smiled briefly, showing yellow horse teeth, one of them missing on the side.

"Thanks. Just a minute. We'll collect a few things." Robert motioned toward the car and glanced at Gaylie. On opposite sides, they opened the front doors and slipped inside. The trucker remained standing in front of the hood, arms folded.

"What do you think?" Gaylie whispered, bending low. The open hood shielded them from view.

"An interesting character."

"He's all right though?"

"I think so. A fellow human." Their eyes locked in silence. Robert's conclusion on species was the best Gaylie could have gathered from external clues, the dry data. She didn't have enough yet to arrive at specifics. Neither did Robert, she sensed. "Ethics of the highway," he added. "These truckers have a need to help their fellow driver."

"Well, we don't have much choice." She looked away

from him and busied herself, gathering her possessions in a battle against apprehension. First, she opened her zippered canvas bag to make sure it contained the essentials and valuables—wallet, checkbook, diary, camera, comb and brush, Chapstick. Hesitating, fingering the door handle, she thought again and leaned over into the back seat to remove a few things from her overnight case. Toothbrush and toothpaste, aspirin, hand lotion. The lotion bottle was big and bulky but seemed necessary in the heat and dry air. Another thin tee shirt and a pair of underwear. Two apples, two oranges, and a bottle of water from the cooler. All these things she put into her canvas bag.

Robert covered his bare chest with a tee shirt but didn't seem to be carrying anything. There was a bulge in the back pocket of his shorts. Gaylie guessed that he had his wallet and little telephone book. Eyeing her bag, he said, "We're coming right back. We'll get help at a service station."

Gaylie could say nothing in defense. Her instincts were valid, another instinct told her.

"I've let you down," he said.

"No, you haven't. No one could help this. Let's just go."

He touched her hand before they slid out opposite doors and locked them.

"Set?" asked the trucker. His mouth was different, pushed into something short of a grin. He led them up to the passenger side of the cab, jumped up and opened the door for them, and jumped down again. As Gaylie climbed up behind Robert, she glanced back. There sat the Tank—alone, useless, forlorn.

The truck driver bounded up on his side, engaged the gears, glanced in the side mirror and started to roll. He shifted again and again, every five feet it seemed. Finally, the noise was manageable.

"I'm Robert and this is Gaylie," announced Robert.

"Pete," said the trucker.

Next to the passenger window, Gaylie clutched her canvas bag resting on bare knees and stared into endless desert. Aloft and bouncing, she remembered the feeling of a carnival ride, the excitement and fear.

"I guess you must travel this highway a lot," suggested Robert.

"Fair amount."

"Is there a service station up ahead?"

"Always one up ahead."

Gaylie glanced past Robert for a brief evaluation of Pete. He seemed innocuous enough, smaller than Robert and almost too slight to be at the controls of a multi-ton rig. Still there was no place to go. The door to their carnival ride had been shut to keep them from falling—or jumping.

"If you know a service station with a tow truck or a mechanic, that would be a big help."

"Would be."

"You think we could get someone to come out to the car? Maybe get it running? Or would they have to tow it?"

"Depends. The block is cracked."

Robert waited for more from Pete. When nothing came, he said, "Right, the block is cracked."

They fell silent beneath the rumble of the engine. The vibrations at least covered Gaylie's building panic, increasing with their distance from the waters of the Pacific and their distance from the Tank, the one possession that fused her and Robert to dry earth. Their helplessness would consume her, she knew, unless she acted against it.

She found her voice and spoke. "Are you from Arizona, Pete?"

He turned his eye on her with that expression he'd shown earlier, something she couldn't quite call a grin. "No," he said.

"Do you drive cross-country or locally?"

"Some of everything. This is my rig." The statement might have been self-congratulatory. He didn't look at her when he said it, but glanced alternately in the side mirror, at his hands and the road ahead.

"Quite a truck," offered Robert. "Sleek chrome, a shining star."

"Mine all right," said Pete.

"Must be hard to be away from home so much," said Gaylie.

"Home?" Pete let the word hang. Gaylie wanted to ask more but sensed the futility. They lapsed into silence, a wasteland stretching ahead and behind. No towns, service stations, or buildings of any kind in sight.

Miles later, moments before Pete spoke again, Gaylie anticipated something coming. His eyes darted double time at the mirror, his hands, the road, and the mirror again. He glanced out the corner of his eye at Robert, at Gaylie, then each of them again. He cleared his throat. "A lot goin' on out there in California."

"We like it," said Robert.

Pete quickly appraised Robert from head to waist, then glanced at Gaylie. "Any kind with any other kind. Bi and tri and all that."

"Well, I don't know…"

"Love power, flower power, all that."

"You can tap the power of love anywhere, not just California."

Pete's eyes darted again at Robert and he emitted a single syllable laugh. "Even in Arizona!"

"Sure. This is the land for it. Orange sun, cactus bloom, desert beauty…"

"Where *are* you headed with this truck, Pete?" Gaylie cut in. Pete turned his eyes from the road and looked at her, too long for comfort even though the highway was straight and empty. "East," he said, his face blank.

"What kind of cargo are you carrying?"

"This and that."

"Like, goods for stores."

"Yeah, goods." He cleared his throat again. "Just another mile up, there's a truck stop."

"Great!" exclaimed Robert a bit too loudly. "A service station, you mean."

"Sure. They got a service station."

"They have a mechanic you know of?"

"Could have."

Pete began to downshift just as the outcropping of buildings came into view: a long, low diner and a service station with two gas pumps. In anticipation of their stop, Gaylie clutched at her canvas bag, ready to grab it and descend. She saw half a dozen trucks lined up in the dust at some distance from the restaurant door. Pete pulled up alongside and stopped without killing the engine. Gaylie pulled at the door handle, discovered it wasn't locked, and jumped down from the cab. Suddenly she was surrounded by the steady, thundering rumble of powerful engines, every one left to idle.

Pete got down and came up alongside Robert and Gaylie. "Thanks for the ride," yelled Robert before they'd walked clear of the parking area. Pete just shrugged his shoulders and stayed two feet behind as they walked to the service station. "We really appreciate it," said Robert, yelling a little less. Pete tagged along. Gaylie looked over her shoulder at him and caught his eye. Nothing could be read on his face. She forced a small, appreciative smile and turned to look toward their destination.

The service station pumps, one with diesel fuel for trucks, were outdated yet remarkably well preserved. Gaylie didn't recognize the brand of gas. A handful of beat up cars decorated the exterior of a service building containing a small office and a single bay for repairs.

With some hope, Gaylie appraised the man working on a car in the service bay. He saw them coming and walked outside, rubbing oil-stained hands on a blackened rag. He was middle-aged with a military crew cut, a face and neck the color of medium-rare beef. A half-smoked cigarette, stubbed out, hung from the corner of his mouth.

Pete, acting as interpreter, opened his mouth first. "These folks havin' some car trouble."

The man said nothing and remained planted ten feet

from them, rubbing his hands.

Robert said, "The car's about, what would you say, Pete, seven or eight miles back?"

"More like fifteen or twenty."

The mechanic shrugged his shoulders, unimpressed. A rim of yellowish-white showed under the light blue balls of his eyes, trained on Pete's. Gaylie looked at the trucker, standing slightly behind them and to the side. His face bore that illusive non-grin, a spark of light in his eyes. Her focus shifted from trucker to mechanic and back again, an instinct forming without objective data to support it. These men weren't strangers. Maybe they even said something to each other with their eyes.

"Could you drive back with us and take a look?" asked Robert.

The trucker and mechanic disengaged their eyes. "Couldn't do that," said the mechanic.

"The block's cracked anyway," threw in Pete.

The mechanic raised his eyebrows while his lips curled and rolled snakelike, sending the cigarette stub from one side of his mouth to the other. "So, the block's cracked. You should've said." He looked hard at Robert.

"Well, I'm sure it can be fixed," said Robert.

"Depends," said Pete.

"Depends," said the mechanic.

"Depends on what?" asked Gaylie.

"We'd have to take a look."

"Can you send a tow truck out?" she asked.

The mechanic, his eyes rolling between Robert and Gaylie, hesitated before answering. "Not for you, I can't."

"Well, you *have* a tow truck, right?"

"Not here today."

"Can we use your phone? Maybe we can get another tow truck to bring it here," Gaylie suggested.

"Could try it. Course, I'm booked as it is." The mechanic threw an arm in the direction of the parked cars. Gaylie evaluated them. Dents and rust, baked-on dirt, flat tires here and there—cars that hadn't moved for years.

"I guess we're out of luck then," said Robert.

"Outta luck then." His lips curled up around the stub.

"Guess you better come get some coffee then," said Pete in Robert's direction.

"No thanks," said Gaylie.

"Guess you better come along."

The trucker and the mechanic exchanged another look before Pete turned toward the diner, expecting Robert and Gaylie to follow. Robert took Gaylie's hand and gave it a small tug, meant to convey a request that she come along. "Maybe we'll use the phone in the diner."

"Suit yourself," said the mechanic, wiping his hands and staring after them as they walked away.

Halfway to the diner, Gaylie looked back and saw the mechanic unmoved from his spot of dirt. From this angle she could see, for the first time, a tow truck parked behind the service building. Behind Pete's back, Gaylie flashed Robert a look of eroding trust. He withstood the glare with deliberate, calm eyes and a blink of reassurance. She understood. After all, the choice between Pete and the mechanic was easy. They would have to follow Pete into the diner.

"Good coffee here," said Pete as he pushed open the glass door.

"I don't drink coffee," said Gaylie.

Pete didn't respond but led them to the first empty booth and slid in. Robert and Gaylie took the opposite side. They sat in silence against a background medley of tinny silverware and thick coffee cups on saucers, the cool, conditioned air gradually lifting their moods. Pete sat like a man without a timetable, slumped into the cushioned bench, eyes slowly scanning the dining room.

"Actually, I think I'll use the ladies' room," said Gaylie.

"Good idea. The men's room, I mean," said Robert. "If the waitress comes, we just want something to drink."

Pete touched a finger to his forehead under the toupee. Magically, it sat straighter now. As they turned toward the "Restroom" sign in the back, Gaylie felt oddly panicked with the thought that Pete might be gone when they returned, leaving them to face the desert alone.

"Only twenty-five miles to Kingman, you know," Gaylie heard behind her. She glanced over her shoulder to see Pete eyeing her backside, the non-grin on his lips.

Enclosed in a little vestibule next to the restrooms, in the company of two pay phones, they talked in hushed tones. The air was warmer, heavy with disinfectant and stale cigarette smoke.

"I'm really not interested in going any farther with this man," said Gaylie.

"Kingman's a bigger town. We'll get help there."

"Who's going to help us?"

"Pete seems to be trying."

"Did you see the way that mechanic looked at us? He had a tow truck, you know."

"I know. I saw it." He shook his head. "The idea of brother helping brother was lost on *that* man. A pitiable soul, vision blighted—the scourge of the underclass."

"What underclass are you talking about?"

"That mechanic. He's poor. We're poor."

"We're not poor, Robert. We have some cash and I brought my checkbook." Gaylie, who'd never thought of money as a limitation, thrust her hand into the canvas bag, fingers seeking the reassuring outline of her checkbook.

"And what in the bank? A few *centimes*? Hardly enough to tow a car twenty miles and fix a cracked block."

"Whatever *that* is."

"Right, whatever. Something serious, that much is clear."

"But he doesn't know what kind of money we have. He didn't even ask."

"True." Robert fell silent for a moment, his mind working while he searched his love's countenance. Gaylie dipped her chin to avoid his eyes, not willing to show her apprehension and annoyance.

"But I'm afraid this is more than a class problem," he added. "I don't think it matters what he thought about our money." Robert paused. Gaylie lifted her eyes. He explained. "Money wouldn't change his attitude. Not with this face." He squeezed his cheeks between thumb and fingers of one hand. "This hair." He pulled at a lock. "The etch of ebony, distant drum of slavery…"

"What *are* you *talking* about?"

A barrel-chested patron emerged from the men's room, shirttail dangling. Gaylie closed her mouth, immediately aware that her voice had risen. The man squeezed past them and out of the vestibule.

Robert looked at Gaylie with eyes meant to impress an important truth. "I have a grandmother of mixed parentage. Some of that darkness has come down to me. I've never mentioned it, I suppose, because…"

Yes, because why? He would have assumed she recognized it and didn't care. Gaylie examined his face, trying to see it. Robert had always been just Robert, no one to pigeonhole. "I don't think," she started, then stopped. *Bi and tri. Any kind with any other kind.* Pete had seen it, the mechanic had seen it, but Gaylie, the closest person to Robert, had been blind. She considered it now. They were not a fluke of nature, orca mating beluga. They were just Robert and Gaylie. "You're saying it's dangerous. With Pete, I mean."

"I don't think with Pete. I doubt it. That mechanic was hostile, sure, but Pete…"

True, they had the hard evidence against the mechanic, but what did they have on Pete? His silence: was it deviousness or an inability to communicate? His comments about California: perversion or curiosity? The non-grin, the toupee? They all pointed to something, just what, neither Robert nor Gaylie could say.

Unable to name their doubts, they decided to stick with Pete, easily discarding less attractive ideas: telephone calls to parents or friends, hitchhiking. Counting up the cash between them, they believed they had enough for a bus trip back to California. Robert's return home and Gaylie's exploration of his roots would have to wait. They would leave the Tank to rust in the desert, abandon it along with their suitcase of summer clothing and cooler of rotting food. This much accepted, Gaylie felt awash in relief and discovered she could, once again, look Robert squarely, lovingly, in the eye.

They used the facilities and returned to the booth, where Pete still slouched into the vinyl bench, drinking from a coffee cup. Two identical cups of transparent brown liquid sat on the table across from him. Gaylie and Robert slid in. "My second cup," said Pete with a mild air of accusation.

"Sorry we took so long," said Gaylie. "It was my fault. I had to wash up." Pete eyed her face, neck, and shoulders, apparently looking for signs of washing, but his own curiosity seemed to embarrass him and he looked down again. He took a sip from his cup. "Good coffee," he said.

Gaylie said nothing, not wishing to offend him with another reminder of her aversion to coffee. Politely, she took a sip. Cold, weak.

"We were thinking, Pete," said Robert. "Is there a bus station in Kingman?"

At that, Pete looked up from his coffee and gazed out into the aisle, brow lowering over deep-set eyes that registered surprise, then disappointment. He remained silent for a long time, as if the question took a great deal of thought. Gaylie and Robert exchanged looks. "You think there's a station?" repeated Robert.

"Sure," Pete blurted. "But I told you, I'm going east.

Better than a bus."

"Right, well, thank you, but you know, we decided we're going to turn around and go back to California."

"California?" Pete rolled the word over in thought, as though Robert had made a proposal. "You said you were goin' east."

"Right, but we changed our mind. Can you get us to Kingman?"

"Sure, well…" He glanced briefly at Robert, then Gaylie, then back into the aisle. No one said anything for seconds until a thought visibly crossed Pete's face and he said, "What about your car?"

"The block's cracked," said Robert with a big smile.

Pete turned to him with the non-grin. "Right about that," said Pete, biting the inside of his cheeks against a smile and looking down.

The twenty-five miles to Kingman lasted twice the necessary time. Pete's driving noticeably slowed, and the desolate highway unaccountably produced two truck stops on the way, each one providing an excuse for Pete to pull over. "Can't get enough coffee, drivin' a rig." Gaylie and Robert politely sat across from him two more times, sipping soft drinks and avoiding food to conserve their meager cash supply. Dutch both times, Pete refusing Robert's offer to treat. Coffee was nothing, but they hoped Robert's gesture was proof enough of their gratitude, having no other way to pay for the ride. Between truck stops they ate the fruit in Gaylie's bag, Pete declining their offer to share.

With all the coffee drinking, Pete still didn't use the

men's room, as if reluctant to let them out of his sight. Conversation was sparse but increasingly needful and desperate, thoughts crossing Pete's face in painful waves, producing jerks of phrases and twitching expositions of yellow teeth. The toupee slipped once more.

By the second truck stop, night had fallen. Its descent timed the slow diffusion of Gaylie's anxiety about Pete, particles of it gradually filtering outward through the gray, vanishing behind the boundary of dark. Only then did she understand completely what she'd sensed all along about him. In the sparse light cast from the truck's control panel, Gaylie looked to Robert for confirmation. His eyes told her what she knew.

Despite their protestations, Pete got off the highway at Kingman and drove through town, looking for the Greyhound station. "Not too late to go east," he kept saying, right up to the door. By then he should have given up, but he followed them inside, heeling like a stray dog as they walked to the booth and bought their tickets to California. The bus wouldn't be leaving until morning.

Tickets in hand, they turned to face Pete. "Messenger of mercy," said Robert. "We don't know how to thank you." He extended his hand and Pete's timidly rose to meet it. Even then, he didn't budge.

"Thank you for everything," said Gaylie.

With two fingers, Pete touched his forehead in a fumbling salute, catching an edge of the toupee. Gaylie's heart jumped for him. But the hairpiece didn't fly, only shifted slightly. With that and a non-grin, Pete turned and was gone.

They settled onto a wooden bench, rubbed smooth

with wear and marred by etchings of initials and profanity. A long wait and a long journey lay ahead. Robert's eyes glazed over with fatigue. "Dark, cold blanket. Night." He put his arm around Gaylie's shoulder and she settled into him. "One day," he said, "when you leave me, I'll be as lonely as Pete."

"Why would I ever leave you?"

"After everything I put you through with the Tank and—"

"Never," said Gaylie. "Never."

For she'd decided by then that she belonged with Robert. She never did leave him, and though her decision to stay had nothing to do with Arizona or cracked blocks or truckers, her constancy remained forever cast alongside her vision of Pete, driving miles of endless highway, never changing, never finding home.

———————

✍ *Dear Reader*

As I write the afterword to this updated edition, I'm celebrating a few book birthdays.

A little more than a decade ago, I gathered up all the stories I had written in the '90s and the '00s and arranged them in three volumes by theme: *Everyone But Us, tales of women*, *Dust of the Universe, tales of family*, and *Malocclusion, tales of misdemeanor*. Since the publication of these collections in 2012-2013, many readers have let me know how much they've enjoyed my stories.

During the same decade, I've published six novels of legal suspense in the Dana Hargrove series. Each one is a stand-alone, finding Dana at a discrete stage of her family life and career. If you enjoy courtroom drama, legal thrillers, mystery, and police procedurals, these novels may be for you, starting with the first one, *Thursday's List*. The sixth, *Power Blind*, releases in January 2022.

Let me know your impressions of my stories by posting a reader review of any length with your online book retailer. You can also drop me a line through the contact page on my website, vskemanis.com, and I'll respond directly. The contact page also has a link to a free e-book offer.

To keep up with the latest on my books and life, find me on Goodreads, YouTube, BookBub, Facebook, Twitter, and Instagram, and subscribe to the blog on my website.

Thanks for reading!

V.S.K.

January 2022

℘ *Opus Nine Books*

All works published by Opus Nine Books are dedicated
to the nine members of the family headed by John and
Kate Swackhamer at 3 South Trail, Orinda, California—a
large world under one small roof.